THE TAMINA GORGE AT RAGATZ

The
Playground of Europe

By

Leslie Stephen

"We complain of the mountains as rubbish, as not only disfiguring the face of the earth, but also to us useless and inconvenient ; and yet, without these, neither rivers nor fountains nor the weather for producing and ripening fruits could regularly be produced."

Abp. King *On the Origin of Evil.*

Illustrated

G. P. Putnam's Sons
New York and London
The Knickerbocker Press
1909

TO M. GABRIEL LOPPE

Gabriel Loppé (1825–1913) was a French painter, photographer and mountaineer. He became the first foreigner to be made a member of the Alpine Club in London. His father was a captain in the French Engineers and Loppé's childhood was spent in many different towns in south-eastern France. Aged twenty-one Loppé climbed a small mountain in the Languedoc and found a group of painters sketching on the summit. He had found his calling and subsequently went off to Geneva where he met the reputed leading Swiss landscapist, Alexandre Calame (1810 -1864). Loppé took up mountaineering in Grindelwald in the 1850s and made friends easily with the many English climbers in France and Switzerland. Although he was frequently labelled as a pupil of Calame and his rival Francois Diday, Loppé was almost an entirely self-taught artist. He became the first painter to work at higher altitudes during climbing expeditions earning the right to be considered the founder of the peintres-alpinistes school, which became established in the Savoie at the turn of the nineteenth century.

MY DEAR LOPPE,

Twenty-one years ago we climbed Mont Blanc together to watch the sunset from the summit. Less than a year ago we observed the same phenomenon from the foot of the mountain. The intervening years have probably made little difference in the sunset. If they have made some difference in our powers of reaching the best point of view, they have, I hope, diminished neither our admiration of such spectacles, nor our pleasure in each other's companionship. If, indeed, I have retained my love of the Alps, it has been in no small degree owing to you. Many walks in your company, some of which arc described in this volume, have confirmed both our friendship and our common worship of the mountains. I wish, therefore, to connect your name with this new edition of my old attempt to set forth the delights of Alpine rambling. Xo one understands the delights better than you, and no one, I am sure, will be a more lenient critic of the work of an old friend.

Yours ever,
Leslie Stephen.

PREFACE TO THE FIRST EDITION

This volume is a collection, with certain additions and alterations, of articles which have appeared in Fraser's Magazine, in the publications of the Alpine Club, and in the Cornhill Magazine. I call attention to the alterations and additions, not because I imagine that any large number of Alpine enthusiasts have learnt my writings by heart, or will resent changes as I have sometimes resented a fresh touch in one of Mr. Tennyson's familiar poems, but by way of making one of those apologies which we all know to be useless, and which yet have an inexpressible attraction for a writer. One does not make a bad book good by giving notice of its faults, nor can one hope to soften the inexorable ferocity of critics. And yet I am possessed with a nervous feeling, like that of a gentleman entering an evening party with a consciousness that his neckcloth is badly tied, and endeavouring by an utterly futile contortion to put it right at the last moment. With my eyes open to the weakness of my conduct, I do what I have often condemned in others, and

make a statement which I might more wisely leave to my enemies. The case, then, is this. I have endeavoured to remove from these papers one glaring fault. Most of them were originally written for a small and very friendly audience; and whilst the pen was in my hand, I had a vision before my eyes of a few companions sitting at the door of some Swiss inn, smoking the pipe of peace after a hard day's walk, and talking what everybody talks, from archbishops to navvies; that is to say, what is ordinarily called "shop." I was simply prolonging pleasant chats about guides and snow-slopes and aretes, and ropes and crevasses, which had a strange interest at the time, and were delightful even in the recollection. As some often-cited painter used to work at his pictures in a court dress by way of maintaining a dignified frame of mind, I could hardly scribble my undignified narratives in anything but a rusty old shooting-coat perfumed with tobacco, and still marked by the rope that had often been fastened round it. It was perhaps excusable that there should intrude into my pages a certain quantity of slang, and a large allowance of exceedingly bad jokes. On presenting myself to a larger public I have endeavoured to perform the painful operation of self-mutilation. The slang, I would fain hope, has been ruthlessly excised; but the pain of

dismissing a poor old joke, at which its author has smiled with parental affection, and which his friends have condescended to accept as more or less facetious, inflicts so cruel a pang, that I fear some intolerable specimens may remain. Moreover one cannot alter the tone of a narrative, though one may remove its most palpable blemishes ; and I fear that there will be in the following chapters a certain suspicious flavour as of conversation not quite fitted for polite society, which no use of literary disinfectants has quite removed. If so, I must try to console myself for the blame which I shall incur. The book is offered chiefly to those fellow-lunatics—if they will forgive the expression—who love the Alps too well not to pardon something to the harmless monomaniac who shares their passion. And I would fain hope that with the indecorum there will remain some sense of the pleasure with which these pages were first written. The way to make others feel is to feel oneself; and I will make, shall I call it a boast or a confession? which is perhaps less prudent than the apology. I not only wrote these pages with pleasure, but I have read them over again with some touch of my original feeling. liven benevolent critics may ascribe that pleasure, not to t any merit in the writing, but to the associations connected with the narratives. Somehow, in

reading, London fogs have rolled away, and I have caught glimpses of the everglorious Alps; above the chimney-pots over the way I have seen the solemn cliffs of the Schreckhorn and the Jungfrau. If my pages could summon up the same visions to other people that they have revealed to me, they would indeed be worth reading. As it is, they may perhaps suggest some faint shadows of those visions to fellow-labourers in the same field.

Leslie Stephen.

[In republishing these papers of a young gentleman, whom I shall regard with a certain interest, I have not felt myself at liberty to make any serious corrections. He would possibly have denied the force of some critical remarks which to me appear very obvious; and I do not know that my judgment would be superior to his. I have therefore left all faults of omission and commission in the republished chapters. I have, however, suppressed two chapters, one upon the "Eastern Carpathians," as irrelevant, and one upon "Alpine Dangers," as obsolete. I have substituted for them three papers, written at a rather later period: one upon the "Col des Hirondelles," from the Alpine Journal; and two,

"Sunset on Mont Blanc," and "The Alps in Winter," from the Comhill 'Magazine. The last, I may observe, was written when visits to the Alps in winter were much less common than at present.

L. S.]

Sir Leslie Stephen KCB (28 November 1832 – 22 February 1904) was an English author, critic, historian, biographer, and mountaineer, and father of Virginia Woolf and Vanessa Bell.Stephen was born at Kensington Gore in London, and son of Sir James Stephen and Lady Jane Catherine (née Venn) Stephen. His father was Colonial Undersecretary of State and a noted abolitionist. He was the fourth of five children, his siblings including James Fitzjames Stephen (1829–1894) and Caroline Emilia Stephen (1834–1909).

His family had belonged to the Clapham Sect, the early 19th century group of mainly evangelical Christian social reformers. At his father's house he saw a good deal of the Macaulays, James Spedding, Sir Henry Taylor and Nassau Senior. After studying at Eton College, King's College London and Trinity Hall, Cambridge, where he graduated B.A. (20th wrangler) in 1854 and M.A. in 1857, Stephen remained for several years a fellow and tutor of his college. He recounted some of his experiences in a chapter in his Life of Fawcett as well as in some less formal Sketches from Cambridge: By a Don (1865). These sketches were reprinted from the Pall Mall Gazette, to the proprietor of which, George Murray Smith, he had been introduced by his brother.

MARRIAGE:The family connections included that of William Makepeace Thackeray. His brother, Fitzjames had been a friend of Thackeray's and assisted in the disposition of his estate when he died in 1863. His sister Caroline met Thackeray's daughters, Anny (1837–1919) and Minny (Harriet Marian Thackeray 1840–1875) when they were mutual guests of Julia Margaret Cameron (of whom, see later). This led to an invitation to visit from Leslie Stephen's mother, Lady Stephen, where the sisters met him. They also met at George Murray Smith's house at Hampstead. Minny and Leslie became engaged on December 4, 1866 and married on June 19, 1867. After the wedding they travelled to the Swiss Alps and northern Italy, and on return to England lived at the Thackeray sister's home at 16 Onslow Gardens with Anny, who was a novelist. In the spring of 1868 Minny miscarried but recovered sufficiently for the couple to tour the eastern United States. Minny miscarried again in 1869, but became pregnant again in 1870 and on December 7 gave birth to their daughter, Laura Makepeace Stephen (1870–1945). Laura was premature, weighing three pounds. In March 1873 Thackeray and the Stephens moved to 8 Southwell Gardens. The couple travelled extensively, and by 1875 Minny was pregnant again, but this time was in poor health. On November 27 she developed convulsions, and died the following day of eclampsia.

After Minny's death, Leslie Stephen continued to live with Anny, but they moved to 11 Hyde Park gate South in 1876, next door to her widowed friend and collaborator, Julia Duckworth. Leslie Stephen and his daughter were also cared for by his sister, the writer Caroline Emelia Stephen, although Leslie described her as "Silly Milly" and her books as "little works".Meanwhile, Anny was falling in love with her younger cousin Richmond Ritchie, to Leslie Stephen's consternation. Ritchie became a constant visitor and they became engaged in May 1877, and were married on August 2. At the same time Leslie Stephen was seeing more and more of Julia Duckworth.

Contents

THE PLAYGROUND OF EUROPE

The Playground of Europe

CHAPTER I
THE OLD SCHOOL

A highly intelligent Swiss guide once gazed
with me upon the dreary expanse of chimney-pots
through which the South-Western Railway escapes
from this dingy metropolis. Fancying that i rightly interpreted his looks as symptomatic
of the proverbial homesickness of mountaineers, I (remarked with an appropriate sigh, "That is
not " so fine a view as we have seen together from the top of Mont Blanc." "Ah, sir!" was his

pathetic reply, "it is far finer!" This frank avowal set me thinking. Were my most cherished prejudices folly, or was my favourite guide a fool? A question not to 1 >e asked! Yet very similar shocks, as has often been remarked, await the student of early Alpine literature.

Not long ago 1 took up a queer old Swiss guidebook, the predecessor of the long line of similar

productions which have culminated in Murra), Baedeker, and Ball. It was orginally published in 1713, and for half a century or more seems to have been the familiar friend of the travellers who then visited the district of which it treats. It is called by the attractive title of the Delices de la Suisse; but the author is a little startled at his own presumption in using so ambitious a name. He explains that it is merely adopted with a view to a series of similar publications referring to more unequivocally delicious countries. In truth, he says, "si Ton considere les Alpes du cote de leur hauteur prodigieuse, de leurs neiges eternelles, et de l'incommodite et rudesse des chemins qu'on y trouve, il n'y a pas beaucoup de delices a esperer. " However, in spite of the horrors of eternal snow and prodigious height and steep paths, there are many attractions to be f-ind in the towns; and the wisdom of Providence in forming mountains is justified by certain statistics as to the number of cattle supported on the pasturages and the singular crystals to be found in the rocks. This was indeed a favourite argument at a time when the doctrine of the philosophic Pangloss was so generally popular. Everything must be for the best in this best of all possible worlds, and some final cause must be found even for the Alps. Another contemporary writer, after observing

that it is difficult to understand why the Almighty should have raised these "great excrescences of the earth, which to outward appearance indeed have neither use nor comeliness, " discovers a similar solution of the enigma. Not only are the "hideous rocks of the Cevennes, the Vosges, and the Alps " useful as sending down rivers to the sea, but they are an excellent preserve for fur-bearing animals. Thus the infidel who naturally regards such monstrosities as discreditable to the Architect of the universe is satisfactorily confuted; and by calculating the number of cheeses produced in Alpine dairies and the quantity of chamois leather and crystals which may be obtained in the mountain fastnesses, we can penetrate the hidden purposes of the Creator in producing such hideous excrescences as the Jungfrau and Mont Blanc. It is true that this trial of faith is somewhat severe, and that the explanation seems occasionally rather to break down. The French translator of one of the early Swiss travellers has a very short '.nd conclusive answer to the ingenious device by vhich his author proves the necessity of the Alps. In spite of this special pleading, he says, it cannot be denied that France gets on pretty well without everlasting snows, and that which is not wanted in France can certainly not be essential to the rest of the world. If this gentleman had lived in the

days when the French frontier crossed the summit of Mont Blanc his views might have undergone a change, and his patriotism have no longer come into conflict with his piety. Perhaps, however, he was a disciple of Voltaire, and had a general disrespect for final causes. In all the ordinary books we find much the same explanation of the old difficulty. Fur-bearing animals and cheeses and crystals are the missiles with which the unlucky sceptic is overwhelmed, and the ways of Providence satisfactorily vindicated to mankind. Abandoning the discussion of such inscrutable questions as little suited for the temper of the times, it is rather interesting to investigate the state of mind by which they were provoked. Why should the Alps be treated like the smallpox or as "a Borgia or a Catiline"'—as shocking to our belief in a beneficent Providence? What were the feelings with which they were regarded when theologians treated them as puzzling phenomena, only to be fully explained when we understood the origin of evil?

That explanation about the fur-bearing animals is so palpably inadequate as to indicate the grievous straits in which the unfortunate reasoner must have found himself confined. Obviously its inventor hated the mountains as a seasick traveller hates the ocean, though he may feebly remind himself that it is a

good place for the fish. The author, however, of the Dcliccs de la Suisse rinds one or two more intelligible consolations. At intervals he comes across a view which he admits to be pretty, almost, as it would seem, in spite of the mountains. There is, for example, a "fort joli aspect" from the terrace at Bcme, and he admires the lovely coteaux of the Pays de Vaud as seen from the Lake of Geneva, though he has not a word for the glorious mountain parapet which encloses the opposite shores. In this, I may remark, he coincides rather curiously with the higher authority of Addison, who says, speaking of the terrace at Bcme, "There is the noblest summer prospect in the world from this walk, for you have a full view of a noble range of mountains that lie in the country of the Grisons, and are buried in snow." The geography of this remark is singular, but the taste is unimpeachable. That Addison, however, cannot have been a great lover of snow mountains seems to follow from his comparison between the lakes of Constance and Geneva. The Lake of Constance, he says, "appears more beautiful to the eye, but wants the fruitful fields and vineyards that border upon the other." Why, then, should it be more beautiful to the eye? The only obvious reason is that it is not bordered by the wild ranges of Savoy, which he must apparently have reckoned

as a positive disadvantage to its rival. In a paper in the Toiler, the snow mountains are treated by him with a painful degree of disrespect which seems to countenance this conclusion. That the natives have winter in August, and that there are seven wooden legs in one family, seem to be the only remarks which Addison brought back from the "top of the highest mountain in Switzerland." The Lake of Geneva is almost a sacred place to the lover of mountain scenery: whether we hail it as the first introduction to the beauties of the Alps or pay them our last farewell from its shores, it is equally incomparable; its lovely grouping of rock and hanging meadow and distant snow and rich lowland and breadth of deep blue water strikes one as a masterpiece in some great gallery of exquisite landscapes. We now look upon it, or ought to look upon it, as tinged with poetical associations from Rousseau and Byron — if those respectable authors have not become too old-fashioned for the modern generation. But its own intrinsic merits are incomparable, and a man who preserves a stolid indifference in face of such a scene must be, one would think, of the essentially pachydermatous order. It was slow, however, in making its way to public favour. Perhaps we may excuse Bishop Burnet for taking more interest in the theology

than in the scenery of Geneva. He seems to have glanced at the mountains with considerable disgust. He looked at the Mont Maudit—as Mont Blanc was then expressively named—and was assured by a certain incomparable mathematician that it was two miles in perpendicular height; and after meditating a little upon the subject, remarks that "one will be afterwards apt to imagine that these cannot be the primary productions of the Author of Nature, but are the vast ruins of the first world which the deluge broke into so many inequalities." Later writers gradually awoke to its charms. Gibbon admired, though from a safe distance, the noble mountains of Savoy, which looked down upon him on the moonlight night w T hen he put the last stroke to the Decline mid Fall, and Voltaire composed a few smart lines about

ces monts sourcilleux Qui pressent les enfers et qui fendent lcs cieux,

and declared that "mon lac est le premier," principally because it was the residence of the lofty goddess La Liberte. But we should hardly look either to Voltaire or to Gibbon for any genuine enthusiasm in presence of natural sublimity. From Rousseau—the first man, according to Mr. Carlyle (though the expression is not

strictly accurate), who said, Come, let us make a description—we might expect better things; and better things are not altogether wanting. Yet it is curious to find in one of St.-Preux's set descriptions just the same peculiarity which we have noticed in Addison. That enthusiastic gentleman describes the head of the Lake of Geneva with his usual fluency. He points out to Julie the mouth of the Rhone and the "redans of the mountains"; but his great point is the comparison between the rich and charming banks of the Pays de Vaud and the barren heights of the Chablais. The moral is, of course, that freedom has produced vineyards in one case and slavery left bare rocks in the other ; and would seem to imply that even Rousseau had not learnt our modern admiration for barrenness on its own account. He admired the mountains as the barriers which kept luxury from corrupting the simplicity of the native, and in some passages he expresses what may be taken for substantially the modern sympathy with savage scenery; but one still feels an uncomfortable suspicion that his love of rocks may be a particular case of his love of paradox. He admires them, we may fancy, precisely because they are hideous; the mountains, like the noble savage, are a standing protest against the sophisticated modern taste; they are bare and wild and repulsive, but at any rate they

have not taken to wearing wigs and stays and submitted to the conventional taste of the century. To love them is a proof of a singular independence of character, which is admirable because it is eccentric. To this, however, I must presently return. Meanwhile, by way of extreme contrast to this point of view, we may take the last of the Tories, to whom the abuse of luxury was meaningless cant, and London the centre of all interest. Dr. Johnson speculates after his fashion upon the love of mountain scenery, when Boswell has succeeded in lugging him into the wilds of the Highlands. He gets to a place such as a "writer of romance might have been delighted to feign," but he evidently regards it with supreme disgust. He thinks with fond regret of his ideal prospect at Charing Cross, and has a dim conviction that he is rather a fool for suffering himself to be dragged at the tail of a Boswell into these regions of bog and heather. However, it will never do for a philosopher to admit that he has made a mistake, and accordingly he proceeds to moralise in this fashion: "It will readily occur." he says, "that this uniformity of barrenness can afford very little amusement to the traveller; that it is easy to sit at home and conceive rocks, heaths, and waterfalls, and that these journeys are useless labours, which neither

impregnate the imagination nor inform the understanding. " That is obviously the genuine Johnsonese sentiment. Why was he not sitting in the "Mitre" "conceiving rocks and heaths and waterfalls" enough to give additional zest to his comforts, instead of dragging his ponderous bulk into this "uniformity of barrenness"? Of course he finds a reason sufficient to save his philosophical character. Such regions, he says, form a great part of the earth's surface, and he that has never seen them must be unacquainted with one of the great scenes of human existence. On another occasion his reflections have a similar tinge. He admits that he has entered the Highlands by choice, and has no serious cause for alarm; yet the thoughts produced by the "unknown and untravelled wilderness" verge upon the uncomfortable. "The phantoms which haunt the desert are want and misery and danger; the evils of dereliction rush upon the thoughts; man is made unwillingly acquainted with his own weakness; and meditation shows him how little he can sustain, how little he can perform."

I may quote a more curious specimen of this simple-minded abhorrence of mountains from Johnson's friend Richardson. One of the characters in Sir Charles Grandison describes a passage of the Mont Cenis. He describes the chaises-a-porteur and the avalanches with great interest; he shudders at the wind called "The Tormenta," which blows the frozen snow into his face and wounds it as with sharp-pointed needles. But for the scenery he has no words, except frank expressions of horror. He contrasts Savoy, "equally noted for its poverty and rocky mountains," with the smiling fields of France, and admits that "his spirits were great sufferers by the change. " When he arrives at Lans-le-bourg—a place which for three months in the twelve scarcely sees the sun —he declares emphatically that "every object which here presents itself is excessively miserable," and indeed falls so ill that, but for the wonderful skill and kindness of the inimitable Sir Charles, he could never have faced the terrible passage to Italy. What would the hero of a modem novel say to such blasphemy of the charms of mountain scenery?

It would be difficult to imagine a human being more thoroughly out of his element than Dr. Johnson on a mountain; and Richardson was not much better qualified for the position. We may pardon them for expressing frankly sentiments which a considerable number of modern tourists might probably discover at the bottom of their hearts. Indeed, there is a good deal to be said for their opinions. Is there not something rather

12 The Playground of Europe

unnatural in the modern enthusiasm, or affectation of enthusiasm, for" uniformity of barrenness" ? Why should we not prefer the regions which are admirably fitted for human comfort to those in which life must be a continual struggle? Goldsmith, writing from Leyden, speaks contemptuously of the Scottish scenery from which he had just departed. "There," he says, "hills and rocks intercept every prospect; here it is all a continued plain," and very much the better, as he seems to intimate, for the absence of those disagreeable excrescences. Macaulay, commenting upon this passage, suggests a very simple explanation: comfort and security, he thinks, have more to do with our sense of beauty than "people of romantic dispositions" are disposed to admit. A traveller will not be thrown into ecstasies by natural objects which threaten him with actual danger—"by the gloomy grandeur of a pass where he finds a corpse which the marauders have just stripped and mangled, or by the screams of those eagles whose next meal may probably be on his own eyes!" One is sometimes inclined to ask, Is not this beginning at the Avrong end? Undoubtedly the scream of an eagle must be singularly unpleasant when it acts as dinner-bell to a meal of which you are the piece dc resistance; but why should it be pleasant under any circumstances?

The problem should not be stated, Why did Goldsmith (or Addison, or Johnson) hate objeets which made him uncomfortable with so good reason? but Why do we love them? At any rate, the explanation seems to be incomplete. Goldsmith could see Arthur's Seat and the Pentland hills and the Firth of Forth—

Whose isles upon its bosom float Like emeralds chased in gold—

and all the neighbourhood of the most picturesque city in Europe (I do not insist upon the accuracy of the expression) as easily and safely as the weary flats that encircle Leyden. Why did he not admire them? To notice one parallel phenomenon, there has been a similar change in modern taste in regard to objects where Lord Macaulay's theory is obviously inapplicable. Gothic architecture, the influence of which is in many respects analogous to that of mountain scenery, was as accessible in the eighteenth century as it is in the present day. There was no more danger then than now of the cathedral jackdaws dining off the eyes of the spectator, or of any worse robbers than elderly vergers lying in wait for sightseers. Yet it is spoken of in language which reminds one forcibly of the criticism on mountains. Thus, for example——to quote from a writer who has given

us his views on both topics,—Bishop Berkeley was certainly a man of fine taste and keen sensibility. He crossed Mont Cenis on New Year's Day, 1714, and remarks, first, that he was "put out of humour by the most horrible precipices"; secondly, that his life often "depended on a single step"; and thirdly, that his correspondent had much better take the comparatively safe and pleasant route to Italy by sea. In the Minute Philosopher, again, he has occasion to propose a theory of beauty. The Eastern nations and the Greeks, he tells us, "naturally ran into the most becoming dresses, whilst our Gothic gentry have never yet had the luck to stumble on anything that was not absurd and ridiculous." Following out the argument, he speaks of the various graces of Greek buildings, in all of which, according to him, "beauty ariseth from the appearance of use in the imitation of natural things . . . which is indeed the grand difference between Greek and Gothic architecture, the latter being fantastical and for the most part founded neither in nature or reason, necessity or use, the appearance of which accounts for all the beauty, grace, and ornament of the other." Thus Berkeley assumed as a primary axiom, needing no sort of proof, that Gothic architecture was naturally devoid of beauty, as indeed Gothic was generally used in that age as

synonymous with barbarous, or, in other words, as a term of abuse, whether applied to manners or to buildings. Not to dwell upon this, it is sufficient to remark at present that a man who could cite Westminster Abbey or Salisbury Cathedral as a specimen of simple ugliness might very well shudder at the Alps. The second party of tourists that ever visited Chamouni compared the Aiguilles to the spires of a Gothic church, and the comparison has become as hackneyed as other tourist commonplaces. The cathedral and the granite peaks have indeed many qualities in common; the grey walls have caught something of the solemn gloom of the mountain cliff, and the fantastic and almost grotesque shapes of some of the rocky pinnacles rival the daring visions of mediaeval architects. Indeed, it is scarcely possible to describe the wildest mountain scenery without the use of architectural metaphor; and one might venture to predict from a man's taste in human buildings whether he preferred the delicate grace of lowland scenery or the more startling effects only to be seen in the heart of the mountains. It may fairly be inferred that men who held the artistic creed of the eighteenth century were prevented from loving the sublime but irregular shapes of the Alps by something more than the inconveniences or the dangers of

travel. The mountains, like music, require not only the absence of disturbing causes, but the presence of a delicate and cultivated taste. Early travellers might perceive the same objects with their outward sense; but they were affected as a thoroughly unmusical person is affected by the notes of some complex harmony, as a chaos of unmeaning sounds.

We require, therefore, to penetrate a little farther into the question. I have spoken hitherto of sentiments which may be due simply to the material inconveniences of the Alps. They were such as a farmer or a political economist might utter from the purely utilitarian point of view. Mountains, it was said, showed a "uniformity of barrenness"; and patriots replied by counting the number of cows they could feed. The mountains were simply species of the great genus desert. An economist might use them to illustrate the meaning of the "margin of cultivation, " which creeps gradually up their flanks as rent rises in the valleys. But the simple statements that bare rock and everlasting snow are very much in the way of an enlightened agriculturist, and highly inconvenient to roadmakers, with a few necessary amplifications, will pretty well sum up the reflections of the old-fashioned guide-books. There were, however, even in those dark ages, some

observers who could see in the Alps more than inconvenient lumps of objectionable matter; men of science had penetrated their recesses, had hunted for rare herbs upon their slopes, had attempted to account for glacier motion, and had given, as they imagined, a perfectly satisfactory account of the origin of the mountains themselves. It is interesting to see what were the first impressions of those who surmounted their natural terror or disgust, and gave some descriptions of the more striking phenomena which they observed. A few notes from some of the earlier writers will help to illustrate their state of mind. In the Delices de la Suisse —to return for a moment to that excellent work—there is a picture which may catch the eye of the hasty reader. It appears at first sight to represent a croquet-ball. The two poles are dark, but a lighter zone runs round the equator, and is marked by certain singular figures something like the astronomical sign of Pisces. And thereby hangs a tale-—and a very remarkable one. The object in question was the chief ornament of a museum at Lucerne, and for aught I know may still be visible there to enterprising travellers. One of the earlier Swiss travellers, Scheuchzer by name, declares in a fine glow of enthusiasm that there is nothing like it "in regum, principum, privatorumquc museis."

18 The Playground of Europe

Scheuchzer, who made several tours from 1702 to 1711, was a man of some real scientific acquirements, especially as a botanist; he invented a theory of glacier motion, which at any rate opened an interesting question; some of his journals were published at the expense of the Royal Society of London, and two of the quaint illustrations are dedicated to Sir Isaac Newton. He represents the intellectual stage at which a growing scepticism has made a compromise with old-fashioned credulity. His rule, and it is a very convenient one, is always to believe half of what he is told. For example, he does not believe that any chamois possess the quality of "impenetrabilitas," i.e. to musket-shots; but thinks that some of them must have an abnormal toughness of constitution, probably due to the bezoars sometimes found in their intestines. In regard, however, to this marvellous stone, he throws aside his scepticism in favour of unqualified faith. It is, in fact, nothing less than a draconita or dragon-stone, and the rarity of such an object may be inferred from the most approved process of obtaining it. You must first catch a dragon asleep, then scatter soporific herbs about him (which, as Scheuchzer admits, has a fabulous sound), and then cut the stone out of his head, which, however, will be spoilt if he wakes during the process. Consider-

ing the extreme difficulty of securing all these conditions, it must be held as fortunate that in this instance the stone was dropped promiscuously by a flying dragon and picked up by a passing peasant. The authenticity of the stone is proved by several arguments: as, first, a dishonest man would never have invented so simple a story, but would rather have produced some marvellous tale about its coming from the farthest Indies; secondly, there are various depositions of the finder and his family; and, thirdly, the stone not only cures simple haemorrhages (which it might have done if composed of simple jasper or marble) but dysenteries and fevers, and a catalogue of more terrible complaints than were ever relieved by Hollo way's Pills. Scheuchzer then brings forward a quantity of corroborative evidence as to the existence of dragons. There is, indeed, a strong a priori probability that in regions so wild and full of caves as the Rhaetian Alps dragons must exist; but more direct testimony is not wanting and generally conforms to one type. Some "vir quidam probus" comes home in the evening with a swimming in the head and a marked uncertainty about the motions of his legs. He attributes these unprecedented phenomena to the influence of the dragon who encountered him in the forest.

From his

description an accurate portrait of the dragon is composed. The remarkable thing about these diagrams is the singular variety of type in the genus dragon. There are scaly dragons and slimy dragons, dragons with wings and feet, two-legged and four-legged dragons, and at times dragons with neither wings nor legs, but with objectionable heads and semi-human faces of an expression at once humorous and malignant. Scheuchzer divides these dragons by a scientific classification, and is puzzled by the question whether the crest is to be taken as a specific distinction or is merely characteristic of the male or (should we say?) the cock dragon. At any rate "satis superque constat" that there are dragons which differ from serpents in seven respects; amongst which it may be mentioned that they breathe so hard as to draw in not merely air but the birds flying above them.

Half a century before Scheuchzer. or about 1666, the Alps were visited by the learned Jesuit Kircher, and it is rather amusing to compare their views. Kircher believes, as becomes his cloth and his period, in various stories which Scheuchzer summarily puts down amongst "anilia delira-menta." On dragons he is specially emphatic. A certain "clarissimus vir," Herr Schorer, had seen with his own eyes a fiery dragon, which flew

across the Lake of Lucerne from Mount Pilate, emitting sparks like an anvil, and indeed strongly resembling a meteor to less experienced observers. Nay, Ivirchcr is bound by his respect for the Church—though not without a word or two of hinted suspicion—to believe in a legend which is preserved by a public notice in the church of St. Leodegarius in Lucerne. It tells how a man passed some months in a cave with two dragons, who were either naturally amiable or were calmed by his energetic appeals to the Virgin, and finally escaped by holding on to their tails when they ilew away after their period of hibernation. Dragons, it is plain, still flapped their gigantic wings across every retired gorge and haunted all the inaccessible caves of the Alps; and if any one doubts it, he must reckon with Gesncrus, Cysatus, and the learned Stumphius. Indeed, they seem to have been almost as common as Ldmmcrgeicr. Kircher has still more marvellous anecdotes to relate. Pie was evidently a good mountaineer, and made the ascent of Pilatus, upon which Scheuchzer failed " partim propter corporis lassitudinem, partim propter longinquitatem via' adhuc metiendac"; causes which, though seldom so frankly acknowledged, have hindered a good many ascents before and since. Devils,] iennies, and cobolds still lingered like the relics of primaeval populations, slowly decaying before the advance of civilisation. On Pilate, Kircher saw the lake to which the devil drags Pilate every Good Friday to inflict an annual punishment. He was disappointed at finding it only a yard and a half in depth, but was gratified by discovering certain suspicious footsteps in the snow, which might or might not have been those of the diabolical visitant. On this, as on some other points, he leans towards a qualified scepticism, and thinks that most of the damitnculi of which he speaks were due to the credulity of the peasantry. Once, however, he had a more startling adventure. He was climbing the Mons Arnus in Unterwalden, in search of a gold-bearing cave. As he approached the mouth, there issued from it a confused hubbub as of human voices, though no being of mortal flesh and blood could have been within some miles. Poor Kircher narrowly escaped being hurled to the bottom, "like Sisyphus," as he puts it, and we may fancy returned to the nearest village with his appetite for gold-bearing caves considerably damped. I will only add that, in regard to dragons, Kircher had an hypothesis to explain the variety in structure upon which I have already remarked. The dragon, he thought, was the result of spontaneous generation. Eagles left the carcases of their prey

to decay in the neighbourhood of their eyries, and from these savoury hotbeds of corruption there would natural!\'7d" arise dragons partaking in various proportions of the peculiarities of the animals whose carcases happened to form the delectable compost.

The Alps, then, were still haunted, even in the days of Sir Isaac Newton, by portentous dragons. At a rather earlier period they had afforded shelter to goblins and devils of still more portentous nature. These picturesque beings disappeared before the early dawn of science, much as the natives of Tasmania have disappeared before the English immigrants. It is only another stage in the process described in Milton's lines'—

From haunted spring and dale,
Edged with poplar pale,
The parting genius is with sighing sent.

The old gods of the woods and the streams were degraded, as we know, into demons; and their last descendants seem to have been the wretched d&munculi who lingered in Kircher's imagination. The dragons, as having a quasi-scientific existence and having left at least one tangible token of their presence in the museum at Lucerne, lingered yet a little longer; but they, with much that was more beautiful, fled before the earliest approach

of the tourist. Not the vestige of a dragon is now to be found, even in those wildest regions of the Alps which, according to Scheuchzer, were specially adapted for their generation, and which are now thronged and, as some think, desecrated by the bathing guests at St. Moritz. Fairies and elves, and other symbols by which people once interpreted to themselves the awe and wonder produced by natural scenery, have died too thoroughly even for poetical purposes. How much will go with them? and how far will the same process applied in other directions destroy the beauty and the romance of our daily lives?

Old travellers saw a mountain and called it simply a hideous excrescence; but then they peopled it with monsters and demons; gnomes wriggled through its subterranean recesses; mysterious voices spoke in its avalanches; dragons winged their way across its gorges; the devil haled the ghosts of old sinners to its lakes to be tormented; the wild huntsman issued from its deep ravines; and possibly some enchanted king sat waiting for better days in a mysterious hall beneath its rocks. Was not this merely expressing in another way the same sense of awe which we describe by calling the mountain itself sublime and beautiful? The sentiment was projected

into these external images, but in substance it may have been much the same; and every legend which floats round these noble peaks shows as distinctly as the ravings of the modem enthusiast how much they impress the imagination. When the machinery, as old critics used to call it, has finally decayed and dropped to pieces, the feelings to which its rise was due may still survive, and we may admire nature equally or possibly more when the beings by which we accounted to ourselves for our admiration have ceased to exist even in fancy.

At the period, however, of which I am speaking, dragons and goblins were, so to speak, at the fag end of their existence. They had received notice to quit and were submitting without serious opposition. For a short time there was a struggle between scepticism and faith, which is rather odd to observe. Sensible men of course took a middle path and admitted that many dragons were the fictions of credulous peasants, and perhaps even a mythical way of describing waterfalls (that is one of Seheuchzer's suggestions), but they would not fly to the ridiculous extreme of abandoning their dragons altogether. They made a judicious compromise and tried to reconcile the conclusions of faith and science. It is evident that some mental effort was necessarv to belief. When it,

comes to classifying dragons and dividing them into scientific species ("dracones," says one traveller in 1680, "in non alatos et alatos divide-mus, illosque in apodes et pedatos subdividemus "), we feel that their days are doomed; and it is at this period when the old romance is finally slain and science has not as yet created a new interest for itself that the mountains would naturally be most prosaic. Yet there was already a beginning of better things. Kircher, for example, had taken to mountain exploration from his extreme interest in an explosion of Vesuvius, and was eager to solve the curious problems which they presented. The mountains were already interesting in his eyes and from that it is a short step to their becoming beautiful. His explanation, indeed, admits that their occasional beauty is a kind of supplementary cause of their existence. There are, it appears, five main reasons for the existence of mountains: first, they serve as chains to bind the earth together, or as the bones or skeleton of the world, which is illustrated by elaborate diagrams; secondly, they resist the destructive action of the sea; thirdly, they make rivers, and to illustrate this he treats us to singular diagrams, showing how the Alps and other mountain chains are simply lids to vast cisterns of water—"hydrophy-laciae," as he calls them—from which the rivers

are somehow pumped up; fourthly, they restrain the wind and protect plants; and, fifthly, they produce mines. To this he adds cursorily, and, as it were, rather ashamed of so trifling a reason, "non dicam hie de amcenitate prospectus, de utilitate quam umbra sua in subjectis agrorum planis vallibusque conferunt," etc. So that the mountains were not quite without their charms. The most striking passage, however, upon this subject occurs in Burnet's Sacred Theory of the Earth, which in the beginning of the eighteenth century was, as Waterland tells us, a text-book for geological students at Cambridge. People in those days fancied, as people generally fancy when they catch sight for the first time of a new problem, that it was far easier and simpler than was actually the case; they did not know till experience taught them how painfully they would be compelled to advance from step to step, and to unravel the intricate chain of causes which have gone to bring the earth into its present shape; and still less how one principal result of the enquiry would be to prove that the most interesting questions lay outside the reach of human knowledge. With the Book of Genesis for their authority, a happy faculty of guessing to eke out any deficiencies of information, and a few inferences from the Newtonian theories to produce a scientific

tinge, they thought that the whole thing would be explained.

Burnet's view was that the earth resembled a gigantic egg, the shell representing the superficial crust, the white of the egg the subterranean waters, and the yolk the central core. When the fountains of the great deep were broken up the shell was shivered, the waters drowned mankind and then retired into the present sea, leaving the fragments to form the mountain ranges. The conclusions thus obtained as to the past and the probable future of the world coincided in the most charming way with the Book of Genesis and the Apocalypse, and they are enforced with abundant eloquence, if with a rather short allowance of reason. I quote part of the poetical passage in which Burnet describes how he was first induced to approach so tremendous a subject. He says:

The greatest objects of nature are, methinks, the most pleasing to behold; next to the great concave of the heavens, and those boundless regions which the stars inhabit, there is nothing that I look upon with more pleasure than the vide sea and the mountains of the earth. There is something august and stately in the air of these things, that inspires the mind with great thoughts and passions. We do naturally, upon such occasions, think of God and Tlis greatness; whatever hath but a shadow and appearance of die Infinite. as all things have thai arc too big for our compre-

hension, and fill and overbear the mind with their excess, cast it into a pleasing kind of stupor and admiration. And yet these mountains that we are speaking of, to confess the truth, are nothing but great ruins, but such as show a certain magnificence of nature: as from the temples and broken amphitheatres of the Romans, we collect the greatness of that people. But the grandeur of a nation is less sensible to those who never saw the remains and monuments they have left, and those who never see the mountainous parts of the earth scarce ever reflect upon the causes of them or what power in nature could be sufficient to produce them.

Burnet proceeds to say that when he crossed the Alps and Apennines, the "sight of those vast undigested heaps of stone did so strike my fancy that I was not easy till I could give myself some tolerable account of how* that confusion came in nature." He imagines a sleeper suddenly transported from the plains, and paints his astonishment on waking to see "such vast bodies thrown together in confusion."

Look upon these great ranges [he exclaims], in what confusion do they lie; they have neither form nor beauty, neither shape nor order, no more than the clouds in the air. Then how barren, how desolate, how naked art' they! How they stand neglected by nature! Neither the rains can soften them nor the dews from heaven can make them fruitful.

After insisting 'm the chaotic disorder of the

so The Playground of Europe

Alps, he says that if you could get within the mountains,

for they are generally hollow, you would find all things there more rude, if possible, than without. . . . No tempest nor earthquake could put things in more disorder. 'T is true they cannot look as ill now as they did at first. The ruin that is. fresh looks much worse than afterwards when the earth grows discoloured and skinned over, but I fancy if we had seen the mountains when they were new-born and raw, when the earth was first broken and the waters of the deluge newly retired, the fractions and confusions of them would have appeared very ghastly and frightful.

This passage gives a very striking account of the influence of mountains in that day upon a highly imaginative observer. They resembled vast ruins, not so ghastly and frightful as of old, because their deformities have been partially skinned over, yet still without form or beauty, huge chaotic fragments of the tremendous catastrophe that once shook the earth to its foundations, and yet, from the fact that they spoke so forcibly of that inconceivable exhibition of power, intensely interesting and suggestive of elevating thoughts. He felt like a man coming upon the ruins of an imperial city, just sacked by barbarians, with remnants of its former splendour lying heaped in hideous confusion, yet carrying the mind back to the days when they were perfect. The same thought

is expressed in Scott's lines about Ben venue, whose

Knolls, crags, and mounds confusedly hurled, Seemed fragments of an earlier world.

Only Scott is content to play with the fancy which Burnet puts forward with all the seriousness of a scientific enquirer. Think of the mountains as, in sober earnestness, ruins of the antediluvian world, and the\'7d' are really terrible. When they have declined into the romantic stage the same expression is merely a lively image of their apparent chaos. At a later period they gain an interest of a different order, when the mounds are indicative of the action of ancient glacial forces and every rock speaks to the observer of the slow lapse of geological periods.

From this, I think, we may deduce a few obvious conclusions as to the different temper with which the mountains were then regarded. Macau-lay's theory obviously contains much truth, though not the whole truth. The Alps, indeed, were visited without much fear of robbers or of eagles in the eighteenth century. Every young gentleman crossed them in making the grand tour, and no worse incidents are recorded that I know of than the slaughter of Horace Walpole's lapdog by a wolf. But in a wider sense there was precisely the same difference between our view of

Alpine scenery then and now, as between the American backwoodsman's hatred of a tree and that passionate regard for trees which people entertain who live in dread of economical officials and grasping landlords. Ice is a nuisance in Greenland and an inestimable luxury at Calcutta, and we, who are pent for ten months of the year in a crowd of three million cockneys, love our remaining playgrounds of fresh air and unenclosed pasture as naturally as men hated them whose lives were a daily battle with the wilderness. Mountains were once the main fortresses of the tyrannical powers of nature; now they are the last strongholds in which unsophisticated nature holds out: it is not surprising that our sentiments have changed. But we must add, if we would understand the precise nature of the change, some of the considerations which I have endeavoured to suggest.

The judgment passed on mountain scenery in different generations would, I imagine, curiously illustrate the relation between the poetical and the scientific stage of thought characteristic of any given period. When science had exorcised the dcEmuncidi, the mountains were left, like Burnet's unskinned ruins, bare of imaginary beings, and not yet covered by the complicated network of associations which has been gradually produced

by a closer observation of their details. To reproduce the mountains of a hundred and fifty years back we must begin by emptying our idea of nearly everything which gives them interest. The same picture was painted upon the retina of Addison when he stood on the terrace of Berne, and of the modern observer who follows in his footsteps. But when we compare the significance to the mind of the two spectacles, it is the difference between the vague blue films in the background of an ignorant painter and the photograph with all its infinite variety of detail. One man saw nothing but a flat surface bounded by an irregular jagged line; to the other, every minute fragment of the picture has a story and a language of its own. Mr. Ruskin has expounded at great length and with admirable acuteness the difference between the fulness of meaning in a mountain as drawn by Turner and the vague shapeless lumps of earlier artists. The mountains are now intensely real and, so to speak, alive to their fingers' ends; they began by being empty metaphysical concepts, and the difference is simply due to the fact that nobody had then taken the trouble to look at them, and that a great many highly skilled observers have been working at them very carefully ever since and have added their impressions to the existing slock. The hasty and inac-

curate outline has been slowly filled up by the labours of successive generations, and they have come into contact with our sympathies at an incomparably greater number of points.

Now, it is plain that the big chaotic lumps which existed in the beginning of the eighteenth century were comparatively useless for poetical purposes. Burnet has perhaps made the best of them in the passage I have quoted. There is something impressive about his picture of the ruins of an earlier world. But, to say nothing of the unreality of the hypothesis, it is too summary and simple a mode of explanation. It takes us into the most unpoetical sphere of metaphysics, and rather stops enquiry than suggests fresh trains of thought.

Finally, it may be noticed that the contemporaries of Newton had an uncomfortably mathematical way of looking at such problems. They thought that as the earth's orbit was a respectable ellipse, the earth itself should have been a neat oblate spheroid; and any irregularity in figure was rather discreditable than otherwise—perhaps, as Whiston argued, was in some way connected with the fall of man.

We might trace the reflection of these views in poetry, except that the poets had then so little to say of the mountains, or indeed of any natural

objects. When, at a later period, men of science were prying into every detail of Alpine scenery, poets were simultaneously looking at them with a fresh interest. When Saussure had been speculating on the causes of glacier motion, Shelley spoke of the glaciers which creep

Like snakes that watch their prey from their far

fountains, Slow rolling on;

and Bryon told how the

Glacier's cold and restless mass Moves onwards day by day.

Erratic blocks were objects of a poetical as well as of a scientific treatment. Wordsworth describes his leech-gatherer as standing

As a huge stone is sometimes seen to lie Couched on the bald top of an eminence, Wonder to all that do the same espy, By what means it could thither come and whence, So that it seems a thing endued with sense, Like a sea beast crawled forth, which on a shelf Of rock or sand reposeth there to sun itself.

Wordsworth, Byron, and Shelley had evidently observed the rocks and the ice with an interest as keen as that of Saussure, though they turned their observations to a different account. But what was a poor poet to do with the shapeless inorganic lumps of matter which did duty for

mountains to a former generation? We may find one or two feeble attempts to hitch them into verse. Young, for example, of the Night Thoughts, took it into his head to improve some of the celebrated descriptions in Job; 1 but he mentions with some pride that the passage about mountains is entirely his own. This is the whole of it:

Who heaved the mountain, which sublimely stands And casts its shadow into distant lands?

For a more elaborate treatment we may go to Pope, and quote a once celebrated passage in the Essay on Criticism:

So pleased at first, the tow'ring Alps we try, Mount o'er the vales and seem to touch the sky; The eternal snows appear already past, And the first clouds and mountains seem the last. But those attained, Ave tremble to survey The growing labours of the lengthening way; Th' increasing prospect tires our wond'ring eyes— Hills peep o'er hills, and Alps on Alps arise!

The metaphor is not a bad one for a young gentleman who had never seen a higher mountain than Richmond Hill; but it obviously implies no love of the "tow'ring Alps" either in the poet or

Let any one who pays a visit to the Zoological Gardens remark the closeness to nature of the following remark upon the hippop tamus:

" How like a mountain cedar moves his tail! "

the original from whom he copied. And, finally, I will quote a few lines from one of the worst poets of his own or any other generation. They arc, however, curious as an example of the way in which the scientific opinions of the Burnet or Kircher variety could be worked into rhyme. This is Blackmore's account of the mountains:

These strong unshaken mounds resist the shocks
Of tides and seas tempestuous, while the rocks
That secret in a long continued vein
Pass through the earth, the ponderous pile sustain;
These mighty girders which the fabric bind,
These ribs robust and vast in order joined,
These subterranean walls, disposed with art,
Such strength and such stability impart
That storms beneath and earthquakes underground
Break not the pillars nor the work confound.

Bad metaphysics are too easily converted into execrable poetry, and it is not surprising that a dissertation on final causes makes very indifferent verses. Indeed, it would be absurd to expect that poets should make use of raw science or philosophy; though they may turn to account the results obtained by scientific thinkers, and profit by the habits of close observation of nature which they have inculcated. Before anybody had ever looked into the mountains closely, classified their flora and catalogued their strata, it was impossible for a poet to do better than make a few random

allusions to their most obvious features. Even if he had possessed the necessary knowledge, he might as well have written in Hebrew as talked about glaciers or avalanches. Anything which is to be a fit object for poetical management must be already associated with some strong feeling in the mind of the audience as well as of the writer. The speculations in natural theology to which the mountains gave rise were especially unsuitable for poetry. That was the era of applying common sense to theology, from which it has since been banished effectually enough. In other words, the philosophers of that time had an undoubted confidence in their powers of explaining everything, and seem to have considered the Supreme Being as a highly intelligent ruler whose purposes might be very fairly understood and whose legal position in regard to mankind could be accurately defined. Poetry is out of place when mystery disappears, and the deeper religious motives are for the time banished from the world. Our imaginations may be awed when we look at the mountains, from a purely scientific point of view, as monuments of the slow working of stupendous forces of nature through countless millenniums. But when we know precisely, by a metaphysical demonstration, that they were made as very large "girders," they are not much more impressive than the roof

of a railway station. The modes of operation which are within the grasp of the metaphysician's intellect are measured by the scale of his own mind; and an omnipotent Blackmore is only a very strong Blackmore after all. The taste of the generation to which he belonged, though it had many advantages as compared with our anarchical state of sentiment, was certainly not favourable to the emotions due to sublimity of any kind. When Pope's versification, and Vanbrugh's architecture, and Locke's philosophy—all of them admirable things in their way—were the highest ideals of mankind, it was not to be expected that Mont Blanc and the Jungfrau should be duly appreciated. They would hardly have stooped, if they could have been consulted, to the worship of such a generation. They came in with the renewed admiration for Shakespeare, for Gothic architecture, for the romantic school of art and literature, and with all that modern revolutionary spirit which we are as yet hardly in a position to criticise. I will endeavour shortly to point out in the following section the most conspicuous names connected with this great change of taste.

CHAPTER II
THE NEW SCHOOL

We may begin by enquiring at what precise period the taste for mountain scenery became a recognised and vigorous reality. The most direct testimony to this purpose is that of Chateaubriand, who may be considered as the most distinguished devil's advocate who ever protested against the canonisation of the new objects of reverence, and who had the audacity to assert categorically and unequivocally that the Alps were ugly. I would be the last to suggest that any person who maintains such heretical opinions, even at the present day, ought to be summarily stoned or burnt. It is quite possible for a scoffer at the Alps to be an excellent father of a family, an honest politician, and even to have glimmerings of good taste in other departments of the beautiful. When, however, a man utters so bold an opinion, it is worth while asking what he means. He may intend to say that he personally does not like the Alps, which is of course unanswerable; or that other people do not like them, which can only be met by a peremptory

negative; or, finally, that other people ought not to like them—that, in short, a taste for Alpine scenery, like a taste for prize-fighting or pigeon-shooting, is in some way a proof of a depraved state of the faculties. Chateaubriand is bold enough to argue that the Alps do not give pleasure, though his arguments on this head will scarcely trouble the faith of true believers; but he also says in substance, which is to us more interesting, that if you admire the Alps you must be a revolutionist and a materialist. These are ugly names, though the frequency of their use has rather diminished their terrors; but we may glance shortly at his line of argument. He tells us that the mountains do not look so big as they really are. In other words, a Frenchman on his first visit to Chamouni did not appreciate the size of the objects before him. Nothing could be more natural, and for the simple reason that mountains, like all other superlatively beautiful objects, require long and affectionate study before their charms are fully revealed. The cockney who enters the British Museum generally prefers the stuffed hippopotamus to the Elgin marbles; but that is not the fault of the Greek sculptors. Nor is there much in the argument that you cannot see a large part of the sky from a deep valley, or enjoy a sunset at Chamouni. The beauty of

42 The Playground of Europe

the celestial canopy does not depend on the number of square yards plainly visible; if a certain strip is cut off near the horizon, the balance is far more than redressed by the apparent depth of the atmosphere, and the incomparable superiority of the energetic mountain mist to its lazy lowland rival; whilst as for sunsets, nobody can be said to have seen a sunset who has not watched the last Alpine glow dying off the everlasting snow-fields. Chateaubriand's appeals to the ancients who did not care for the mountains, or to the Bible where the Mount of Olives (not, I believe, a very Alpine summit) is mentioned only as the scene of superhuman agony, need little answer. Perhaps the thunders of Sinai might be quoted against him; and one might venture to remark that a certain view from an " exceeding high mountain" must at least have been considered as highly attractive by a very good judge of human pleasures. Chateaubriand admits, in conclusion, that the Alps might do for an anchorite, and that they may form a beautiful background a long way off. "Leurs tetes charnues," he says, " leurs flancs dechames, leurs membres gigan-tesques, hideux quand on les contemple de trop pres, sont admirables lorsqu'au fond d'un horizon vapoureux ils s'arrondissent et se colorent dans une lumiere fluide et doree." And he thinks

they would be a suitable dwelling for an anchorite.

The true motive of Chateaubriand's sacrilegious onslaught on the mountains was, as I have suggested, his dislike to the supposed principles of their adorers. The passion for mountain scenery, whose strength at the time of his writing is attested by the energy of his attack, was in his eyes a symptom of that revolutionary impulse of which Rousseau was the first great exponent. Saussure invented Mont Blanc, he tells us; but Rousseau was the arch-heretic who instituted a regular and avowed worship of the Alps. It was of a piece with his other sentimentalisms and ravings against the orthodox canons, whether of art or religion. Indeed, Rousseau is accused, which at first sight seems rather hard, of a "certain materialism," for exalting the charms of mountain scenery. Pie exaggerates the influence of external nature over the spirit, and falls into raptures over stocks and stones which he should have reserved for less tangible objects of worship.

I imagine that this affiliation of our modern sentiment is substantially correct, and the fact throws some light upon the growth of the new faith. If Rousseau were tried for the crime of setting up mountains as objects of human worship, he would be convicted by any impartial jury. Ie

44 The Playground of Europe

was aided, it is true, by accomplices, none of whom was more conspicuous than Saussure; and he had a few feeble precursors, one or two of whom shall be mentioned directly. Luther was preceded in his attacks upon the ancient Church by such men as Wycliffe and Huss; many inventors had tried their hands on the steam-engine before Watt made the great step towards its perfection; older navigators, it is said, had seen the shores of America before they were reached by Columbus. No great discovery or revolt falls entirely to the share of one leader; many have caught dim glimpses of the light before the rising of the sun. But Rousseau, though partly anticipated, and though his revelation had to be completed by various supplementary prophets, may be called, without too much straining of language, the Columbus of the Alps, or the Luther of the new creed of mountain worship. He showed the promised land distinctly, if he did not himself enter into and possess it. His title may be established by examining the date at which that doctrine first became popular, and in some degree defining the change of sentiment to which it was due.

The date, in the first place, may be fixed by two or three simple facts. The dividing line may be drawn about 1760, and the Alps were fairly inaugurated (in modern phrase) as a public play-

ground by the generation of travellers which succeeded the Seven Years' War. In 1760 Saussure paid his first visit to Chamouni, and says that the route was then both dangerous and difficult; though we may add, with some patriotic pride, that Pocock and Wyndham, the earliest forerunners of the great herd of British tourists, had penetrated so far as early as 1741. In 1761 Saussure offered a reward for the discovery of a route to the summit of Mont Blanc, and the quarter of a century which elapsed between that time and the final accomplishment of his wishes may be regarded as the period of the first great invasion of sightseers. Gibbon tells us that in 1755 the fashion of "climbing the mountains and reviewing the glaciers" had not yet been introduced by foreign travellers. When he retired to Lausanne in 1783, fashion, he says, had "opened us on all sides to the incursions of travellers." We may fix the same period by comparing two sturdy commonplace authors of that class which Mr. Carlyle emphatically describes as "wooden." They cannot be suspected of the least gleam of originality, and are therefore well qualified to be witnesses to the ordinary state of mind of their gen e rati on.

Gruner, whose book, first published in 1760, was for some time a standard authority, represents

the last phase of the old period. He talks freely of the "horrors and beauties" of the Alps, but we can easily see how the terms ought to be distributed. He stands, for example, on theGrimsel, where the traveller looks down upon fertile valleys, and upwards to the wild ranges of Ober-land. The Haslithal and the Valais excite Gruner's unaffected admiration; but the masses of ice and snow to east and west make him openly shudder. The bravest chamois-hunters and crystal-finders will scarcely venture into the terrible valley of the Ober-aar glacier; the region which stretches to its foot is a terrible desert; the mountain ranges lead to a desert, terrible in itself, and inspire fear and horror. "Horror," in short, is always on his lips, though a dash of curiosity, not quite unmixed with admiration, begins to penetrate at intervals. Sixteen years later we find the good solid orthodox British parson admirably represented by Archdeacon Coxe. He was of the type of those appalling members of Parliament who now employ their vacation in amassing materials for blue-books. He differs from his pleasure-seeking successors, by condescending to take an interest in the political institutions of the country; but he has an eye, such as it is, for scenery. He graciously approves the sights provided for him in a respectable though a

foreign region, and is sufficiently candid to prefer the Linththal to Matlock. The Rigi seems to have been still a mere "phenomenon of nature" in a geological point of view; but our other old friends, such as the Rhone glacier, the Handeck, and the Reichenbach Falls, are already established objects of interest. From Lauterbrunnen he "contemplates with rapture" and astonishment part of the great central chain "of the Alps." He even reaches the couvercle on the Mer de Glace, and admires, though he does not visit, the Jar din. He is a little disappointed by the glaciers after the "turgid accounts" which he had heard and read; but finally gives them his distinct approval. Nay, he records the first ascent of the Titlis; and I regret to add, for the credit of Alpine travellers, that the first climber of that charming mountain not only asserted (what seems to have been a common opinion) that it was second in height amongst Alpine peaks, but declared that an amazing valley of ice stretched from its foot "almost to Mont Blanc." When I add that Coxe prints a panorama of the Lake of Thun from the summit of the Niesen, it will be abundantly clear that the career of the modern tourist was fully open about a century ago.

We may say, then, that before the turning-point of the eighteenth century a civilised being

might, if he pleased, regard the Alps with unmitigated horror. After it, even a solid archdeacon, with a firm belief in the British constitution, and Church and State, was compelled to admire, under penalty of general reprobation. It required as much originality to dislike as it had previously required to admire. If we ask by what avenues the beauty of the Alps succeeded in first revealing itself to an unpoetical generation, we shall find two or three leading trains of sentiment wdrich gradually became popular. Rousseau, whose Nouvelle Heloise was first published in 1759, must, as I have said, be considered as the main exponent of the rising sentiment. I have already quoted him as exhibiting a certain indifference to our present objects of admiration. Yet in one sense he is susceptible to the mountain influences; he is in the right frame of mind for a devout worship of the Alps, though the idol has not yet been distinctly revealed to him. The sentiment is diffused throughout the pages of the Nouvelle Heloise, which is ready to crystallise into more definite form so soon as the object is distinctly presented. If he had lived a generation or two later he might have anticipated much of Mr. Ruskin's eloquence. As it is, the absence of distinct reference to the high Alps in one so naturally predisposed to admire them is as signif-

icant of the general indifference of his contemporaries as the predisposition itself is significant of the approaching change. We are in the early dawn, before the diffused light has been concentrated round a definite centre. It follows that Rousseau's sentiments must be gathered rather from the general tone of his writings than from any definite passages. In the Confessions, indeed, there is an explicit avowal of his hatred for the plains, and his love of torrents, rocks, pines, black woods, rough paths to climb and to descend, and precipices to cause a delicious terror; and he describes two amusements so characteristic of the genuine mountaineer that we feel at once that he is in the right track. One is gazing for hours over a parapet at the foam-spotted waters of a torrent, and listening to the cry of the ravens and birds of prey that wheel from rock to rock a hundred fathoms beneath him. The other is a sport whose charms are as unspeakable as they are difficult of analysis. It is fully described somewhere (if I remember rightly) by Sir Walter Scott, and consists in rolling big stones down a cliff to dash themselves to pieces at its foot. No one who cannot contentedly spend hours in that fascinating though simple sport really loves a mountain. The leading passage, however, which was most frequently quoted, and was probably

So The Playground of Europe

in Chateaubriand's mind, occurs in the Nouvelle Heloise, where the lover retires to the Valais and speculates with his usual flow of language upon the causes of his sensations. He finds himself happier than is quite becoming at such a distance from Julie. He attributes this undeniable happiness for a time to the wonderful spectacles before him. However, when it lasts over another night and the following day, he finds a better explanation. Climbing the highest mountain near him, and sitting down with the thunder and storm at his feet, he traces the true cause of his exhilaration to the state of the atmosphere. The pleasure conferred by mountains is resolved into the favourable influence produced upon the digestion, and the tendency to promote insensible perspiration. It must be admitted that this has a rather materialist sound, and tends to justify the accusation above quoted from Chateaubriand. It is, indeed, characteristic of Rousseau to join his most high-flown sentiments with very materialist explanations. Let him throw the first stone who has never felt his taste for scenery affected by the state of his digestion, and whose love of the beautiful is not in some degree measured by the variations of the barometer. We cannot honestly omit from our catalogue of the charms of Alpine scenery the influences whose immediate action is upon the lungs and the stomach.

It matters, however, far less how a great writer accounts for his feelings than how he feels. Rousseau is disappointing when he takes to philosophy; but his sentiment, though often disgusting to modern readers and intolerably long-winded in its expression, was the cause of his extraordinary power over the age. The mode in which, as I imagine, he really taught men to love the mountains was by expressing with unequalled eloquence that eighteenth-century doctrine which has become so faded and old-fashioned for us. The denunciations of luxury, the preference of a savage to a civilised life, and all those paradoxes which our grandfathers discussed so seriously, and which we have agreed to ridicule, though perhaps they had a very real meaning in them, naturally combined themselves with a rather extravagant craving for wild as compared with cultivated scenery; and with a professed admiration, which was not quite insincere, for the simple pastoral life of primitive populations. The love of the mountains came in with the rights of man and the victory of the philosophers; and all the praise of Alpine scenery is curiously connected with praise of the unsophisticated peasant. It seems as if the philosophers fancied that they had found a fragment of the genuine Arcadia still preserved by the Alpine barrier against the encroachments of a corrupt civilisation, and the mountains came in for some of the admiration lavished upon the social forms which they protected. Thus, for example, we may take a poem, which in its day had a certain celebrity, composed by Haller the distinguished physiologist, and published in 1728. It was pronounced to be as sublime, and to bid fair to be as immortal, as the Alps themselves. It contains some descriptions which imply a lively interest in the higher ranges, and an intimate knowledge of their phenomena. There is a striking picture of an Alpine sunrise, and a description of the Staubbach. A wanderer, he exclaims,

Ein Wand'rer sieht erstaunt im Himmel Strome
fliessen, Die aus den Wolken zieh'n und sich in Wolken
giessen;

a bold couplet in defence of which he thinks it necessary to adduce, in a note, the testimony of a native who lived near the then unfrequented wilderness of Lauterbrunnen. The moral, however, which Haller has most at heart is that which fills so large a space in the contemporary literature. The absence of luxury, and the charms of a simple life, are the main theme of his song. In the quiet Alpine valleys, he tells us with great emphasis, there is no learning, but plenty of common sense; there is hard work, but security and comfort; the drink is pure water, and the richest dishes are made of milk. Ambition and the thirst for gold have not corrupted the Arcadian simplicity of the natives, or introduced social inequalities. Every season of the year brings its appropriate labours and its simple pleasures;

there is wrestling and putting of weights and dancing on holidays; marriage is honoured, and the heart always follows the hand. In short, the mountains had still kept that much-abused Luxury at bay; and there, if anywhere, might be found some traces of that state of nature so ardently desired by theorists and poets. The same sentiment, caught up and repeated in various forms, supplies much of the ordinary rhetoric about the Alps for many years to come. Goldsmith expresses it in the graceful verses of The Traveller, when he turns from the Italian plains to survey the country

> Where rougher climes a nobler race display,
> Where the bleak Swiss their stormy mansions spread,
> And force a churlish soil for scanty bread.

Rousseau, though the great teacher, had no monopoly of the doctrine. To us it sounds a very faded and dreary commonplace; partly

54 The Playground of Europe

because our whole point of view on such topics has considerably changed; and partly, it must be said because Switzerland is about the last place to which the hater of luxury would now resort. The Swiss soil in these days is only churlish and bleak enough to give additional zest to the hotels of Chamouni and Interlaken; and the sturdy peasant who then saw

> No costly lord the sumptuous banquet deal To make him loathe his vegetable meal,

has become very well accustomed to that spectacle, and regards the said lord as his most reliable source of Trinkgelder and other pecuniary advantages. Yet the sentiment, though in a somewhat altered form, is by no means extinct. In one sense it is perhaps more lively than ever. If the Swiss have lost something, it may be too much, of their churlishness, the mountains themselves are fortunately impregnable citadels of natural wildness. We may turn with greater eagerness than ever from the increasing crowds of respectable human beings to savage rock and glacier, and the uncontaminated air of the High Alps. Nor, to say the truth, is the charm of the Alpine life really so extinct as cockney travellers would persuade us. There are innumerable valleys which have not yet bowed the knee to Baal, in the shape

of Mr. Cook and his tourists; and within a few hours of one of the most frequented routes in Europe there are retired valleys where Swiss peasants--I mention a fact—will refuse money in exchange for their hospitality. It may be remarked too, in passing, that most describers of scenery seem to dwell too little upon what may be called the more human side of the pleasures of scenery. The snows of Mont Blanc and the cliffs of the Matterhorn would have their charm in the midst of a wilderness; but their beauty is amazingly increased when a weather-stained chalet rises in the foreground; when the sound of cowbells comes down through the thin air; or the little troop of goats returns at sunset to the quiet village. I say nothing of that state of society which has rendered possible the Ammergau mystery ; because, to say the truth, I fear we must have seen nearly the last of it, and am always expecting to hear of a performance taking place at the Crystal Palace. If the mountains could be swept clear of all life which has been growing up amongst them for centuries, and which harmonise them as the lichens mellow the scarred masses of fallen rock, they would be deprived of half their charm. The snowy ranges of California or the more than Alpine heights of the Caucasus may doubtless be beautiful, but to my imagination at

least they seem to be unpleasantly bare and chill, because they are deprived of all those intricate associations which somehow warm the bleak ranges of Switzerland. The early forms of this sentiment gave to the Alps a certain moral value. They were the natural retreat of men disgusted with the existing order of things, profoundly convinced of its rottenness; and turning sometimes in a sufficiently morbid and sentimental frame of mind to the nearest regions which were still unspoilt or unimproved by the aggressive forces of civilisation. If virtue consisted in spinning your own cloth from your own sheep, and confining your diet to black bread and milk, it was to be found in the Alpine valleys. If the sight of towns and palaces, and the "abodes of luxury" generally, was suggestive of nothing but vice and oppression, Paradise might be judiciously sought after amongst the "longues aretes de rochers, les crevasses, les trous, les entor-tillements des vallees des Alpes," for which Chateaubriand expressed his sincere disgust.

This, at any rate, is reckoned amongst the charms of the mountains by another writer of whom something must be said by every one who touches, however lightly, on the subject. Saussure deserves the unfeigned reverence of every true mountaineer. Saussure, indeed, was primarily a man of science; but he was one of the long series of Alpine travellers who have illustrated by example the mode in which the data supplied by science may be turned to account for poetical purposes. Readers of Forbes or Tyndall will not require to be told how the accurate observation of Alpine phenomena, and the patient interpretation of the natural monuments, supplies the mountains with a new language as imposing and sublime as that which is spoken by the ruins of human workmanship. The Pyramids or the broken arches of a Roman amphitheatre are not more impressive to the rightly prepared understanding than the vast obelisks and towers that have been raised and carved and modelled by mysterious forces throughout ages of indefinable antiquity. I have sometimes doubted the justice of Wordsworth's denunciation of the gentleman who would peep and botanise upon his mother's grave. There are obvious objections to the process; but, after all, would not a botanist of any sensibility be more deeply affected by the flowers whose forms he had studied, and whose beauty he had learnt to appreciate, than the ordinary observer who has no special associations with the objects confounded together under the general name of weeds? At any rate, the inquirers who have peeped and botanised under the shadow of Mont

Blanc have proved that their habits had no tendency to deaden their love of nature. Though Saussure seldom indulges in passages of set eloquence, his appreciation of mountain scenery is always breaking through the drier details of scientific pursuits. Two well-known passages record his delight in the calm summer evenings spent during his stay of sixteen days (a feat almost unrivalled) on the summit of the Col du Geant; and mention as the happiest hours of his life those which he spent on the top of the Cramont in contemplation of the southern precipices of Mont Blanc. In the preface to his collected journeys Saussure tries to explain the secret of his pleasure. From his youth, he tells us, he had loved the mountains, and by the age of eighteen had climbed all the hills round Geneva. He afterwards visited the mountain districts of England, France, Germany, and Italy. For years he was prowling round the base of Mont Blanc, till at length he followed Balmat to the summit. The traveller, he says, who has surmounted the labour of an ascent (for Saussure had not quite risen to the purely athletic pleasure) will be overwhelmed for a time with astonishment. Then he will think with wondering awe of the long series of slow changes which have built up the dome of Etna, or raised the primeval ridges of the central

Alps. He will feel the pettiness of man in presence of those tremendous forces to whose action the mountains bear unmistakable testimony. All the natural phenomena, clouds and floods and storms and avalanches, have an intensity of which the lowlander can form no conception. And, finally, he adds, the mountains have a moral interest; the Alpine peasant is far nobler and more independent than his relation in the plains; and he who has only seen the labourer in the neighbourhood of towns knows nothing of the true "man of nature."

Saussure in this passage gives a condensed summary of the great poem of the Alps. They had been preaching in vain to many generations which were obstinately deaf, or had at best caught some faint glimpses of their meaning. The time had come for their voice to fall upon congenial ears. On one hand, they might be regarded as huge inarticulate Sphinxes suggesting problems as to the growth of the world, the barest statement of which affected the scientific imagination with a sense of overpowering sublimit)'. On the other, they served to offer an asylum to dreamers like Rousseau who have tried, sometimes in very inarticulate language, to tell us why the atmosphere of the mountains is soothing to minds out of harmony with the existing

social order. The feeling, which cannot perhaps be very well reduced into logical formula, may be pretty well expressed in a passage from Mr. Matthew Arnold's friend Obermann. In the lowlands, he says, the natural man is corrupted in breathing a social atmosphere made turbid by the sound of the arts, of our noisy ostentatious pleasures, by our cries of hatred, and moans of grief and anxiety.

Mais la, sur ces monts deserts oule eiel est immense, ou l'air est plus fixe, et les temps moins rapides, et la vie plus permanente; la, nature entiere exprime elo-quemment un ordre plus grand, une harmonie plus visible, un ensemble eternel. La, l'homme retrouve sa forme alterable mais indestructible; il respire l'air sauvage loin des emanations sociales; son etre est a, lui comme a l'univers; il vit d'une vie reelle dans l'unite sublime.

If this cannot be reckoned precisely as a philosophical statement of truth, it is a poetical expression of the sentiment more or less dimly present to the minds of all mountain-lovers. It is Rousseau's doctrine in a more spiritual form.

I will turn for a few minutes to another vein of sentiment, which was worked otit by a different school of observers. Even in the depth of the much-vilified eighteenth century there were traces of the tastes which in England first found distinct

utterance in Sir Walter Scott's poetry, and have led to various strange developments in later years. There was even then something which went by the name of the romantic; and which was to our present sentiment what carpenters' Gothic was to our elaborate revivals of mediaeval art.

The correct remark to make about a bit of rough scenery, if it was not too obtrusive or too actively dangerous, was that it reminded \'7d t ou of Salvator Rosa. Every now and then it might be admitted into descriptions, though sparingly and as it were under protest; as a tame rock or so, a bit of grotesque ruin, or a miniature waterfall, might be permitted in a formal garden. There was indeed little trace of that close observation of nature which we now consider to be essential; but the picturesque element could not be altogether excluded. Here, for example, is a bit of what is now called "word-painting" from Shaftes-bu ry' s C*ha ra cterist ics:

Beneath the mountain's feet [he says], the rocky country rises into hills, a proper basis of the ponderous mass above; where huge embodied rocks lie piled on one another, and seem to prop the high arch of heaven. See with what trembling steps poor mankind tread the narrow brink of the deep precipices! From whence with giddy horror they look down, mistrusting even tin; ground that bears them; whilst they hear the hollow sound of torrents under-

neath, and sec the ruin of the impending rock with falling trees which hang with their roots upward and seem to draw more ruin after them.

This is not really a description of a mountain, but of a rather big landslip. A touch or two of similar feeling ought to be discoverable in the letters of Lady Mary Wortley Montagu, who passed some years at Lovere, on the Lago d'Iseo, and deserves some credit for the remark that it is a place "the most beautifully romantic I ever saw in my life." The enthusiasm rather loses its effect when we find her discovering a close resemblance between Lovere and Tunbridge Wells, and afterwards comparing the gardens to those on Richmond Hill. We come to more distinct indications of the modem tendencies in the following generation. Horace Walpole anticipated the taste of later times in this as in many other ways. Walpole had ventured to declare explicitly that Gothic architecture was at once "magnificent and genteel"; and we might expect that he would bestow equally judicious praise upon the grander effects of Alpine scenery. The following-passage, written in 1739, may show that a fine gentleman of the rising generation could even then manufacture a very fair imitation of modern raptures. "But the road, West, the road!" he exclaims, on his way to the Grande Chartreuse,

winding round a prodigious mountain and surrounded with others, all shagged with hanging woods, obscured with pines and lost in clouds! Below, a torrent breaking through cliffs, and tumbling through fragments of rocks! Sheets of cascade forcing their silver speed, and hasting into the roughened river at the bottom! Now and then an old foot-bridge, with a broken rail, a leaning cross, a cottage, or the ruins of a hermitage! This sounds too bombast and romantic for one that has not seen it, too cold for one that has. If I could send you my letter post between two lovely tempests that echoed each other's wrath, you might have some idea of this noble roaring scene, as you were reading it.

This is at least equal to the modern guide-book. Walpole's friend Conway, a year or two later, declares that the Rhine shows the "most rude romantic scenery, the most Salvator Rosa you ever saw." And Gray wrote a Latin ode at the Chartreuse, which later travellers frequently quote as sublime, about the "niveas rupes" and "fera juga,"

Clivosque pracruptos, sonantes Inter aquas, nemorumque noctem.

Gray, indeed, has had the credit, on the strength of his letters from the Lakes in 1769, of having set the fashion of mountaineering. The claim is clearly untenable; but, to do him justice, I may quote one aspiration for which we may give him due credit. Speaking of a young Swiss traveller, he says, "I

64 The Playground of Europe

have a partiality for him because he was burn amongst mountains, and talks of them with enthusiasm; of the forests of pines which grow darker and darker as you ascend, till the nemorum nox is completed and you are forced to grope your way; of the cries of eagles and other birds of prey adding to the horror; in short, of all the wonders of his country which disturb my slumbers in Lovingland." The traveller, he adds, must stay a month at Zurich to learn German, "and the mountains must be traversed on foot, avec des grimpons aux mains and shoes of a peculiar construction. I 'd give my ears to try!" Perhaps it is as well that he did not try with "grimpons" on his hands; but Gray may have the credit of at least aspiring to become a genuine tourist at a period when the journey involved such serious preparations.

In Walpole's ecstasies there is, it may be, something of an artificial ring. We feel that he would have been capable of erecting a sham mountain at Strawberry Hill, or manufacturing a toy cascade, and thinking his playthings pretty nearly as good as the originals. Some men, who might perhaps have shown a deeper feeling, were incapacitated by the simple want of opportunity. There is a melancholy passage in Cowper's Task where lie describes the view from an "eminence" in

the neighbourhood of Olney. Nobody can doubt that Cowper was the very man to love mountain scenery; but what is a poor poet to do with such mountains as rise on the banks of the Ouse? A commentator informs us that the view from this, the nearest approach to the Alps in that district, was "bounded on the north by a lofty quickset hedge." The imagination that would not be cramped by a quickset hedge would be capable of raising the Serpentine to the dignity of the

Atlantic, or painting Niagara from Tedding-ton Weir. Amongst the earlier poets of the century there is at least one who had the benefit of nobler models. It is proper, I hold, to admire Thomson's Seasons, and there is a certain number of persons who are capable of working admiringly through many hundred lines of descriptive blank verse. Even Wordsworth admits that Thomson was a genuine observer of nature, though of course he takes care to add that he was admired rather for his faults than for his beauties. Now Thomson knew the Scotch hills; or, to use his own dialect, his Muse had seen

Caledonia in romantic view, Her airy mountains from the waving main Invested with a keen diffusive sky, Breathing the soul acute; her forests huge, Incult, robust, and tall, by nature's hand s

Planted of old; her azure lakes between, Poured out extensive and of watery wealth Full; winding deep and green her fertile vales.

And so on; which, if not very exalted poetry, bears at least some traces of first-hand touches from the land of lochs and moors. These and other verses deserve more credit when we remember that they were written just at the same time when Captain Burt (quoted by Lord Macaulay as a specimen of the contemporary taste) was declaring his decided preference of Richmond Hill to the Grampians. Moreover Thomson had to struggle against a disqualification only less serious than that of the general indifference of the time. He was, we know, "more fat than bard beseems," and, many as are the virtues which naturally fall to the lot of the fat, a true appreciation of mountain scenery can hardly be reckoned among them. When a man's circumference bears more than a certain ratio to his altitude, he prefers the plains in the bottom of his soul. Such admiration, therefore, as Thomson could express is doubly valuable. I will venture to quote one more passage as a fair specimen, which may be put alongside of Byron's often quoted thunderstorm, where

Jura answers from her misty shroud
Back to the laughing Alps that call to her aloud.
Thomson's version is as follows:
Amidst Carnarvon's mountains rages loud The repercussive roar; with mighty crash Into the flashing deep from the huge rocks Of Penmaenmawr heaped hideous to the sky, Tumble the smitten cliffs, and Snowdon's peak Dissolving, instant yields his wintry load; Far-seen the heights of heathy Cheviot blaze, And Thule bellows through her utmost isles.

These, if I mistake not, are good sonorous lines; though the expressions savour rather strongly of the gigantesque; and the storm is made to roar a little too much in "Ercles' vein." The mountains are, so to speak, still in the background. The poetry may remind us of an honest citizen of Berne who had been in the habit of consuming his evening pipe on the terrace above the Aar. He sees huge forms in the distance, almost beautiful when lighted by the setting sun, but more often looming in vague sublimity through a distinct haze, and gathering storms about their mysterious summits. He never thinks of approaching more closely, and holds that

The pikes, of darkness named and fear and storms,
well deserve their titles. Thomson could admire his native hills, but he liked them best a long way off, and could meditate most cheerfully on the frosty Caucasus when it warmed his imagination by a comfortable fireside. His mountains are

always vague, gloomy, and distant; and his wanderings do not stretch beyond the cultivated regions at their feet. It is a melancholy fact, too, that in one description he makes the summit of a certain hypothetical mountain in Abyssinia "stretch for many a league."

The growth of the modern spirit might probably be further illustrated from Ossian—if it were now possible for any human being raised south of the Tweed to read more than a page or two of that strange twaddle whose amazing popularity throughout Europe is a curious puzzle to our generation. Wordsworth labours to prove, what seems to be sufficiently palpable, that his mountains are wretched daubs, and utterly unsatisfactory to any original observer. Still a taste for daubs may be the precursor of an appreciation of more genuine portraits. Certainly there is something significant in the amazing appetite of men in that generation for trash which the humblest stomach now rejects with indignation. Even Goethe, for example, condescends to illustrate some remarks about the scenery at Scharlhausen by a reference to MacPherson's bombast. Of Goethe's original remarks on the same subject it would be impertinent to offer any specimens. It is enough to say that he has made some philosophical remarks on the beauties of Alpine seen-

ery in his letters from Switzerland, and that his enthusiasm about the " wunderschones Wallisthal" and the appalling dangers of the Furka rather outruns the zeal of the present generation. It would be equally absurd to quote passages from the great English poets of the beginning of this century and to prove that Scott, Wordsworth, Shelley, and Byron loved the mountains and expounded their teaching with a power which has met with no rivalry. We are in broad daylight, and have no need to remark that the sun is shining. I need only remark how much their poetry is affected, not only by mountain beauty in general, but by the special districts which were most congenial to them.

The Lake mountains discourse very excellent music, and sometimes in favourable moments can rise to the sublimity of the great ode on the Intimations of Immortality, or the song at the feast of Brougham Castle. But it must be confessed that they are a little too much infested by the "sleep that is among the lonely hills," and can even at times drop into the flat prose which fills certain pages of the Excursion. We can understand how a poet brought up at their feet should labour under a permanent confusion of ideas between Providence and the late Duke of Wellington—a delusion which would have been

70 The Playground of Europe

scarcely conceivable amongst the great central ridges which have shaped a continent and fashioned the history of the world. Scott, too, might have been stimulated to a loftier strain by the tonic of a few good glaciers and avalanches in place of his dumpy heather-clad hills.

Coleridge, Byron, and Shelley have each sung hymns, after their fashion, to Mont Blanc. Coleridge makes the monarch of mountains preach a very excellent sermon, though I fear it is a plagiarism. There are some good touches, as in the lines

Around thee and above Deep is the air and dark, substantially black, An ebon mass; methinks thou picrcest it As with a wedge:

but we feel him to be more at home in the fantastic and gloomy scenery of Kubla Khan or the magical icebergs of the Ancient Mariner. The mountain air is not congenial to opium-eating. Byron's mountains treat us to some fine vigorous poetry, and have filled popular guide-books with appropriate quotations, but they are just a little too anxious to express their contempt for mankind. To my taste, though I speak with diffidence, Shelley's poetry is in the most complete harmony with the scenery of the higher Alps; and I think it highly creditable to the mountains that they

should agree so admirably with the most poetical of poets. He tells us that his familiarity with such scenery was one of his qualifications. "I have been familiar," he says, "from boyhood with mountains and lakes and the sea and the solitude of forests; danger which sports upon the brink of precipices has been my playmate; I have trodden the glaciers of the Alps and lived under the eye of Mont Blanc." Besides the lines written in the Vale of Chamouni, his exquisite sense for the ethereal beauty of the high mountains pervades his whole poetry. There is something essentially congenial to his imagination in the thin atmosphere of the upper regions, with its delicate hues and absence of tangible human interest. He loves the clouds, and watches them folding and sunning, lighted up by the "sanguine sunrise with his meteor eyes," or gathered into solid masses, hanging "sunbeam proof, over a torrent sea," with unflagging enthusiasm. Now the special glory of mountain scenery, as Goethe has told us, is that the clouds do not there present themselves as flat carpets spread over the sky, but enable us to watch them as they form and disperse, and roll up the sides of the gigantic peaks. All through the Prometheus Unbound we feel ourselves to be really looking out from the top of some "eagle-baffling" peak, not yet vulgarised

by associations with guides and picnics. We are where

The keen sky-cleaving mountains From icy spires of sunlike radiance fling The dawn, as lifted Ocean's dazzling spray, From some Atlantic islet scattered up, Spangles the wind with lamplike waterdrops.

And can hear

the rushing snow, The sun-awakened avalanche—whose mass Thrice sifted by the storm had gathered here, Flake after flake, in heaven-defying minds As thought by thought is piled, till some great

truth Is loosened, and the nations echo round, Shaken to their roots, as do the mountains now.

Coleridge's mountains of course adduce excellent arguments in favour of theism; Byron's indulge in a few sneers at the insignificance of mankind; and Shelley's have "a voice to repeal large codes of fraud and woe, not understood by all," and, it is to be feared, not very clearly by the poet himself. But all of them are genuine mountains, so to speak, of flesh and blood, not mere theatrical properties constructed at second-hand from old poetical commonplaces. It is curious from this point of view to compare them with the mountains of another great poet, which were unluckily constructed according to his natural method, out

of his own self-consciousness, or, rather, by the more really characteristic method of indefatigable cram. Schiller endeavours to give the local colour to William Tell by dint of inserting little bits of guide-book information about Switzerland. But Schiller had never seen the Alps, and, in spite of certain criticisms in the true conventional spirit, I venture to assert that the fact is evident to every reader who in that respect has the advantage over him. He is aware, indeed, that certain forests maintained for protection against avalanches are called Bannwald, that there is a thing called a Staublawine, that hay-cutting is a dangerous trade, that chamois-hunters do (or do not) cut their feet to glue themselves to the rocks with their blood, and so on. Some of his elaborate cram is brought in by the rather clumsy device of making an Alpine peasant give information to his sons about matters which are as familiar to them as the nature of an omnibus to a young cockney; but that is a pardonable error in a playwright. Neither can I complain that an innocent reader would probably infer, from Schiller's account, that one of the most dangerous feats in vSwiss travelling is to cross the Lake of Lucerne in a very big barge, for that is naturally suggested by the incident in Tell's story. But I confess that I am rather amazed by the story

74 The Playground of Europe

of the gallant Arnold von Melchthal, who recounts his tremendous adventures to the conspirators at the Rutli. He made, it seems, an expedition

Durch der Surennen furchtbares Gebirg,

and there he is driven to the direst expedients. He has actually to drink glacier-water, and to sleep in abandoned chalets. If a chamois-hunter should endeavour to excite the compassion of his comrades by the recital of such expedients, I very much fear that he would be strongly advised to abandon his profession. Glacier-water used to be considered as a remedy for many diseases, and though the popular superstition is now in the opposite direction, any traveller, poet or peasant, is too glad to have an occasional draught. Sleeping in a deserted chalet is the height of luxury, unless we must suppose that the brave conspirator was daunted at the thought of fleas. The passage strikes us rather as if a man who had never seen the ocean should represent Columbus as deterred from crossing the Atlantic chiefly by the thought of seasickness. That William Tell is an admirable play in other respects may be undeniable; but I confess it appears to me to be a practical warning that the genuine local colouring cannot be extracted from books; and that, in short,

even a poet had better see a place before he attempts to describe it.

I will not undertake to sum up the conclusions which might be drawn from these rather desultory-remarks. My readers-—for I may assume that my readers are mountain-lovers—will agree that the love of mountains is intimately connected with all that is noblest in human nature. If no formal demonstration of that truth be possible our faith in it will be not the less firm, and all the more meritorious. The true faith in these matters is not indeed a bigoted or exclusive creed. I love everything in the shape of a mountain, from Mont Blanc down to Hampstead Hill; but I also have some regard for the Fen Country and the flats of Holland. Mountain scenery is the antithesis not so much of the plains as of the commonplace. Its charm lies in its vigorous originality; and if political philosophers speak the truth, which I admit to be an exceedingly doubtful proposition, the great danger of modern times consists in our loss of that quality. One man, so it is said, grows more like another; national costumes die out before monotonous black hats and coats; we all read the same newspapers, talk the same twaddle, are bound by the same laws of propriety, and are submitting to a uniform imposition of dull respectability. Some day, it is supposed, we

shall all bo under the orders of a Prussian drill-sergeant; and, as M. Michelet declares in his book on the mountains, la vulgar ite prevaudra. I do not enter upon these wide social questions beyond expressing, by way of parenthesis, a general disbelief in all human predictions; but I confess that, especially as regards scenery, there is something to be said for such melancholy forebodings. Lord Macaulay, for example, announces with extreme satisfaction the advent of a happy day, when cultivation will spread to the top of Helvellyn, and England, we must suppose, will be one gigantic ploughed field, with occasional patches of coal-smoke. Still more appalling is the prospect revealed to us by some American patriots. Their statistical prophecies about the Mississippi valley have given me occasional nightmares. Conceive of a gigantic chess-board many hundreds of miles in length and breadth, with each square so like its neighbours that any two might be changed in the night without its inhabitants detecting the difference; suppose each square to be inhabited by several millions of human beings as like as the denizens of an ant-hill; all of them highly educated persons, brought up under school boards and public meetings and church organisations, with no political or social grievances; and, in short, as somebody calls them, intelligent and God-fearing citizens.

The imagination fairly recoils from the prospect in horror. We long to believe that some earthquake may throw up a few mountain-ranges and partition off the country, so as to give its wretched inhabitants a chance of developing a few distinctive peculiarities. Yet everywhere the same phenomenon is being repeated on a smaller scale. Life, we shall soon be saying, would be tolerable if it were not for our fellow-creatures. They come about us like bees, and as we cannot well destroy them, we are driven to fly to some safe asylum. The Alps, as yet, remain. They are places of refuge where we may escape from ourselves and from our neighbours. There we can breathe air that has not passed through a million pair of lungs; and drink water in which the acutest philosophers cannot discover the germs of indescribable diseases. There the blessed fields are in no danger of being "huzzed and mazed with the devil's own team." Those detestable parallelograms, which cut up English scenery with their monotonous hedgerows, are sternly confined to the valley. The rocks and the glaciers have a character of their own, and are not undergoing the wearisome process of civilisation. They look down upon us as they looked down upon Hannibal, and despise our wretched burrowings at their base. Human society has been adapted to the scenery, and has

not forced the scenery to wear its livery. It is true, and it is sad, that the mountains themselves are coming down; day by day the stones are rattling in multitudes from the flanks of the mighty cliffs; and even the glaciers, it would seem, are retreating sulkily into the deeper fastnesses of the high valleys. And yet we may safely say, as we can say of little else, that the Alps will last our time. They have seen out a good many generations, and poets yet unborn will try to find something new to say in their honour. Meanwhile it should be——I can hardly say it is——the purpose of the following pages to prove that whilst all good and wise men necessarily love the mountains, those love them best who have wandered longest in their recesses, and have most endangered their own lives and those of their guides in the attempt to open out routes amongst them.

CHAPTER III

ASCENT OF THE SCHRECKHORN

Most people, I imagine, have occasionally sympathised with the presumptuous gentleman who wished that he had been consulted at the creation of the world. It is painfully easy for a dweller in Bedfordshire or the Great Sahara to suggest material improvements in the form of the earth's surface. There are, however, two or three districts in which the architecture of nature displays so marvellous a fertility of design, and such exquisite powers of grouping the various elements of beauty, that the builders of the Parthenon or of the noblest Gothic cathedrals could scarcely have altered them for the better. Faults may of course be found with many of the details: a landscape gardener would throw in a lake here, there he would substitute a precipice for a gentle incline, and elsewhere he would crown a mountain by a more aspiring summit, or base it on a more imposing mass. Still I will venture to maintain that there arc districts where it is captious to find fault; and foremost amongst them I should

place the three best-known glacier systems of the Alps. Each of them is distinguished by characteristic beauties. The mighty dome of Mont Blanc, soaring high above the ranges of aiguilles, much as St. Paul's rises above the spires of the City churches, is perhaps the noblest of single mountain masses. The intricate labyrinths of ice and snow that spread westwards from the Monte Rosa, amongst the high peaks of the Pennine range, are worthy of their central monument, the unrivalled obelisk of the Matterhorn. But neither Chamouni nor Zermatt, in my opinion, is equal in grandeur and originality of design to the Bernese Oberland. No earthly object that I have seen approaches in grandeur to the stupendous mountain wall whose battlements overhang in mid-air the villages of Lauterbrunnen and Grindelwald; the lower hills that rise beneath it, like the long Atlantic rollers beaten back from the granite cliffs on our western coast, are a most effective contrast to its stern magnificence; in the whole Alps there is no ice-stream to be compared to the noble Aletsch glacier, sweeping in one majestic curve from the crest of the ridge down to the forests of the Rhone valley; no mountains, not even the aiguilles of Mont Blanc, or the Matterhorn itself, can show a more graceful outline than the Eiger—that monster, as we may fancy, in the act of bounding from

Ascent of the Schreckhorn Si

the earth; and the Wetterhom, with its huge basement of cliffs contrasted with the snowy cone that soars so lightly into the air above, seems to me to be a very masterpiece in a singularly difficult style; but indeed every one of the seven familiar summits, whose very names stand alone in the Alps for poetical significance—the Maiden, the Monk, the Ogre, the Storm Pike, the Terror Pike, and the Dark Aar Pike—would each repay the most careful study of the youthful designer. Four of these, the Jungfrau, Mdnch, Eiger, and Wetterhom, stand like watchhouses on the edge of the cliffs. The Jungfrau was the second of the higher peaks to be climbed; its summit was reached in 1828, more than forty years after Saussure's first ascent of Mont Blanc. The others, together with the Fiiisteraamorn and Aletschhorn, had fallen before the zeal of Swiss, German, and English travellers; but in 1861 the Schreckhorn, the most savage and forbidding of all in its aspect, still frowned defiance upon all comers.

The Schreckhorner form a ridge of rock\'7d' peaks, forking into two ridges about its centre, the ground-plan of which may thus be compared to the letter Y. The foot of this Y represents the northern extremity, and is formed by the massive Mettenberg, whose broad faces of cliff divide the two glaciers at Grindehvald. Ilalf-wav along the

82 The Playground of Europe

stem rises the point called the Little Schreckhorn. The two chief summits rise close together at the point where the Y forks. The thicker of the two branches represents the black line of cliffs running down to the Abschwung; the thinner represents the range of the Strahlhorner, crossed by the Strahleck pass close to its origin. Mr. Anderson, in the first series of Peaks and Passes, describes an attempt to ascend the Schreckhorn, made by him under most unfavourable circumstances; one of his guides, amongst other misfortunes, being knocked down by a falling stone, whilst the whole party were nearly swept away by an avalanche. His courage, however, did not meet with the reward it fully deserved, as bad weather made it impossible for him to attempt more than the Little Schreckhorn, the summit of whch he succeeded in reaching. A more successful attack had been made by MM. Desor and Escher von der Linth, in 1842. Starting from the Strahleck, they had climbed, with considerable difficulty, to a ridge leading apparently to the summit of the Schreckhorn. After following this for some distance, they were brought to a standstill by a sudden depression some ten or twelve feet in depth, which was succeeded by a very sharp arete of snow. Whilst they were hesitating what to do, one of the guides, in spite of a warning shriek from

his companions, and without waiting for a rope, suddenly sprang down so as to alight astride of the ridge. They followed him more cautiously, and, animated to the task by a full view of the summit, forced their way slowly along a very narrow and dangerous arete. They reached the top at last triumphantly, and, looking round at the view, discovered, to their no small disgust, that to the north of them was another summit. They had indeed proved, by a trigonometrical observation, that that on which they stood was the highest; but in spite of trigonometry, the northern peak persisted in looking down on them. As it was cut off from them by a long and impracticable arete some three hundred yards (in my opinion more) in length, they could do nothing but return, and obtain another trigonometrical observation. This time the northern peak came out twenty-seven metres (about eighty-eight feet) the higher. It was, apparently, the harder piece of work. Even big Ulrich Lauener (who, I must admit, is rather given to croaking) once said to me, it was like the Matterhorn, big above and little below, and he would have nothing to do with it. In 1861, however, the prestige of the mountains was rapidly declining. Many a noble peak, which a few years before had written itself inaccessible in all guide-books, hotel registers, and poetical descriptions of the Alps, had fallen an easy victim to the skill and courage of Swiss guides, and the ambition of their employers. In spite, therefore, of the supposed difficulties, I was strongly attracted by the charms of this last unconquered stronghold of the Oberland. Was there not some infinitesimal niche in history to be occupied by its successful assailant? The Schreckhorn will probably outlast even the British Constitution and the Thirty-nine Articles: so long as it lasts, and so long as Murray and Baedeker describe its wonders for the benefit of successive generations of tourists, its first conqueror may be carried down to posterity by clinging to its skirts. If ambition whispered some such nonsense to my ear, and if I did not reply that we are all destined to immortal fame so long as parish registers and the second column of the Times survives, I hope to be not too severely blamed. I was old enough to know better, it is true; but this happened some years ago: and since then I have had time to repent of many things.

Accordingly, on the night of August 13, 1861, I found myself the occupant of a small hole under a big rock near the northern foot of the Strahleck. Owing to bad diplomacy, I was encumbered with three guides—Peter and Christian Michel, and Christian Kaufmann—all of them good men, but

one, if not two, too many. As the grey morning light gradually stole into our burrow, I woke up with a sense of lively impatience—not diminished, perhaps, by the fact that one side of me seemed to be permanently impressed with every knob in a singularly cross-grained bit of rock, and the other with every bone in Kaufmann's body. Swallowing a bit of bread, I declared myself ready. An early start is of course always desirable before a hard day's work, but it rises to be almost agreeable after a hard night's rest. This did not seem to be old Peter Michel's opinion. He is the very model of a short, thick, broad mountaineer, with the constitution of a piece of seasoned oak; a placid, not to say stolid, temper; and an illimitable appetite. He sat opposite me for some half-hour, calmly munching bread and cheese, and meat and butter, at four in the morning, on a frozen bit of turf, under a big stone, as if it were the most reasonable thing a man could do under the circumstances, and as though such things as the Schreckhorn and impatient tourists had no existence. A fortnight before, as I was told, he had calmly sat out all night, half-way up the Eiger, with a stream of freezing water trickling over him, accompanied by an unlucky German, whose feel received frost-bites on thai occasion from which they were still in danger, while old .Michel had not a chilblain.

And here let me make one remark, to save repetition in the following pages. I utterly repudiate the doctrine that Alpine travellers are or ought to be the heroes of Alpine adventures. The true way at least to describe all my Alpine ascents is that Michel or Anderegg or Lauener succeeded in performing a feat requiring skill, strength, and courage, the difficulty of which was much increased by the difficulty of taking with him his knapsack and his employer. If any passages in the succeeding pages convey the impression that I claim any credit except that of following better men than myself with decent ability, I disavow them in advance and do penance for them in my heart. Other travellers have been more independent: I speak for myself alone. Meanwhile I will only delay my narrative to denounce one other heresy —that, namely, which asserts that guides are a nuisance. Amongst the greatest of Alpine pleasures is that of learning to appreciate the capacities and cultivate the good-will of a singularly intelligent and worthy class of men. I wish that all men of the same class, in England and elsewhere, were as independent, well-informed, and trustworthy as Swiss mountaineers! And now, having discharged my conscience, I turn to my story.

At last, about half-past four, we got deliberately

under way. Our first two or three hours' work was easy enough. The two summits of the Schreckhorn form as it were the horns of a vast crescent of precipice which runs round a secondary glacier, on the eastern bank of the Grindelwald glacier. This glacier is skirted on the south by the ordinary Strahleck route. The cliffs above it are for the most part bare of snow, and scored by deep trenches or gullies, the paths of avalanches, and of the still more terrible showers of stones which, in the later part of the day, may be seen every five minutes discharged down the flank of the mountain. I was very sanguine that we should reach the arete connecting the two peaks. I felt doubtful, however, whether we could pass along it to the summit, as it might be interrupted by some of those gaps which so nearly stopped Desor's party. Old Michel indeed had declared, on a reconnoitring expedition I had made with him the day before, that he believed, "steif unci jest," that we could get up. But as we climbed the glacier my faith in Michel and Co. began to sink, not from any failing in their skill as guides, but from the enormous appetites which they Still chose to exhibit. Every driblet of water seemed to be inseparably connected in their minds with a drop of brandy, and every fiat stone suggested an open-air picnic. Perhaps my impatience rather

exaggerated their delinquencies in this direction; but it was not till past seven, when we had deposited the heavy part of our baggage and, to my delight, most of the provisions on a ledge near the foot of the rocks, that they fairly woke up, and settled to their task. From that time I had no more complaints to make. We soon got hard and steadily at work, climbing the rocks which form the southern bank of one of the deeply-carved gullies of which I have spoken. It seemed clear to me that the summit of the Schreckhorn, which was invisible to us at present, was on the other side of this ravine, its northern bank being in fact formed by a huge buttress running straight down from the peak. This buttress was cut into steps, by cliffs so steep as to be perfectly impracticable; in fact, I believe that in one place it absolutely overhung. It was therefore necessary to keep to the other side; but I felt an unpleasant suspicion that the head of the ravine might correspond with an impracticable gap in the arete.

Meanwhile we had simply a steady piece of rock-climbing. Christian Michel, a first-rate cragsman, led the way. Kaufmann followed, and, as we clung to the crannies and ledges of the rock, relieved his mind by sundry sarcasms as to the length of arm and leg which enabled me to reach points of support without putting my limbs out of

joint'—an advantage, to say the truth, which he could well afford to give away. The rocks were steep and slippery, and occasionally covered with a coat of ice. We were frequently flattened out against the rocks, like beasts of ill repute nailed to a barn, with fingers and toes inserted into four different cracks which tested the elasticity of our frames to the uttermost. Still our progress though slow was steady, and would have been agreeable if only our minds could have been at ease with regard to that detestable ravine. We could not obtain a glimpse of the final ridge, and we might be hopelessly stopped at the last step. Meanwhile, as we looked round, we could see the glacier basins gradually sinking, and the sharp pyramid of the Finstcraarhom shooting upwards above them. Gradually, too, the distant ranges of Alps climbed higher and higher up the southern horizon. From Mont Blanc to Monte Rosa, and away to the distant Bernina, ridge beyond ridge rose into the sky, with many a well-remembered old friend amongst them. In two or three hours' work we had risen high enough to look over the ridge connecting the two peaks, down the long reaches of the Aar glaciers. A few minutes afterwards we caught sight of a row of black dots creeping over the snows of the Strah-leck. With a telescope 1 could just distinguish a friend whom I had met the day before at Grindel-wald. A loud shout from us brought back a faint reply or echo. We were already high above the pass. Still, however, that last arete remained pertinaciously invisible. A few more steps, if steps is a word applicable to progression by hands as well as feet, placed us at last on the great ridge of the mountain, looking down upon the Lauteraar Sattel. But the ridge rose between us and the peak into a kind of knob, which allowed only a few yards of it to be visible. The present route, as I believe, leads to the ridge at a point farther from the summit of the mountain. We were, however, near the point where a late melancholy accident will, it is to be hoped, impress upon future travellers the necessity of a scrupulous adherence to all recognised precautions. The scene was in itself significant enough for men of weak nerves. Taking a drop of brandy all round, we turned to the assault, feeling that a few yards more would decide the question. On our right hand the long slopes of snow ran down towards the Lauteraar Sattel, as straight as if the long furrows on their surface had been drawn by a ruler. They were in a most ticklish state. The snow seemed to be piled up like loose sand, at the highest angle of rest, and almost without cohesion. The fall of a pebble or a handful of snow was sufficient to

detach a layer, which slid smoothly down the long slopes with a low ominous hiss. Clinging, however, to the rocks which formed the crest of the ridge, we dug our feet as far as possible into the older snow beneath, and crept cautiously along. As soon as there was room on the arete, we took to the rocks again, and began with breathless expectation climbing the knob of which I have spoken. The top of the mountain could not remain much longer concealed. A few yards more, and it came full in view. The next step revealed to me not only the mountain top, but a lovely and almost level ridge which connected it with our standing-point. We had won the victory, and, with a sense of intense satisfaction, attacked the short ridge which still divided us from our object. It is melancholy to observe the shockingly bad state of repair of the higher peaks, and the present was no exception to the rule. Loose stones rattled down the mountain sides at every step, and the ridge itself might be compared to the ingenious contrivance which surmounts the walls of gaols with a nicely balanced pile of loose bricks-—supposing the interstices in this case to be filled with snow. We crept, however, cautiously along the parapet, glancing down the mighty cliffs beneath us, and then, at two steps more, we proudly stepped (at 11.40) on to the little level

platform which forms the " allerhochste Spitzc" of the Sehreckhorn.

I need hardly remark that our first proceeding was to give a hearty cheer, which was faintly returned by the friends who were still watching us from the Strahleck. My next was to sit down, in the warm and perfectly calm summer air, to enjoy a pipe and the beauties of nature, whilst my guides erected a cairn of stones round a large black flag which we had brought up to confute cavillers. Mountain tops are always more or less impressive in one way-—namely, from the giddy cliffs which surround them. But the more distant prospects from them may be divided into two classes: those from the Wetterhorn, Jungfrau, or Monte Rosa, and other similar mountains, which include on one side the lowland countries, forming a contrast to the rough mountain ranges; and those from mountains standing, not on the edge, but in the very centre of the regions of frost and desolation. The Sehreckhorn (like the Fin-steraarhorn) is a grand example of this latter kind. Four great glaciers seem to radiate from its base. The great Oberland peaks—the Finsteraarhorn, Jungfrau, Monch, Eiger, and Wetterhorn—stand round in a grim circle, showing their bare faces of precipitous rock across the dreary wastes of snow. At your feet are the "urns of the silent snow,"

from which the glaciers of Grindelwald draw the supplies that enable them to descend far into the regions of cultivated land, trickling down like great damp icicles, of insignificant mass compared with these mighty reservoirs. You are in the centre of a whole district of desolation, suggesting a landscape from Greenland, or an imaginary picture of England in the glacial epoch, with shores yet unvisited by the irrepressible Gulf Stream. The charm of such views——little as they are generally appreciated by professed admirers of the picturesque——is to my taste unique, though not easily explained to unbelievers. They have a certain soothing influence like slow and stately music, or one of the strange opium dreams described by De Quincey. If his journey in the mail-coach could have led. him through an Alpine pass instead of the quiet Cumberland hills, he would have seen visions still more poetical than that of the minister in the "dream fugue."
Unable as I am to bend his bow, I can only say that there is something almost unearthly in the sight of enormous spaces of hill and plain, apparently unsubstantial as a mountain mist, glimmering away to the indistinct horizon, and as it were spellbound by an absolute and eternal silence. The sentiment may be very different when a storm is rainmi and nothing is visible but the black ribs

of the mountains glaring at you through rents in the clouds; but on that perfect day on the top of the Schreckhorn, where not a wreath of vapour was to be seen under the whole vast canopy of the sky, a delicious lazy sense of calm repose was the appropriate frame of mind. One felt as if some immortal being, with no particular duties upon his hands, might be calmly sitting upon those desolate rocks and watching the little shadowy wrinkles of the plain, that were really mountain ranges, rise and fall through slow geological epochs. I had no companion to disturb my reverie or introduce discordant associations. An hour passed like a few minutes, but there were still difficulties to be encountered which would have made any longer delay unadvisable. I therefore added a few touches to our cairn, and then turned to the descent.

It is a general opinion, with which I do not agree, that the descent of slippery or difficult rock is harder than the ascent. My guides, however, seemed to be fully convinced of it; or perhaps they merely wished to prove, in opposition to my sceptical remarks, that there was some use in having three guides. Accordingly, whilst Christian Michel led the way, old Peter and Kaufmann persisted in planting themselves steadily in some safe nook, and then hauling at the rope round

my waist. By a violent exertion and throwing all my weight on to the rope, I gradually got myself paid slowly out, and descended to the next ledge, feeling as if I should be impressed with a permanent groove to which ropes might be fixed in future. The process was laborious, not to say painful, and I was sincerely glad when the idea dawned upon the good fellows that I might be trusted to use my limbs more freely. Surtout point de zelc is occasionally a good motto for guides as well as ministers.

I have suffered worse things on awkward places from the irregular enthusiasm of my companions. Never shall I forget a venerable guide at Kippel, whose glory depended on the fact that his name was mentioned in The Book, viz., Murray's Guide. Having done nothing all day to maintain his reputation, he seized a favourable opportunity as we were descending a narrow arete of snow, and suddenly clutching my coat-tails, on pretence of steadying me, brought me with a jerk into a sitting position. My urgent remonstrances only produced bursts of patois^ mixed with complacent chucklings, and I was forced to resign myself to the fate of being pulled backwards, all in a heap, about every third step along the arete. The process gave the old gentleman such evident pleasure that 1 eeased to complain.

On the present occasion my guides were far more reasonable, and I would never complain of a little extra caution. We were soon going along steadily enough, though the slippery nature of the rocks, and the precautions necessary to avoid dislodging loose stones, made our progress rather slow. At length, however, with that instinct which good guides always show, and in which amateurs are most deficient, we came exactly to the point where we had left our knapsacks. We were now standing close to the ravine I have mentioned. Suddenly I heard a low hiss close by me, and looking round saw a stream of snow shooting rapidly down the gully, like a long white serpent. It was the most insidious enemy of the mountaineer—an avalanche; not such as thunders down the cliffs of the Jungfrau, ready to break every bone in your body, but the calm malicious avalanche which would take you quietly off your legs, wrap you up in a sheet of snow, and bury you in a crevasse for a few hundred years, without making any noise about it. The stream was so narrow and well defined that I could easily have stepped across it; still it was rather annoying, inasmuch as immediately below us was a broad fringe of snow ending in a bergsehrund, the whole being in what travellers used to represent as the normal condition of mountain snow—such that

a stone, or even a hasty expression, rashly dropped, would probably start an avalanche. Christian Michel showed himself equal to the occasion. Choosing a deep trench in the snow——the channel of one of these avalanches——from which the upper layer of snow was cut away, he turned his face to the slope and dug his toes deeply into the firmer snow beneath. We followed, trying in every way to secure our hold of the treacherous footing. Every little bit of snow that we kicked aside started a young avalanche on its own account. By degrees, however, we reached the edge of a very broad and repulsive-looking bergschrund. Unfixing the rope, we gave Kaufmann one end, and sent him carefully across a long and very shaky-looking bridge of snow. He got safely across, and we cautiously followed him, one by one. As the last man reached the other side, we felt that our dangers were over. It was now about five o'clock.

We agreed to descend by the Strahleck. Great delay was caused by our discovering that even on the nearly level surface there was a sheet of ice formed, which required many a weary step to be cut. It was long before we could reach the rocks and take off the rope for a race home down the slopes of snow.

As we reached our burrow we were "ratified

with one of the most glorious sights of the mountains. A huge eloud, which looked at least as lofty as the Eiger, rested with one extremity of its base on the Eiger, and the other on the Mettenberg, shooting its white pinnacles high up into the sunshine above. Through the mighty arched gateway thus formed, we could see far over the successive ranges of inferior mountains, standing like flat shades one behind another. The lower slopes of the Mettenberg glowed with a deep blood-red, and the more distant hills passed through every shade of blue, purple, and rose-coloured hues, into the faint blue of the distant Jura, with one gleam of green sky beyond. In the midst of the hills the Lake of Thun lay, shining like gold. A few peals of thunder echoed along the glacier valley, telling us of the storm that was raging over Grindelwald

It was half-past seven when we reached our lair. We consequently had to pass another night there—a necessity which would have been easily avoided by a little more activity in the morning.

It is a laudable custom to conclude narratives of mountain ascents by a compliment to the guides who have displayed their skill and courage. Here, however, I shall venture to deviate from the ordinary practice by recording an anecdote, which may be instructive, and which well deserves

to be remembered by visitors to Grindelwald. The guides of the Oberland have an occasional weakness, which Englishmen cannot condemn with a very clear conscience, for the consumption of strong drink; and it happened that the younger Michel was one day descending the well-known path which leads from the chalet above the so-called Eismeer to Grindelwald in an unduly convivial frame of mind. Just above the point where mules are generally left, the path runs close to the edge of an overhanging cliff, the rocks below having been scooped out by the glacier in old days, when the glacier was several hundred feet above its present level. The dangerous place is guarded by a wooden rail, which unluckily terminates before the cliff is quite passed. Michel, guiding himself as it may be supposed by the rail, very naturally stepped over the cliff when the guidance was prematurely withdrawn. I cannot state the vertical height through which he must have fallen on to a bed of hard uncompromising rock. I think, however, that I am within the mark in saying that it cannot have been much less than a hundred feet. It would have been a less dangerous experiment to step from the roof of the tallest house in London to the kerbstone below. Michel lay at the bottom all night, and next morning shook himself, got up, and walked

home sober, and with no broken bones. I submit two morals for the choice of my readers, being quite unable, after much reflection, to decide which is the more appropriate. The first is, Don't get drunk when you have to walk along the edge of an Alpine cliff; the second is, Get drunk if you are likely to fall over an Alpine cliff. In any case, see that Michel is in his normal state of sobriety when you take him for a guide, and carry the brandy-flask in your own pocket.

CHAPTER IV

THE ROTHHORN

The little village of Zinal lies, as I need hardly inform my readers, deep in the recesses of the Pennine chain. Some time in the Middle Ages (I speak on the indisputable authority of Murray) the inhabitants of the surrounding valleys were converted to Christianity by the efforts of a bishop of Sion. From that time till the year 1864 I know little of its history, with the exception of two facts—one, that till lately the natives used holes in their tables as a substitute for plates, each member of the family depositing promiscuously his share of the family meals in his own particular cavity; the other, that a German traveller was murdered between Zinal and Evolena in 1863. This information, however, meagre as it is, illustrates the singular retirement from the world of these exquisite valleys. The great road of the Simplon has for years carried crowds of travellers past the opening of their gorges. Before its construction, Rousseau and Goethe had celebrated the charms of the main valley. During the last

twenty years Zermatt has been the centre of attraction for thousands of tourists. And yet, so feeble is the curiosity of mankind, and so sheeplike are the habits of the ordinary traveller, that these remote fastnesses still retain much of their primitive seclusion. Evolena, Zinal, and the head of the Turtman Thai are still visited only by a few enthusiasts. Even the Saas valley, easily accessible as it is, and leading to one of the most justly celebrated of Alpine passes, attracts scarcely one in a hundred of the many visitors to the twin valley of Zermatt. And yet those who have climbed the slopes behind the village and seen the huge curtain of ice let down from the summits of the mighty range between the Dom and Monte Rosa, cutting off half the horizon as with a more than gigantic screen, will admit that its beauties are almost unique in the Alps. Mr. Wills did justice to them long ago; but, in spite of all that can be said, the tourist stream flows in its old channels and leaves on either side regions of enchanting beauty, but almost as little visited as the remote valleys of Norway. I remember a striking scene near Griiben, in the Turtman Thai, which curiously exemplified this fact. We were in a little glade surrounded by pine forest, and with the Alpine rose clustering in full bloom round the scattered boulders. Above us rose the Weisshorn in one of

the most sublime aspects of that almost faultless mountain. The Turtman glacier, broad and white, with deep regular crevasses, formed a noble approach, like the staircase of some superb palace. Above this rose the huge mass of the mountain, firm and solid as though its architect had wished to eclipse the Pyramids. And, higher still, its lofty crest, jagged and apparently swaying from side to side, seemed to be tossed into the blue atmosphere far above the reach of mortal man. Nowhere have I seen a more delicate combination of mountain massiveness, with soaring and delicately carved pinnacles pushed to the verge of extravagance. Yet few people know this side of a peak, which every one has admired from the Riff el. The only persons who shared our view, though they could hardly share our wonder, were a little group of peasants standing round a small chalet. A herd of cows had been collected, and a priest in tattered garments was sprinkling them with hoi\'7d- water. They received us much as we might have been received in the least frequented of European districts, and it was hard to remember that we were within a short walk of the main post route and Mr. Cook's tourists. We seemed to have stepped into the Middle Ages, though I fancied that some shade of annoyance showed itself on the faces of the party, as of men

surprised in a rather superstitious observance. Perhaps they had a dim impression that we might be smiling in our sleeves, and knew that beyond their mountain wall were sometimes to be seen daring sceptics, who doubted the efficacy of holy water as a remedy for rinderpest. We of course expressed no opinion upon the subject, and passed on with a friendly greeting, reflecting how a trifling inequality in the earth's surface may be the means of preserving the relics of extinct modes of thought. But, for that matter, a London lane or an old college wall may be as effectual a prophylactic: even a properly cut coat is powerful in repelling contagion.

Leaving such meditations, I may remark that Swiss enterprise has begun to penetrate these retired valleys. It is a mystery, of difficult solution, how the spiders which live in certain retired and, as we would think, flyless corners of ancient libraries, preserve their existence; but it is still harder to discover how innkeepers in these rarely trodden valleys derive sufficient supplies from the mere waifs and strays that are thrown, as it were, from the main body of tourists. However that may be, a certain M. Epinay maintains a hospitable inn at Zinal, which has since been much enlarged; and the arrival of Grove, Macdonald, and myself, with our guides Melchior and Jacob Ander-my

egg, in August, 1864, rather more than doubled the resident population. M. Epinay's inn, I may remark, is worthy of the highest praise. It is true that the accommodation was then limited. Mac-donald and Grove had to sleep in two cupboards opening out of the coffee-room, whilst I occupied a bed which was the most conspicuous object of furniture in the coffee-room itself. The only thing I could complain of was that whenever I sat up suddenly I brought my head into violent contact with the ceiling. This peculiarity was owing to a fourth bed, which generally lurked beneath the legs of my rather lofty couch, but could be drawn out on due occasion. The merits of the establishment in other respects were manifold. Above all, M. Epinay is an excellent cook, and provided us daily with dinners which— I almost shrink from saying it—were decidedly superior to those of my excellent friend M. Seiler, at Zermatt. Inns, however, change almost as rapidly as dynasties, and I do not extend these remarks to the present day. Finally, the room boasted of one of the few decent sofas in Switzerland. It is true that it was only four feet long, and terminated by two lofty barriers; but it was soft, and had cushions—an unprecedented luxury, so far as my Alpine knowledge extends. The minute criticism of M. Epinay's establishment

is due to the fact that we spent there three days of enforced idleness.

Nothing is more delightful than fine weather in the Alps; but, as a general rule, the next thing to it is bad weather in the Alps. There is scarcely a day in summer when a man in ordinary health need be confined to the house; and even in the dreariest state of the atmosphere, when the view is limited to a few yards by driving mists on some lofty pasturage, there are infinite beauties of detail to be discovered by persons of humble minds. Indeed, on looking back to days spent in the mountains, I sometimes think that the most enjoyable have been, not those of unbroken sunshine, but those on which one was forcibly confined to admiring some little vignette of scenery strangely transfigured by the background of changing cloud. The huge boulder under which you take refuge, the angry glacier torrent dashing out of obscurity and disappearing in a few yards, and the cliff whose summit and base are equally concealed by the clouds, gain wonderfully in dignity and mystery. Yet I must confess that when one is suffering from an acute attack of the climbing fever, and panting for an opportunity which will not come, the patience is tried for the moment, even though striking fragments of scenery may be accumulating in the memory.

A persistent screen of storm\'7d' cloud drove up the valley, and clung stubbornly to the higher peaks. We lounged lazily in the wooden gallery, smoking our pipes and contemplating the principal street of the village. Once, as I sat there peacefully, a little pack of mountain stoats dashed in full cry across the village street; the object of chase was invisible; one might easily fancy that some quaint mountain goblin was the master of the hounds; if so, he did not reveal himself to the unworthy eyes of one of those tourists who are frightening him and his like from their native haunts. Once or twice an alarm of natives was raised; and we argued long whether they were inhabitants, or merely visitors from the neighbouring Alps come to see life in Zinal. I incline to the latter hypothesis, being led thereto from a consideration of the following circumstance:—One of our desperate efforts at amusement was playing cricket in the high street, with a rail for a bat, and a small granite boulder for a ball. My first performance was a brilliant hit to leg (the only one I ever made in my life) off Macdonald's bowling. To my horror I sent the ball clean through the western window of the chapel, which looks upon the grande place of the village—the scene of our match. As no one ever could be found to receive damages, I doubt much whether there are any

permanent inhabitants. Tired of cricket, I learnt the visitors' book by heart; I studied earnestly the remarks of a deaf and dumb gentleman, who, for some mysterious reason, has selected this book as the chief medium of communication with the outer world. I made, I fear, rather ill-tempered annotations on some of my predecessors' remarks. I even turned a table of heights expressed in metres into feet, and have thereby contributed richly to the fund of amusement provided for scientific visitors who may have a taste for correcting arithmetical blunders. On Sunday the weather was improving, and after breakfast we lounged up the Diablons—an easy walk, if taken from the right direction. The view met with our decided disapproval—principally, perhaps, because we did not see it, and partly because we had taken no provisions; a thunderstorm drenched us during our descent, and I began to think the weather hopeless. The same evening, as I was reclining on the sofa, in the graceful attitude of a V, whose extremities were represented by my head and feet, and whose apex was plunged in the before-mentioned cushions, the sanguine Macdonald said that the weather was clearing up. My reply was expressive of that utter disbelief with which a passenger in a Channel steamboat resents the steward's assurance that Calais is in sight. Next

morning, however, at 1.50 a.m., I found myself actually crossing the meadows which form the upper level of the Zinal valley. It was a cloudless night, except that a slight haze obscured the distant Oberland ridges. But for the disheartening influence of a prolonged sojourn in Zinal, I might have been sanguine. As it was, I walked in that temper of gloomy disgust which I find to be a frequent concomitant of early rising. Another accident soon happened to damp our spirits. Macdonald was forced to give in to a sharp attack of illness, which totally incapacitated him for a difficult expedition. We parted with him with great regret, and proceeded gloomily on our way. Poor Macdonald spent the day dismally enough. I fear, in the little inn, in the company of M. Epinay and certain German tourists.

We followed the usual track for the Trift pass as far as the top of the great icefall of the Durand glacier. Here we turned sharply to the left, and crossed the wilderness of decaying rock at the foot of Lo Besso. It is a strangely wild scene. The buttress-like mass of Lo Besso cut off our view of the lower country. Our path led across a mass of huge loose rocks, which I can only compare to a continuous series of the singular monuments known as rocking-stones. For a second or two you balanced yourself on a mass as big as a cottage, and balanced not only yourself but the mass on which you stood. As it canted slowly over, you made a convulsive spring, and lighted upon another rock in an equally unstable position. If you were lucky you recovered yourself by a sudden jerk, and prepared for the next leap. If unlucky, you landed with your knees, nose, and other parts of your person in contact with various lumps of rock, and rose into an erect posture by another series of gymnastic contortions. In fact, my attitudes, at least, were as unlike as possible to that of Mercury—

New lighted on a heaven-kissing hill.

They were more like Mercury shot out of a cart on to a heap of rubbish. An hour or so of this work brought us to a smooth patch of rocks, from which we obtained our first view of the Rothhorn, hitherto shut out by a secondary spur of the Besso. And here, at 5.50 a.m., we halted for breakfast. "How beautiful those clouds are!" was Grove's enthusiastic remark as we sat down to our frozen meal. The rest of the party gave a very qualified response to his admiration of a phenomenon beautiful in itself, but ominous of bad weather. For my part, I never profess to be in a good temper at six o'clock in the morning. Christian morality appears to me to become binding every

morning at breakfast-time, that is, about 9.30 a.m. Macdonald's departure had annoyed me. A more selfish dislike to the stones over which we had been stumbling had put me out still further. But the bitterest drop in my cup was the state of the weather. The sky overhead, indeed, was still cloudless; but just before the Besso eclipsed the Oberland ridges, an offensive mist had blotted out their serrated outline. I did not like the way in which the stars winked at us just before their disappearance in the sunlight. But worst of all was a heavy mass of cloud which clung to the ridge between the Dent Blanche and the Gabel-horn, and seemed to be crossing the Col de Zinal, under the influence of a strong south wind. The clouds to which Grove unfeelingly alluded were a detachment rising like steam from a cauldron above this lower mass. They seemed to gather to leeward of the vast cliffs of the Dent Blanche, and streamed out from their shelter into the current of the gale which evidently raged above our heads. At this moment they were tinged with every shade of colour that an Al ine sunrise can supply. I have heard such clouds described as "mashed rainbow"; and whatever the nature of the culinary process, their glorious beauty is undeniable. But for the time the ambition of climbing the Rothhorn had quenched all

aesthetic influences, and a sulky growl was the only homage I could pay them.

Yet one more vexatious element was here intruded into our lot. We were in full view of the Rothhorn, to which we had previously given a careful examination from the foot of the Trift-Joch. As this is the most favourable moment for explaining our geography, I will observe that we were now within the hollow embraced by the spur which terminates in the great promontory of Lo Besso. This spur has its origin in the main ridge which runs from the Rothhorn towards the Weisshorn, the point of articulation being immediately under the final cliffs of the Rothhorn. It divides the Morning glacier from the upper snows of the Durand glacier. The mighty 1 ' cirque" enclosed by the mountain wall—studded in succession by the peaks of the Besso, the Rothhorn, the Gabelhorner, the Dent Blanche, and the Grand Cornier'—is one of the very noblest in the Alps. From the point we had now reached it appeared to form a complete amphitheatre, the narrow gorge through which the Durand glacier emerges into the Einfischthal being invisible. Our plan of operations was to climb the spur (of which I have already spoken) about half-way between Lo Besso and the Rothhorn, and thence to follow it up to the top of the mountain. The difficulty t

as we had early foreseen, would begin just after the place where the spur blended with the northern ridge of the Rothhorn. We had already examined with our telescopes the narrow and broken arete which led upwards from this point to the summit. Its scarped and perpendicular sides, and the rocky teeth which struck up from its back, were sufficiently threatening. Melchior had, notwithstanding, spoken with unusual confidence of our chance. But at this moment the weakest point in his character developed itself. He began to take a gloomy view of his prospects, and to confide his opinion to Jacob Anderegg in what he fondly imagined to be unintelligible patois. I understood him only too well. "Jacob," he said,

"we shall get up to that rock, and then " an

ominous shake of the head supplied the remainder of the sentence. It was therefore in sulky silence that, after half an hour's halt, I crossed the snow-field, reached the top of the spur at 7.55 a.m., and thence ascended the arete to within a short distance of the anticipated difficulty. Our progress was tolerably rapid, being only delayed by the necessity of cutting some half-dozen steps. We were at a great height, and the eye plunged into the Zinal valley on one side, and to the little inn upon the Riffel on the other, whilst on looking round it commanded the glacier basin from which

H4 The Playground of Europe

we had just ascended. Close beneath us, to the north, was the col by which Messrs. Moore and Whymper had passed from the Morning to the Schallenberg glacier. It was now 9 a.m. We cowered under the rocky parapet which here strikes up through the snow like a fin from a fish's back, and guarded us from the assaults of a fierce southern gale. All along the arete to this point I had distinctly felt a keen icy blast penetrate my coat as though it had been made of gossamer, pierce my skin, whistle merrily through my ribs, and, after chilling the internal organs, pass out at the other side with unabated vigour. My hands were numb, my nose was doubtless purple, and my teeth played involuntary airs, like the bones of a negro minstrel. Grove seemed to me to be more cheerful than circumstances justified. By way, therefore, of reducing his spirits nearer to freezing-point— or, let me hope, in the more laudable desire of breaking his too probable disappointment—I invented for his benefit a depressing prophecy supposed to have been just uttered by Melchior; and, if faces can speak without words, my gloomy prediction was not entirely without justification. We were on a ledge of snow which formed a kind of lean-to against the highest crest of precipitous rock. A little farther on the arete made a slight elbow, beyond which we could see nothing. If the

snowy shelf continued beyond the elbow, all might yet be well. If not, we should have to trust ourselves to the tender mercies of the seamed and distorted rocks. A very few paces settled the question. The snow thinned out. We turned to examine the singular ridge along which the only practicable path must lie. From its formation it was impossible to see more than a very short way ahead. So steep were the precipices on each side that to our imaginations it had all the effect of a thin wall, bending in its gradual decay first towards one and then towards the other valley. The steep faces of rock thus appeared to overhang the Schallenberg and Zinal glaciers alternately. The same process of decay had gradually carved the parapet which surmounted it into fantastic pinnacles, and occasionally scored deep channels in its sides. It was covered with the rocky fragments rent off by the frost, and now lying in treacherous repose, frequently masked by cushions of fresh-fallen snow. The cliffs were, at times, as smooth as if they had been literally cut out by the sweep of a gigantic knife. But the smooth faces were separated by deep gullies, down which the artillery of falling stones was evidently accustomed to play. I fear that I can very imperfectly describe the incidents of our assault upon this formidable fortress. Melchior led us with unfaltering skill—his spirits, as usual, rising in proportion to the difficulty when the die had once been cast. Three principal pinnacles rose in front of us, each of which it was necessary to turn or to surmount. The first of these was steepest upon the Zinal side. Two deep gullies on the Zermatt side started from points in the ridge immediately in front and in rear of the obstacle, and converged at some distance beneath. The pinnacle itself was thus shaped like a tooth protruding from a jaw and exposed down to the sockets, and the two gullies afforded means for circumventing it. We carefully descended by one of these for some distance, considerably inconvenienced by the snow which lodged in the deeply-cut channels and concealed the loose stones. With every care it was impossible not occasionally to start crumbling masses of rock. The most ticklish part of the operation was in crossing to the other gull) ; a sheet of hard ice some two or three inches thick covered the steeply-inclined slabs. It was impossible to cut steps in it deep enough to afford secure foothold. The few knobs of projecting stone seemed all to be too loose either for hand or foot. We crept along in as gingerly a fashion as might be, endeavouring to distribute our weight over the maximum number of insecure supports until one of the party had got sounder footing. A severe

piece of chimney-sweep practice then landed us once more upon the razor edge of the arete. The second pinnacle demanded different tactics. On the Zermatt side it was impractically steep, whilst on the other it fell away in one of the smooth sheets of rock already mentioned. The rock, however, was here seamed by deep fissures approximately horizontal. It was possible to insert toes or fingers into these, so as to present to telescopic vision (if any one had been watching our ascent) much the appearance of a fly on a pane of glass. Or, to make another comparison, our method of progression was not unlike that of the caterpillars, who may be observed first doubled up into a loop and then stretched out at full length. When two crevices approximated, we were in danger of treading on our own fingers, and the next moment we were extended as though on the rack, clutching one crack with the last joints of our fingers, and feeling for another with the extreme points of our toes. The hold was generally firm when the fissures were not filled with ice, and we gradually succeeded in outflanking the second hostile position. The third, which now rose within a few yards, was of far more threatening appearance than its predecessors. After a brief inspection, we advanced along the ridge to its base. In doing so we had to perform a manoeuvre which,

though not very difficult, I never remember to have previously tried. One of the plates to Berlepsch's description of the Alps represents a mountain-top, with the national flag of Switzerland waving from the summit and a group of enthusiastic mountaineers swarming round it. One of them approaches, astride of a sharp ridge, with one leg hanging over each precipice. Our position was similar, except that the ridge by which we approached consisted of rock instead of snow. The attitude adopted had the merit of safety, but was deficient in comfort. The rock was so smooth and its edge so sharp, that as I crept along it, supported entirely on my hands, I was in momentary fear that a slip might send one half of me to the Durand and the other to the Schallenberg glacier. It was, however, pleasing to find a genuine example of the arete in its normal state— so often described in books and so seldom found in real life. We landed on a small platform at the other end of our razor of Al Sir at, hoping for the paradise of a new mountain summit as our reward; but as we looked upwards at the last of the three pinnacles, I felt doubtful of the result. The rock above us was, if I am not mistaken, the one which, by its sharp inclination to the east, gives to the Rothhorn, from some points of view, the appearance of actually curling over in that direction, like the crest of a sea-wave on the point of breaking. To creep along the eastern face was totally impossible. The western slopes, though not equally steep, were still frightfully precipitous, and presented scarcely a ledge whereby to cling to their slippery surface. In front of us the rocks rose steeply in a very narrow crest, rounded and smooth at the top, and with all foothold, if foothold there were, completely concealed by a layer of fresh snow. After a glance at this somewhat unpromising path, Melchior examined for a moment the western cliff. The difficulties there seeming even greater, he immediately proceeded to the direct assault. In a few minutes I was scrambling desperately upwards, utterly insensible to the promptings of the self-esteem which would generally induce me to refuse assistance and to preserve a workmanlike attitude. So steeply did the precipice sink on our left hand, that along the whole of this part of the shelf the glacier, at a vast distance below, formed the immediate background to a sloping rocky ledge, some foot or two in width, and covered by slippery snow. In a few paces I found myself fumbling vaguely with my fingers at imaginary excrescences, my feet resting upon rotten projections of crumbling stone, whilst a large pointed slab of rock pressed against my stomach, and threatened to force my centre of

gravity backwards beyond the point of support. My chief reliance was upon the rope; and with a graceful flounder I was presently landed in safety upon a comparatively sound ledge. Looking backwards, I was gratified by a picture which has since remained fixed in my imagination. Some feet down the steep ridge was Grove, in one of those picturesque attitudes which a man involuntarily adopts when the various points to which he trusts his weight have been distributed without the least regard to the exigencies of the human figure, when they are of a slippery and crumbling nature, and when the violent downward strain of the rope behind him is only just counterbalanced by the upward strain of the rope in front. Below Grove appeared the head, shoulders, and arms of Jacob. His fingers were exploring the rock in search of infinitesimal crannies, and his face presented the expression of modified good humour which in him supplies the place of extreme discontent in other guides. Jacob's head and shoulders were relieved against the snows of the Schallenberg glacier many hundred feet below. Our view of continuous rock was thus limited to a few yards of narrow ridge, tilted up at a steep angle apparently in mid-air; and Jacob resembled a man in the act of clambering into a balloon far above the earth. I had but little time for con-

templation before turning again to our fierce strife with the various impediments to our march. Suddenly Melchior, who had left the highest ridge to follow a shelf of rock on the right, turned to me with the words, " In half an hour we shall be on the top." My first impulse was to express an utter scepticism. My perturbed imagination was unable to realise the fact that we should ever get off the arete any more. We seemed to be condemned to a fate which Dante might have reserved for faithless guides—to be everlastingly climbing a hopeless arete, in a high wind, and never getting any nearer the summit. Turning an angle of the rock, I saw that Melchior had spoken the truth, and for the first time that day it occurred to me that life was not altogether a mistake. We had reached the top of what I have called the third pinnacle, and with it our difficulties were over. In the words of the poet, modified to the necessary extent'—

He that with toil of heart and knees and hands
Up the long ridge to the far height hath won
His path upwards, and prevailed,
Shall find the toppling crags of the Rothhorn scaled—
are close to what, by a somewhat forced metaphor, we may call "a shining tableland." It

is not a particularly level nor a very extensive tableland; but, compared with the ridges up which we had

been forcing our precarious way, it was luxurious in the extreme. 'T was not so wide as Piccadilly nor so level as the Bedford River, but 't would serve; I might almost add, if the metaphor were not somewhat strained, that it made "worm's meat" of the Rothhorn. At any rate it was sound under foot, and broad enough for practical purposes ; and within less than Melchior's half-hour, viz., 11.15 a.m., we reachd'—I had almost said the top; but the Rothhorn has no top. It has a place where a top manifestly ought to have been, but the work had been left unfinished. It ended in a flat circular area a few feet broad, as though it had been a perfect cone, with the apex cleanly struck off. Melchior and Jacob set to work at once to remedy this deficiency of nature, whilst Grove and I cowered down in a little hole cut out of the last rocks, which sheltered us from the bitter wind. Here, in good temper with each other and our guides, and everything but Macdonald's absence, we sat down for some twenty minutes, with muscles still quivering from the strain.

No doubt some enthusiast will ask me about the view. I have several times been asked what the Matterhorn looked like; and I wish I could give an answer. But I will make a clean breast of it, and confess that I only remember two things: one, that we saw the Riffelberg, looking like a

flat green carpet; the other, that the gigantic mass of the Weisshorn seemed to frown right above our heads, and shut out a large segment from the view. Seen from this point it is more massive and of less elegant shape than from most others. It looked like an enormous bastion, with an angle turned towards us. Whether I was absorbed in the worship of this noblest of Alpine peaks, or whether the clouds had concealed much of the rest of the panorama, or whether we were thinking too much of the ascent that was past and the descent that was to come, or whether, as I rather believe, the view is really an inferior one, certain it is that I thought very little of it. "And what philosophical observations did you make?" will be the inquiry of one of those fanatics who, by a reasoning process to me utterly inscrutable, have somehow irrevocably associated Alpine travelling with science. To them I answer, that the temperature was approximately (1 had no thermometer) 212 0 (Fahrenheit) below freezing-point. As for ozone, if any existed in the atmosphere, it was a greater fool than I take it for. As we had, unluckily, no barometer, I am unable to give the usual information as to the extent of our deviation from the correct altitude; but the Federal map fixes the height at 13,855 feet. Twenty minutes of freezing satisfied me with the prospect, and I

willingly turned to the descent. I will not trouble my readers with a repetition in inverse order of the description of our previous adventures. I will not tell at length how I was sometimes half-suspended like a bundle of goods by the rope; how I was sometimes curled up into a ball, and sometimes stretched over eight or nine feet of rock; how the rope got twisted round my legs and arms and body, into knots which would have puzzled the Davenport Brothers; how, at one point, I conceived myself to be resting entirely on the point of one toe upon a stone coated with ice and fixed very loosely in the face of a tremendous cliff, whilst Melchior absurdly told me I was "ganz sicher," and encouraged me to jump; how Jacob seemed perfectly at his ease; how Grove managed to lend a hand whenever I wanted one; and how Melchior, rising into absurdly high spirits, pirouetted and capered and struck attitudes on the worst places, and, in short, indulged himself in a display of fancy mountaineering as a partial relief to his spirits. We reached the snow safely at 1.15 p.m., and looked back triumphantly at the nastiest piece of climbing I had ever accomplished. The next traveller who makes the ascent will probably charge me with exaggeration. It is, I know, very difficult to avoid giving just cause for that charge. I must therefore apologise before-

hand, and only beg my anticipated critic to remember two things: one, that on the first ascent a mountain, in obedience to some mysterious law, always is more difficult than at any succeeding ascent; secondly, that nothing can be less like a mountain at one time than the same mountain at another. The fresh snow and the bitter gale told heavily in the scale against us. Some of the hardest ascents I remember have been up places easy in fine weather, but rendered difficult by accidental circumstances. Making allowance, however, for this, I still believe that the last rocks of the Rothhorn will always count among the decidedly mauvais pas of the Alps.

We ran rapidly down the snow without much adventure, except that I selected the steepest part of the snow arete to execute what, but for the rope, would have been a complete somersault—an involuntary but appropriate performance. Leaving the stony base of the Besso well to our right, we struck the route from the Trift-Joch at the point where a little patch of verdure behind a moraine generally serves for a halting and feeding place. Here we stretched ourselves luxuriously on the soft green moss in the afternoon sun. We emptied the last drops of the wine bag, lighted the pipe of peace—the first that day—and enjoyed the well-earned climbers' reward. Some mountaineers

126 The Playground of Europe

do not smoke—such is the darkness which lurks amidst our boasted civilisation. To them the words I have just penned convey no sympathetic thrill. With the ignorance of those who have never shared a blessing, they probably affect even to despise the pleasure it confers. I can, at any rate, say that I have seldom known a happier half-hour than that in which I basked on the mossy turf in the shadow of the conquered Rothhorn—all my internal sensations of present comfort, of hard-won victory, and of lovely scenery, delicately harmonised by the hallowing influence of tobacco. We enjoyed what the lotos-eaters would have enjoyed, had they been making an ascent of one of the "silent pinnacles of aged snow," instead of suffering from seasickness, and partaking of a less injurious stimulant than lotos. Melchior pointed out during our stay eleven different ways of ascending the hitherto unconquered Grand Cornier. Grove and Jacob speculated on adding its summit also to our trophies, whilst I observed, not without secret satisfaction, that the gathering clouds would enforce at least a day's rest. We started homewards with a reluctant effort. I diversified the descent by an act of gallantry on my own account. Melchior had just skipped over a crevasse and turned to hold out a hand. With a contemptuous wave of my own I put his offer aside, remark-

ing something about people who had done the Rothhorn. Next moment I was, it was true, on the other side of the crevasse, but, I regret to say, flat on my back, and gliding rapidly downwards into its depths. Melchior ignominiously hooked me under the arm with his axe and jerked me back, with a suitable warning for the future. We soon left the glacier, and on descending the path towards Zinal were exposed to the last danger of the day. Certain natives had sprung apparently from the bowels of the earth, and hailed us with a strange dialect, composed in equal proportions of French, German, and Italian patois. Not understanding their remarks, I ran onwards, when a big stone whizzed close past my head. My first impression was that I was about to be converted into the victim of another Zinal murder, the gentleman by whom the last was committed being, as it was reported, still wandering amongst the mountains. I looked up, and saw that the offender was one of a large herd of cows, which were browsing in the charge of the natives, and managed, by kicking down loose stones, to keep up a lively fire along some distance of our path. We ran on all the faster, reached the meadows, and ascended the path to the village. Just as we reached the first houses, a melancholy figure advanced to meet us. Friendly greetings, how-

ever, proceeded from its lips, and we were soon shaking hands with poor Macdonald. We reached M. Epinay's inn at 6.45 p.m., the whole expedition occupying 16 h. 50 m., including about two hours' halts. A pleasant dinner succeeded, notwithstanding the clatter of sundry German tourists, who had flooded the little coffee-room and occupied my beloved sofa, and who kept up a ceaseless conversation. Soon afterwards, Macdonald having generously abandoned to me the cupboard in which he slept, I was trying to solve the problem of placing a length of six feet on a bed measuring about 3 ft. 6 in. by 2 ft. As its solution appeared to me to be inextricably mixed up with some question about the highest rocks of the Rothhorn, and as I heard no symptoms of my neighbour's slumbers in the next cupboard, which was divided from mine by a sort of paper partition, I incline to think that I was not long awake.

CHAPTER V

THE EIGER-JOCH

On August 3, 1859, I was travelling on the Swiss railway, between Basle and Olten, with my friends Messrs. William and George Mathews. As we shot out of the long tunnel above Olten, and descended into the valley of the Aar, the glorious range of the Bernese Oberland rose majestically into sight, some fifty miles away. While telling over the names of our gigantic friends, our eyes were caught by the broad flat top of the Monch, which no Englishman had yet reached. It occurred to us that an attack upon this hoary pillar of the mid-aerial church would be a worthy commencement of our expedition, and it struck us at the same time that by ascending, as a first step, the ridge called by Mr. Bun-bury J the Col de la Jungfrau, which connects the Monch with the Jungfrau, we should, so to speak, be killing two birds with one stone. A problem which at that time offered itself to

: In the first series of Peaks, Passes, a>td Glaciers. 9 I2 9

Alpine travellers, was to discover a direct route from the waters of the Lutschine to those of the Rhone. A glance at the map will show five possible routes between the Finsteraarhorn and the Gletscherhorn, corresponding to five depressions in the main ridge of the Oberland. The most direct and obvious route is across the gap between the Monch and the Jungfrau. This is obtrusively, and almost offensively, a genuine pass. Unlike some passes, falsely so called, whose summit levels are either huge plains, like the Theodule, or, still worse, tops of mountains, like one or two that might be mentioned, the Jungfrau-Joch presents a well-defined depression between the two highest mountains in the district. Moreover, the summit of the pass and the two ends of the journey lie in a straight line, from which no part of the route deviates considerably. In fact, were it not for the mountains, the line of the pass would be the most direct route from the Wengern Alp to the JEg-gischhorn. It shows itself, therefore, as the very normal type of a pass to the whole middle land of Switzerland. And but for a certain affectation of inaccessibility, it must long ago have been adopted as one of the main Alpine routes. There are, however, several alternatives which may be adopted in order to turn its obvious difficulties.

To the east of the Monch lie three passes, each with its characteristic peculiarities. The most obvious route is that between the Monch and the Viescherhorn: it was first made in historic times by Messrs. Hudson and Birkbeck, in 1858; but the legend goes that it was used two or three centuries back, when certain Valaisan Protestants were in the habit of crossing the range to attend the services of their fellow-believers at Grindel-wald. Religious zeal must have been greater, or the glaciers materially less, than at present. The same point, again, may be reached by climbing the ridge between the Monch and the Eiger, from the summit of which, as will presently appear, the col may be easily reached. By keeping still farther to the east, the ridge connecting the Viescherhorn with the Finsteraar-horn may again be crossed, and a descent effected upon the higher snows of the Viescher glacier. And, finally, it is possible to cross the chain to the west of the Jungfrau. This was first accomplished by Messrs. Hawkins and Tyndall, in i860; and in 1864 I had the good fortune, in company with Messrs. Grove and Macdonald, to find an easier route over the same depression, which brought us close to the shoulder of the Jungfrau. We were singularly lucky in the weather, and had the satisfaction of reaching

132 The Playground of Europe

the iEggischhorn in eighteen hours from Lauter-brunnen, ascending the Jungfrau en route. This is one of the very noblest expeditions in the Alps.

Till 1859, however, none of these passages had been made, with the single exception of the Monch-Joch. Accordingly, on August 7th, we assembled, with an eager desire to attempt the new passage, at the lower of the two little inns on the ever-glorious Wengern Alp.

The Mathews were accompanied by two Cha-mouni men, Jean-Baptiste Croz and Charlet, whilst I had secured the gigantic Ulrich Lauener, the most picturesque of guides. Tall, spare, blue-eyed, long-limbed, and square-shouldered, with a jovial laugh and a not ungraceful swagger, he is the very model of a true mountaineer; and, except that his rule is apt to be rather autocratic, I would not wish for a pleasanter companion. He has, however, certain views as to the superiority of the Teutonic over the Latin races, which rather interfered with the harmony of the party at a later period. Meanwhile, we examined the work before us more closely. The Monch is connected, by two snow ridges, with the Jungfrau on the west and the Eiger on the east. From the first of these ridges descends the Guggi glacier, and from the second the Eiger glacier, both of them pouring their torrents into

the gloomy Triimleten valley, the trench which also receives the snow avalanches of the Jungfrau. These two glaciers are separated by the huge northern buttress of the Monch, which, I believe, is generally supposed by tourists to be perpendicular; but the long slopes of debris by which it is faced prove the fallacy of this idea to an experienced eye, and it is, in fact, easy to ascend. Both glaciers are much crevassed; the Guggi, however, expands into a kind of level plateau, about half-way up the mountain, connected by long and broken snow-slopes with the Jungfrau-Joch.

The morning of the 6th having been gloomy, we spent the later part of the day in a reconnoitring expedition up to this plateau and a little beyond it. The result of our observations was not encouraging. We mounted some way above the plateau on a great heap of debris that had been disgorged by a glacier above. The blue crevasses which were drawn across the protruding nose of ice showed that at any minute we might be surprised by the descent of new masses, which would convert us into debris ourselves. Even if we surmounted this danger in the early morning, the steep slopes of neve above us, which occasionally bulged out into huge overhanging masses, looked far from pro-

134 The Playground of Europe

mising. Retreating to the buttress of the Monch, we turned our attention to the Eiger glacier. Though some difficulties were obviously to be encountered, its aspect was generally more auspicious, and we accordingly resolved to modify our plans by ascending the eastern instead of the western shoulder of the Monch. We hoped afterwards to attack the Monch, but in any case meant to descend to the Aletsch glacier on the other side.

An additional result of our expedition had been to develop a more decided rivalry between Lauener and the Chamouni men. We had already had one or two little races and disputations in consequence, and Lauener was disposed to take a disparaging view of the merits of these foreign competitors on his own peculiar ground. As, however, he could not speak a word of French, nor they of German, he was obliged to convey this sentiment in pantomime, which perhaps did not soften its vigour. I was accordingly prepared for a few disputes the next day—an annoyance which occasionally attends a combination of Swiss and Chamouni guides.

About four on the morning of August 7th, we got off from the inn on the Wengern Alp, notwithstanding a few delays, and steered straight for the foot of the Eiger. In the early morning the rocks around the glacier and the lateral moraines were hard and slippery. Before long, however, we found ourselves well on the ice, near the central axis of the Eiger glacier, and looking up at the great terrace-shaped ice-masses, separated by deep crevasses, which rose threateningly over our heads, one above another, like the defences of some vast fortification. And here began the first little dispute between Ober-land and Chamouni. The Chamouni men proposed a direct assault on the network of crevasses above us. Lauener said that we ought to turn them by crossing to the south-west side, immediately below the Monch. My friends and their guides forming a majority, and seeming to have little respect for the arguments urged by the minority, we gave in and followed them, with many muttered remarks from Lauener. We soon found ourselves performing a series of manoeuvres like those required for the ascent of the Col du Geant. At times we were lying-flat in little gutters on the faces of the seracs, worming ourselves along like boa-constrictors. At the next moment we were balancing ourselves on a knife-edge of ice between two crevasses, or plunging into the very bowels of the glacier, with a natural arch of ice meeting above our heads. I need not attempt to describe difficulties

136 The Playground of Europe

and dangers familiar to all ice-travellers. Like other such difficulties, they were exciting and even rather amusing for a time, but unfortunately they seemed inclined to last rather too long. Some of the deep crevasses apparently stretched almost from side to side of the glacier, rending its whole mass into distorted fragments. In attempting to find a way through them, we seemed to be going nearly as far backwards as forwards, and the labyrinth in which we were involved was as hopelessly intricate after a long struggle as it had been at first. Moreover, the sun had long touched the higher snow-fields, and was creeping down to us step by step. As soon as it reached the huge masses amongst which we were painfully toiling, some of them would begin to jump about like hailstones in a shower, and our position would become really dangerous. The Chamouni guides, in fact, declared it to be dangerous already, and warned us not to speak, for fear of bringing some of the nicely poised ice-masses down on our heads. On my translating this well-meant piece of advice to Lauener, he immediately selected the most dangerous-looking pinnacle in sight, and mounting to the top of it sent forth a series of screams, loud enough, I should have thought, to bring down the top of the Monch. They failed, however, to dislodge

any seracs, and Lauener, going to the front, called to us to follow him. By this time we were all glad to follow any one who was confident enough to lead. Turning to our right, we crossed the glacier in a direction parallel to the deep crevasses, and therefore unobstructed by any serious obstacles, till we found ourselves immediately beneath the great cliffs of the Monch. Our prospects changed at once. A great fold in the glacier produces a kind of diagonal pathway, stretching upwards from the point where we stood towards the rocks of the Eiger. It was not, indeed, exactly a carriage-road, but along the line which divides two different systems of crevasse the glacier seemed to have been crushed into smaller fragments, producing, as it were, a kind of incipient macadamisation. The masses, instead of being divided by long regular trenches, were crumbled and jammed together so as to form a road, easy and pleasant enough by comparison with our former difficulties. Pressing rapidly up this rough path, we soon found ourselves in the very heart of the glacier, with a broken wilderness of ice on every side. We were in one of the grandest positions I have ever seen for observing the wonders of the ice-world; but those wonders were not all of an encouraging nature. For, looking up to the snow-fields now

close above us, an obstacle appeared which made us think that all our previous labours had been in vain. From side to side of the glacier a vast palisade of blue ice-pinnacles struck up through the white layers of neve formed by the first plunge of the glacier down its waterfall of ice. Some of them rose in fantastic shapes—huge blocks balanced on narrow footstalks, and only waiting for the first touch of the sun to fall in ruins down the slope below. Others rose like church spires, or like square towers, defended by trenches of unfathomable depth. Once beyond this barrier, we should be safe upon the highest plateau of the glacier at the foot of the last snow-slope. But it was obviously necessary to turn them by some judicious strategical movement. One plan was to climb the lower rocks of the Eiger; but, after a moment's hesitation, we fortunately followed Lauener towards the other side of the glacier, where a small gap, between the seracs and the lower slopes of the Monch, seemed to be the entrance to a ravine that might lead us upwards. Such it turned out to be. Instead of the rough footing to which we had hitherto been unwillingly restricted, we found ourselves ascending a narrow gorge, with the giant cliffs of the Monch on our right, and the toppling ice-pinnacles on our left. A beautifully

even surface of snow, scarcely marked by a single crevasse, lay beneath our feet. We pressed rapidly up this strange little pathway, as it wound steeply upwards between the rocks and the ice, expecting at every moment to see it thin out, or break off at some impassable crevasse. It was, I presume, formed by the sliding of avalanches from the slopes of the Monch. At any rate, to our delight, it led us gradually round the barrier of seracs, till in a few minutes we found ourselves on the highest plateau of the glacier, the crevasses fairly beaten, and a level plain of snow stretching from our feet to the last snow-slope.

We were now standing on the edge of a small level plateau. One, and only one, gigantic crevasse of really surpassing beauty stretched right across it. This was, we guessed, some three hundred feet deep, and its sides passed gradually into the lovely blues and greens of semi-transparent ice, whilst long rows and clusters of huge icicles imitated (as Lauener remarked) the carvings and ecclesiastical furniture of some great cathedral. The opposite side of the plain was bounded by a great snow-ridge, which swept round it in a long semicircular curve from the Monch to the Eiger. This ridge, in fact, forms the connecting isthmus by which the great promontory of the

Eiger is joined to its brethren of the Oberland. Close to the Monch the slopes are of great height and steepness, whilst, owing to the gradual rise of the snow-fields and the sinking of the ridge, they become very insignificant at the end next to the Eiger. A reference to the map will explain the geography of our position. The pass which we were attempting would naturally lie over the shoulder, where the connecting, isthmus I have mentioned articulates with the lower ridges of the Monch. Lauener had, in fact, reached this exact point from the other side. And we knew that, once there, we should be on the edge of a nearly level basin of snow, which stretches across the Monch-Joch, or ridge connecting the Monch with the Walcherenhorner. This basin is, in fact, the common source of the Aletsch and Viescher 1 glaciers, and the mound of the Monch-Joch which divides them is very slightly defined across the undulating beds of neve. From this basin, however, the Viescher glacier sinks very rapidly, and consequently the ridge between the Monch and Eiger, which rises above it in bare rock cliffs, is much loftier near the Eiger

    1 The best known Viescher glacier is, of course, that which descends from the Oberaar-Joch towards Viesch. The glacier mentioned in the text is the great tributary of the lower Grindelwald glacier, called "Viescher" glacier in the Carte Dufour.

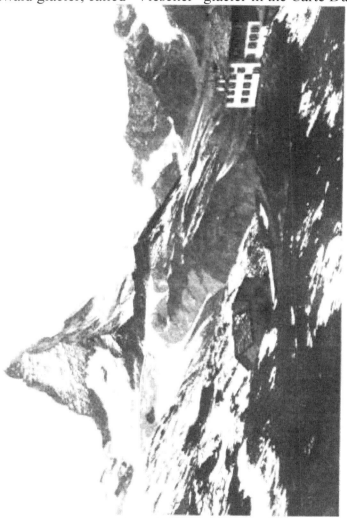

    than near the Monch on its south-eastern side— the exact opposite of its form on the northwestern side, as already mentioned. Hence, to reach our pass, we had the choice either of at once attacking the long steep slopes which led directly to the desired point on the shoulder of the Monch, or of first climbing the gentle slopes near the Eiger, and then forcing our way along the backbone of the ridge. We resolved to try the last plan first.

    Accordingly, after a hasty breakfast at 9.30, we started across our little snow-plain and commenced the ascent. After a short climb of no great difficulty, merely pausing to chip a few steps out of the hard crust of snow, we successively stepped safely on to the top of the ridge. As each of my predecessors did so, I observed that he first looked along the arete, then down the cliffs before him, and then turned with a very blank expression of face to his neighbour. From our feet the bare cliffs sank down, covered with loose rocks, but too steep to hold more than patches of snow, and presenting right dangerous climbing for many hundred feet towards the Grindelwald glaciers. The arete offered a prospect not much bettor: a long ridge of snow, sharp as the blade of a knife, was playfully alternated with great rocky teeth, striking up through their

icy covering, like the edge of a saw. We held a council standing, and considered the following propositions:—First, Lauener coolly proposed, and nobody seconded, a descent of the precipices towards Grindelwald. This proposition produced a subdued shudder from the travellers and a volley of unreportable language from the Cha-mouni guides. It was liable, amongst other things, to the trifling objection that it would take us just the way we did not want to go. The Cha-mouni men now proposed that we should follow the arete. This was disposed of by Lauener's objection that it would take at least six hours. We should have had to cut steps down the slope and up again round each of the rocky teeth I have mentioned; and I believe that this calculation of time was very probably correct. Finally, we unanimously resolved upon the only course open to us—to descend once more into our little valley, and thence to cut our way straight up the long slopes to the shoulder of the Monch.

Considerably disappointed at this unexpected check, we retired to the foot of the slopes, feeling that we had no time to lose, but still hoping that a couple of hours more might sec us at the top of the pass. It was just eleven as we crossed a small bergschrund and began the ascent. Laue-

ner led the way to cut the steps, followed by the two other guides, who deepened and polished them up. Just as we started, I remarked a kind of bright track drawn down the ice in front of us, apparently by the frozen remains of some small rivulet which had been trickling down it. I guessed that it would take some fifty steps and half-an-hour's work to reach it. We cut about fifty steps, however, in the first half-hour, and were not a quarter of the way to my mark; and as even when there we should not be halfway to the top, matters began to look serious. The ice was very hard, and it was necessary, as Lauener observed, to cut steps in it as big as soup-tureens, for the result of a slip would in all probability have been that the rest of our lives would have been spent in sliding down a snow-slope, and that that employment would not have lasted long enough to become at all monotonous. Time slipped by, and I gradually became weary of a sound to which at first I always listen with pleasure—the chipping of the axe, and the hiss of the fragments as they skip down the long incline below us. Moreover, the sun was very hot, and reflected with oppressive power from the bright and polished surface of the ice. I could see that a certain flask was circulating with great steadiness amongst

the guides, and the work of cutting the steps seemed to be extremely severe. I was counting the 250th step, when we at last reached the little line I had been so long watching, and it even then required a glance back at the long line of steps behind to convince me that we had in fact made any progress. The action of resting one's whole weight on one leg for about a minute, and then slowly transferring it to the other, becomes wearisome when protracted for hours. Still the excitement and interest made the time pass quickly. I was in constant suspense lest Lauener should pronounce for a retreat, which would have been not merely humiliating, but not improbably dangerous, amidst the crumbling seracs in the afternoon sun. I listened with some amusement to the low moanings of little Charlet, who was apparently bewailing his position to Croz, and being heartlessly chaffed in return. One or two measurements with a clinometer of

Mathews' gave inclinations of 51 0 or 52 0 , and the slope was perhaps occasionally a little more.

At last, as I was counting the 580th step, we reached a little patch of rock, and felt ourselves once more on solid ground, with no small satisfaction. Not that the ground was specially solid. It was a small crumbling patch of rock, and every stone we dislodged went bounding

rapidly down the side of the slope, diminishing in apparent size till it disappeared in the berg-schrund, hundreds of feet below. However, each of us managed to find some nook in which he could stow himself away, whilst the Chamouni men took their turn in front, and cut steps straight upwards to the top of the slope. By this means they kept along a kind of rocky rib, of which our patch was the lowest point, and we thus could occasionally get a footstep on rock instead of ice. Once on the top of the slope, we could see no obstacle intervening between us and the point over which our pass must lie.

Meanwhile we meditated on our position. It was already four o'clock. After twelve hours' unceasing labour, we were still a long way on the wrong side of the pass. We were clinging to a ledge in the mighty snow-wall which sank sheer down below us and rose steeply above our heads. Beneath our feet the whole plain of Switzerland lay with a faint purple haze drawn over it like a veil, a few green sparkles just pointing out the Lake of Thun. Nearer, and apparently almost immediately below us, lay the Wengern Alp, and the little inn we had left twelve hours before, whilst we could just see the back of the labyrinth of crevasses where we had wandered so long. Through a telescope I could even dis-

tinguish people standing about the inn, who no doubt were contemplating our motions. As we rested the Chamouni guides had cut a staircase up the slope, and we prepared to follow. It was harder work than before, for the whole slope was now covered with a kind of granular snow, and resembled a huge pile of hailstones. The hailstones poured into every footstep as it was cut, and had to be cleared out with hands and feet before we could get even a slippery foothold. As we crept cautiously up this treacherous staircase, I could not help reflecting on the lively bounds with which the stones and fragments of ice had gone spinning from our last halting-place down to the yawning berg-schrund below. We succeeded, however, in avoiding their example, and a staircase of about one hundred steps brought us to the top of the ridge, but at a point still at some distance from the pass. It was necessary to turn along the arete towards the Monch. We were preparing to do this by keeping on the snow-ridge, when Lauener, jumping down about six feet on the side opposite to that by which we had ascended, alighted upon a little ledge of rock, and called to us to follow. He assured us that it was granite, and that therefore there was no danger of slipping. The sun had melted

the snow on the southern side of the ridge, so that it no longer quite covered the inclined plane of rock upon which it rested. The path thus exposed was narrow and treacherous enough in appearance at first; soon, however, it grew broader, and, compared with our ice-climb, afforded capital footing. The precipice beneath us thinned out as the Viescher glacier rose towards our pass, and at last we found ourselves at the edge of a little mound of snow through which a few plunging steps brought us, just at six o'clock, to the long-desired shoulder of the Monch. I cannot describe the pleasure with which we stepped at last on to the little saddle of snow, and felt that we had won the victory. We had made a pass equal in beauty and difficulty to any first-rate pass in the Alps—I should rather say to any pass and a half. For, whereas most such passes can show but two fine views, we here enjoyed three. From the time of our reaching the summit of the ridge we had been enveloped in a light mist. Shortly after we had gained the col, this mist suddenly drew up like a curtain; and as mountain after mountain came out in every direction from a point of view quite new to me I felt perfectly bewildered. We were on the edge of three great basins. Behind us the plain of Switzerland stretched away to the Jura. On

our left a huge amphitheatre of glacier sank down, marked in long concentric curves by tier after tier of crevasses to the level of the Grindelwald glacier. Beyond rose the sheer cliffs of the Wetterhorn, and farther back from the plain the black cluster of rocks of the Schreck-horner. This view is invisible from the Col de la Jungfrau, and is so eminently beautiful that I should recommend visitors from the ^ggisch-horn to prefer this col to the other. It is as easily reached from the southern side, and is alone worth the trouble, if it be not profane to speak of the trouble, of such a walk. But the finest part of the view remains. We were standing at the edge of a great basin of snow. From its farther side the great Aletsch glacier stretched away from our feet like the reach of some gigantic river frozen over, and covered from side to side with a level sheet of pure white snow, sweeping gradually away in one grand curve till it was lost to sight in the distance. Beyond it rose the Monte Leone and the ranges that look down on Italy. On each side rose some of the noblest mountains in Switzerland—the Jungfrau, Monch, Alctschhorn, and the long jagged range of the Viescherhorner, with the needle-point of the Finsteraarhorn overlooking them. So noble and varied a sweep of glacier is visible nowhere else

in the Alps. Is it visible on the Eiger-Joch? Did we really see the Monte Leone, the Jung-frau, and the Aletschhorn with our bodily eyes, or were they revealed only to the eye of faith? Have I, in short, written down accurately what I saw at a given moment, or have I quietly assumed that we saw everything which was visible during the remainder of our walk to the /Eggisch-horn? I regret to say that I have undoubtedly used a certain poetic license——a fact which I ascertained by once more reaching the Eiger-Joch in 1870, though not from the same side. The Monch and Trugberg cut off a large part of the view, and only a limited part of the great sweep of the Aletsch glacier is visible from the col itself. Without adding to the weakness of a blunder the folly of an apology, I will simply remark that he who sees only what is before his eyes sees the worst part of every view. Let the imagination remove the Monch and Trugberg and everything that I have described will be visible; whilst even the prosaic persons who carry note-books to bind themselves down to what Clough calls "the merest it was," and thus cramp their excursions to the "great might have been," will find that perch on the shoulder of the Monch to be almost incomparable in variety and magnificence. I will add that though

150 The Playground of Europe

the pass has, for some reason, never been repeated, I see no reason to suppose it to be specially difficult. My guide on the later occasion maintained that we could have descended the long slopes, which took us seven hours to climb in 1859, in an hour and a half. But they were now snow instead of ice. We saw, too, a route along the cliffs which fall from the ridge towards the Grindel-wald glacier which may turn out to be practicable when there is little snow. I leave the task to another generation of climbers.

Meanwhile our thoughts pardonably concentrated themselves on the important question of food. Of the two requisites for a satisfactory meal, one, viz., the provisions, was abundantly present. I fancied too, at first, that my appetite would do its part; but, on trying to swallow some meat, I found that our long fast since the last meal, combined with the baking we had undergone, had so parched my mouth that the effort was useless. My thoughts turned to a refreshing cup of tea and a bed at the ^Eggisch-horn. But, alas! the inn was seven hours off; it was 6 p.m., and the sun near setting. Lauener mentioned certain wolldecken and some coffee, which he believed to be at the Faulberg; and the Faulberg, though we knew it to be one of those caves from which the whole of one side

and the roof have been removed, immediately seemed to us to be the pleasantest hotel in Switzerland. We started off with enthusiasm to gain it. Passing rapidly round the great snow-basin between the Monch and the Trugberg, we easily reached the summit of the M6nch-Joch; whence a rather steep slope leads to the head of the glacier called the Ewiger Schnee. At foot of the fall, which is perhaps some fifty feet high, is a bergschrund. Lauener, planting his feet in the snow above, prepared to lower each of us by the rope. Suddenly G. Mathews lost his footing, shot down the slope like a flash of lightning, and disappeared over the edge of the bergschrund. To our great relief we immediately heard him call out "All right!" and the next moment he appeared, full of snow, but otherwise none the worse for his involuntary glissade. We followed with the help of the rope, and started down the glacier once more. We were scarcely off when the broad reach before us turned first to a glorious rose-colour, and then faded to a livid hue as the light crept up the sides of the mountains. Soon they, too, turned pale; the glow lingered a little on the loftiest peaks, then faded too, and left us to the light of the moon, which was still clear enough to guide us.

Lauener took this opportunity of remarking

that he had been very unwell for three days before, and was consequently rather tired. He added presently that he could not see, and did not in the least know where he was going. I do not implicitly believe either of these statements, which struck me as being rather ill-timed. However, we marched steadily forwards in a long straggling line over the beautifully even surface of the glacier, already crisp with the evening frost, anxiously watching the sinking moon, and calculating whether her light would enable us to reach the Faulberg.

We were making good progress, and the hospitable Faulberg was coming almost into sight, when we reached the point where the glacier curls over for a steep descent, just above the confluence of the glaciers from the Lotschsattel and Griinhornlucke. Here a few concealed crevasses, causing the partial disappearance of some of our party, made a resort to the rope necessary. Fastening ourselves together, we again pressed on as fast as we could. But the crevasses grew more numerous and broader, and the surface of the ice more steeply inclined. In the faint moonlight we could hardly tell what we were treading upon—treacherous snow-bridges or slippery slides of ice. A stumble or two nearly brought us all in a heap together. Moreover

the Aletschhorn had chosen to shove its head up just in the way of the moon; and at last, as we were all getting rather puzzled how to proceed, the moon suddenly dipped behind it, the great shadow of the mountain shot out over us, and we were left all alone in the dark. Looking hastily round in the faint twilight, we could just make out a great mass of rock on our right hand. This forms part of the great promontory which divides the two main branches of the Aletsch glacier. We made for it at once, found no crevasses to stop us, and stepped once more off the ice on to dry land. We unanimously resolved to stay where we were till daylight should appear. W T e unfastened the ropes, took a glass of wine all round, and determined to make ourselves comfortable. Having drunk my wine, and made a perfectly futile attempt to swallow a bit of bread, I put on a pair of dry stockings which I had in my pocket over my wet ones, stuck my feet into a knapsack, and sat down on some sharp stones under a big rock. My companions most obligingly sat down on each side of me, which tended materially to keep off the cold night wind, and one of them shared my knapsack. My seat may very easily be imitated by any one who will take the trouble to fill one of the gutters by the side of a paved street with a heap of granite stones prepared for macadamising a road. If he will sit down there for a frosty night, and induce a couple of friends to sit with him, he will doubtless learn to sympathise with us. Lauener carefully warned us not to go to sleep, and I think I may say we fulfilled our promise of obeying his injunctions, with the exception of a doze or two towards morning. Lauener himself rose at once into exuberant spirits. His good temper and fun seemed to rise with the occasion; and after telling us a variety of anecdotes, beginning with chamois-hunting and ending (of all things in the world) with examinations—for it seems that Swiss guides share, with undergraduates, this particular form of misery—he retired to the nook which the Chamouni guides had selected, and, to the best of my belief, passed the rest of the night in chaffing them.

There is, of course, something disagreeable in passing a night "squirming" (to use an Americanism) on a heap of stones, and making fruitless endeavours to arrange their sharp corners into a soft surface to sit upon, by a series of scientific wriggles. I fully expected to get up in the morning stuck all over with pebbles, like a large pat of butter dropped into a sugar basin. In other respects I believe I really enjoyed the night. The cold was not intense, and in fact I rarely

felt it at all. Partly the excitement, and partly the beauty of the perfectly still and silent night prevented its seeming long. The huge snow-covered mountains that glimmered faintly through the darkness, the long glorious glacier, half seen as it swept away from our feet, and the perfect stillness of the scene, were very striking. We felt that our little party was in absolute solitude in the very centre of the greatest waste of ice and bare rock in the Alps. I will not, however, deny that towards morning I got a little chilly, not to say sulky. Gradually the mountain forms became more distinct, the outlines of rock and snow showed themselves more plainly, and I was quite surprised, on looking at my watch for the first time, to find that it was half-past two, and to see Lauener coming to tell us it was time to start.

We jumped up, shook ourselves, struggled into our frozen boots, and made a futile attempt at breakfast. The dangers of the darkness had disappeared; but the pleasure and excitement had gone too, and it was a right dreary walk that morning to the /Eggischhorn. The Aletsch glacier is intersected by a number of little crevasses, just too broad to step and wide enough to tire weary men. As we walked on down its broad monotonous surface. I was surprised to

find how extremely ugly everything looked. It was a beautiful day, and before us, as we approached the Marjelen See, rose one of the loveliest of Alpine views—the Matterhorn, flanked by the noble pyramids of the Mischabel and Weisshorn. I looked at it with utter indifference, and thought what I should order for breakfast. Bodily fatigue and appreciation of natural scenery are simply incompatible. We somehow contrived to split into three parties, and the rapidity with which we lost sight of each other was a curious proof of the vast size of the glacier. A party of our friends passed us on their way from the yEggischhorn to the Jung-frau-Joch, but we failed to see them. The utter insignificance of a human figure on these wastes of ice is one of the first things by which we learn to appreciate their vast size.

Lauener and I found our way to some chalets, where a draught of warm milk was truly refreshing. I need hardly say that after it we managed to lose our way over the abominable slopes of the yEggischhorn. Shoulder after shoulder of that dreary mountain came out in endless succession, and I was glad enough to see the friendly little white house a little before nine o'clock, and to rejoin my friends over a luxurious breakfast provided by its admirable landlord.

CHAPTER VI

THE JUNGFRAU-JOCH

Three years afterwards I was once more standing upon the Wengern Alp, and gazing longingly at the Jungfrau-Joch. Surely the Wengern Alp must be precisely the loveliest place in this world. To hurry past it, and listen to the roar of the avalanches, is a very unsatisfactory mode of enjoyment; it reminds one too much of letting off crackers in a cathedral. The mountains seem to be accomplices of the people who charge fifty centimes for an echo. But it does one's moral nature good to linger there at sunset or in the early morning, when tourists have ceased from travelling and the jaded cockney may enjoy a kind of spiritual bath in the soothing calmness of the scenery. It is delicious to lie upon the short crisp turf under the Lauberhorn, to listen to the distant cow-bells, and to try to catch the moment at which the last glow dies off the summit of the Jungfrau; or to watch a light summer mist driving by, and the great mountains look through

its rents at intervals from an apparently impossible height above the clouds. It is pleasant to look out in the early morning from one of the narrow windows, when the Jungfrau seems gradually to mould itself out of darkness, slowly to reveal every fold of its torn glaciers, and then to light up with an ethereal fire. The mountain might almost be taken for the original of the exquisite lines in Tithonus:

Once more the old mysterious glimmer steals From thy pure brows, and from thy shoulders pure And bosom beating with a heart renewed. Thy sweet eyes brighten slowly close to mine E'er yet they blind the stars; and the wild team That love thee, yearning for thy yoke, arise And shake the darkness from their loosened manes, And beat the sunlight into flakes of fire.

We, that is a little party of six Englishmen with six Oberland guides, who left the inn at 3 a.m., on July 20, 1862, were not, perhaps, in a specially poetical mood. Yet as the sun rose whilst we were climbing the huge buttress of the Monch, the dullest of us—I refer of course to myself—felt something of the spirit of the scenery. The day was cloudless, and a vast inverted cone of dazzling rays suddenly struck upwards into the sky through the gap between the Monch and the Eiger; which, as some effect

of perspective shifted its apparent position, looked like a glory streaming from the very summit of the Eiger. It was a good omen, if not in any more remote sense, yet as promising a fine day. After a short climb we descended upon the Guggi glacier, most lamentably un-poetical of names, and mounted by it to the great plateau which lies below the cliffs immediately under the col. We reached this at about seven, and, after a short meal, carefully examined the route above us. Half-way between us and the col lay a small and apparently level plateau of snow. Once upon it we felt confident that we could get to the top. But between us and it lay a broken and distorted mass of crevassed glacier, the passage of which seemed very doubtful. We might, however, turn part of this by creeping up a mass of icy debris, which lay at the foot of a cliff of protruding ice, the abrupt end of a glacier crawling down over the cliffs above us. The process would be precisely equivalent to walking in front of a battery of cannon which might open fire at any moment. There is something about the apparent repose of the icy masses, and, it must be added, the rarity of a fall, which tempts one strongly to run an occasional risk of the kind. In the present instance our guides were certainly awake to the danger.

So unpromising, however, was the appearance of the distorted glacier upon our right, that three of them went forwards to examine this smoother but more treacherous route. We sat down and watched them, not without some anxiety. But after the pleasant process of cutting steps for half an hour under a mass of glacier in an uncertain condition of equilibrium, they returned to us with the news that farther ascent by this route was impracticable as well as dangerous. No alternative was now left but to examine the maze of crevasses on our right. Christian Michel, Christian Aimer, and Kauf-mami accordingly went forwards to try to penetrate it. We watched them creeping forwards round the base of a huge pinnacle of ice, at the other side of which they disappeared. We sat quietly on the snow, finished our breakfast, and smoked our pipes. Morgan sang us some of the songs of his native land (Wales); somebody occasionally struck in with an English chorus; Baumann irrelevantly contributed a few German verses. Gradually our songs died away, and we took to contemplating the scenery. Morgan, who had spoken very disparagingly of the Wengem Alp as compared with the scenery of Pcn-y-Gwryd, admitted that our present view was not unlike that above the Llyn Llydaw,

on the side of Snowdon, though, as he urged, the quantity of snow rather spoilt it. Gradually our conversation slackened. The only sound was the barking of an invisible dog at the Wengern Alp, which came sharp and distinct through the clear mountain air from the distant inn. Nothing could be heard or seen of the three guides who had gone forwards. A very long interval seemed to have passed away.

We all sat looking at each other in an uncomfortable frame of mind, feeling an amount of anxiety which we were unwilling to express. I could not avoid the recollection that the last time Christian Aimer had left me on a glacier, I had only found him again with two of his ribs broken. When George said something about going to look for our lost guides, we scouted his proposition with a determination proportioned to our wish not to believe in its necessity. Our nervousness was, however, gradually becoming intolerable, and we were about to decide that something must be done. Suddenly, after at least two hours' waiting, we heard a faint shout. Looking upwards, we could just distinguish three black figures at the edge of the small snow plateau. "What do they say, Michel? Are we to come?" "Nein, 11 err." "And what is it that they are saying now?" "Something about

162 The Playground of Europe

a heilloser schrund" which I take to be a schrund of such enormity as to be past praying for. They were evidently repulsed. We sat down on the snow in what I may call a ruffled frame of mind, and waited for their return. Morgan quoted a proverb in Welsh—the only literary remains of one of the greatest of Welsh sages, Anarawd, so he informed us—the translation of it being "For the impatient patience is needful," or words to that effect. Whilst we were discussing the least ignominious way of getting to the JEggisch-horn under the circumstances, our guides reappeared. They had been stopped, they told us, by a huge crevasse, thirty feet broad in places, and running right across the glacier, dividing it into two distinct fragments; once beyond it, we should have won the day, and by means of a ladder twenty-five feet long they thought it might be possible to get over it at one point. All our despondency was over. We unanimously resolved to go back to the Wengem Alp and send down for a ladder; and, accordingly, the same evening, the ladder appeared in charge of one Peter Rubi, a man who possesses in great perfection the weight-carrying powers of the Oberland guides in general.

The next morning, starting at 3.05, we had arrived at the same place as before, at 6.12.

We plunged at once into the maze of crevasses, finding our passage much facilitated by the previous efforts of our guides. We had to wind round towers of ice intrenched by deep crevasses, carefully treading in our guides' well-cut footholds. A clinometer, which showed various symptoms of eccentricity throughout the day, made some specially strong statements at this point. By interrogating one of these instruments judiciously, the inclination of Holborn Hill may be brought to approximate to 90 0 . A more serious inconvenience was derived from the extremely unsteady condition of the towering ice-pinnacles around us. We were constantly walking over ground strewed with crumbling blocks of ice, the recent fall of which was proved by their sharp white fractures, and with a thing like an infirm toadstool twenty feet high towering above our heads. Once we passed under a natural arch of ice, built in evident disregard of all principles of architectural stability. Hurrying judiciously at such critical points, and creeping slowly round those where the footing was difficult, we managed to thread the labyrinth safely, whilst Rubi appeared to think it rather pleasant than otherwise in such places to have his head fixed in a kind of pillory between two rungs of a ladder, with twelve feet of it sticking out behind

and twelve feet before him. We reached the gigantic crevasse at 7.35. We passed along it to a point where its two lips nearly joined, and the side farthest from us was considerably higher than that upon which we stood. Fixing the foot of the ladder upon this ledge, we swung the top over, and found that it rested satisfactorily against the opposite bank. Aimer crept up it, and made the top firmer by driving his axe into the snow underneath the highest step. The rest of us followed, carefully roped, and with the caution to rest our knees on the sides of the ladder, as several of the steps were extremely weak—-a remark which was equally applicable to one, at least, of the sides. We crept up the rickety old machine, however, looking down between our legs into the blue depths of the crevasse, and at 8.15 the whole party found itself satisfactorily perched on the edge of the nearly level snow plateau, looking up at the long slopes of broken neve that led to the col.

A little discussion now T ensued as to the route to be taken. The most obvious way was through the steep seracs immediately under the snowy col. The guides, however, determined upon trying to turn these by cutting their way up the steady slopes more to the right. Aimer and Michel accordingly went forward and set to

work, whilst we indulged in a second anomalous meal. For a time they went on merrily. The snow was in good order, and required only a single blow from the axe. The fragments which rolled down upon us were soft and harmless. Soon, however, they began to be mixed with suspicious lumps of hard blue ice. Aimer and Michel seemed to be crawling forwards more and more slowly. The labour was evidently considerable for every foot of progress won. I began to remember, with increasing distinctness, our experience of the exactly corresponding place on the Eiger-Joch. The slopes through which we had there cut our way were neither so long nor so steep as those now before us, and the snow here was equally hard. Fortune seemed to be turning against us. Our spirits, which had risen with the successful passage of the crevasse, began to fall again. The prospect of a return through unsteady seracs in the heat of the day, to present ourselves a second time to the jeers of tourists on the Wengern Alp, was not attractive. Our cheerful reflections were arrested by the return of Michel and Aimer. They agreed that the staircase on which they had now spent an hour's work must be abandoned ; but we might still try the great wall of seracs on the left. It would be very hard to give to any

but Alpine readers the least notion of what the task before us was like. I reject unhesitatingly Morgan's statement that it was exactly similar to the ascent of the Glydirs from Llyn Ogwen. We had to climb a wall built of seracs, their interstices plastered up with snow, and the whole inclined at an angle of between 50 0 and 6o°. Every now and then, where the masonry had been inferior, a great knob of serac protruded, tilting up the snow to a steep angle, and giving us a block of solid ice to circumvent. Deep crevasses, arranged on no particular principle, intersected this charming wall in every direction where they were not wanted. It may be tolerably represented by imagining the seracs of the Col du Geant filled up, and jammed together by their weight at a steep angle. Michel and Aimer led the way rapidly and eagerly. Sometimes we could get on for a few paces in snow: sometimes the axe was called into play. But we all pushed forwards as fast as we could, and in dangerous places those who had passed professed to help the others, by hauling in the rope as hard as they could. When the man behind was also engaged in hauling himself up by the rope attached to your waist, when the two portions of the rope formed an acute angle, when your footing was confined to the insecure grip of one

toe on a slippery bit of ice, and when a great hummock of hard serac was pressing against the pit of your stomach and reducing you to a position of neutral equilibrium, the result was a feeling of qualified acquiescence in Michel or Aimer's lively suggestion of "Vorwarts! vorwarts!"

Somehow or other we did ascend. The excitement made the time seem short; and after what seemed to me to be half an hour, which was in fact nearly two hours, we had crept, crawled, climbed, and wormed our way through various obstacles, till we found ourselves brought up by a huge overhanging wall of blue ice. This wall was no doubt the upper side of a crevasse, the lower part of which had been filled by snowdrift. Its face was honeycombed by the usual hemispherical chippings, and somehow always reminds me of the fretted walls of the Alhambra; and it was actually hollowed out so that its upper edge overhung our heads at a height of some twenty or thirty feet; the long fringe of icicles which adorned it had made a slippery pathway of ice two or three feet distant from the foot of the wall by the freezing water which dripped from them; and along this we crept, in the hope that none of the icicles would come down bodily. The wall seemed to thin out and become much

lower towards our left, and we moved cautiously towards its lowest point. The edge upon which we walked was itself very narrow, and ran down at a steep angle to the top of a lower icefall which repeated the form of the upper. It almost thinned out at the point where the upper wall was lowest. Upon this inclined ledge, however, we fixed the foot of our ladder. The difficulty of doing so conveniently was increased by a transverse crevasse which here intersected the other system. The foot, however, was fixed and rendered tolerably safe by driving in firmly several of our alpenstocks and axes under the lowest step. Aimer, then, amidst great excitement, went forward to mount it. Should we still find an impassable system of crevasses above us, or were we close to the top? A gentle breeze which had been playing along the last ledge gave me hope that we were really not far off. As Aimer reached the top about twelve o'clock, a loud jodel gave notice to all the party that our prospects were good. I soon followed, and saw, to my great delight, a stretch of smooth white snow, without a single crevasse, rising in a gentle curve from our feet io the top of the col.

The people who had been watching us from the Wengem Alp had been firing salutes all day, whenever the idea struck them, and when-

ever we surmounted a difficulty, such as the first great crevasse. We heard the faint sound of two or three guns as we reached the final plateau. We should, properly speaking, have been uproariously triumphant over our victory. To say the truth, our party of that summer was only too apt to break out into undignified explosions of animal spirits, bordering at times upon horseplay. I can imagine that a sentimental worshipper of the beauties of nature would have been rather shocked at the execrable jokes which excited our laughter in the grandest scenery, and would have better become schoolboys than respectable college authorities. There are purists who hold that the outside limits of becoming mirth should be a certain decorous cheerfulness; Milton, they think, has indicated the tone of sentiment appropriate to the contemplation of nature by making the Allegro as sober as the Penseroso; and they would have set us down as heartless despisers of the charms of sublime scenery. I will not undertake our defence at present, and only beg my readers to excuse us, if they can, on the ground of that national reticence which is so great a convenience for people who have no sentiment to hide. Let them believe, or try to believe, that we were as sensitive as Mr. Ruskin himself to the charms of the raoun-

tains, and put on a mask of outward mirth only by way of concealing our "great disposition to cry." At this point of our journey, however, neither emotion made itself manifest. The top of the Jungfrau-Joch comes rather like a bathos in poetry. It rises so gently above the steep ice wall, and it is so difficult to determine the precise culminating point, that our enthusiasm oozed out gradually instead of producing a sudden explosion; and that instead of giving three cheers, singing "God Save the Queen," or observing any of the traditional ceremonial of a simpler generation of travellers, we calmly walked forwards as though we had been crossing Westminster Bridge, and on catching sight of a small patch of rocks near the foot of the Monch, rushed precipitately down to it and partook of our third breakfast. Which things, like most others, might easily be made into an allegory. The great dramatic moments of life are very apt to fall singularly flat. We manage to discount all their interest beforehand; and are amazed to find that the day to which we have looked forward so long—the day, it may be, of our marriage, or ordination, or election to be Lord Mayor—finds us curiously unconscious of any sudden transformation and as strongly in-inclined to prosaic eating and drinking as usual.

At a later period we may become conscious of its true significance, and perhaps the satisfactory conquest of this new pass has given us more pleasure in later years than it did at the moment. However that may be, we got under way again after a meal and a chat, our friends Messrs. George and Moore descending the Aletsch glacier to the . z Eggischhorn, whose summit was already in sight, and deceptively near in appearance. The remainder of the party soon turned off to the left, and ascended the snow-slopes to the gap between the Monch and Trugberg. As we passed these huge masses, rising in solitary grandeur from the centre of one of the noblest snowy wastes of the Alps, Morgan reluctantly confessed for the first time that he knew nothing exactly like it in Wales. We ploughed on in the mid-day sun, Rubi trailing the ladder behind us with singular cease and content. We were not sorry to reach the top of the Monch-Joch, and dropped down through the complicated crevasses beyond to the Grindelwald side. Rubi deposited his ladder at the foot of the great icefall after thirteen hours' companionship; and at nine o'clock we returned to the Adler at Grindelwald, having made a new and interesting high-level route from the Wengern Alp.

On sitting down to supper, T discovered a

large wound in my ankle. On exhibiting this to a medical friend next morning, he asked for my clasp-knife. Extracting from it a very blunt and rusty lancet, and observing that it would probably hurt me very much, he quietly took hold of my leg, and, as it appeared to me, drove the aforesaid lancet right through my ankle with a pleasant grin. He then recommended me to lie down on the sofa, and keep my foot higher than my head. I obeyed his directions, and remained in this attitude (which is rather commodious than elegant) for eight consecutive days of glorious summer weather. I had the pleasure (through a telescope) of seeing my friends one day on the Wetterhorn and another on the Eiger. I read through the whole literature of the village, consisting of an odd number of the Illustrated, half a Bells Life, and Tennyson's Princess, about a dozen times, and occasionally induced two faithful companions to trot me round the house in a chaise-ti-porteiir.

I studied with a philosophic eye the nature of that offensive variety of the genus of primates, the common tourist. His main specialities, as it seems to me from many observations, are, first and chiefly, a rooted aversion to mountain scenery; secondly, a total incapacity to live without the Times; and thirdly, a deeply-seated

conviction that foreigners generally are members of a secret society intended to extort money on false pretences. The cause of his travelling is wrapped in mystery. Sometimes I have regarded him as a missionary intended to show by example the delights of a British Sunday. Never, at least, does he shine with such obvious complacency as when, armed with an assortment of hymn-books and Bibles, he evicts all the inferior races from the dining-room of an hotel. Perhaps he is doing penance for sharp practices at home; and offers himself up for a time to be the victim of the despised native, as a trifling expiation of his offences. This view is confirmed by the spirit in which he visits the better known places of pilgrimage. He likes a panoramic view in proportion to the number of peaks which he can count, which, I take it, is a method of telling his beads; he is doomed to see a certain number of objects, and the more he can take in at one dose, the better. Further, he comforts himself for his sufferings under sublime scenery by enjoying those conundrums in stone—if they may be so called—which are to be found even in the mountains. A rock that imitates the shape of the Duke of Wellington's nose gives him unspeakable delight; and he is very fond of a place near Grindelwald where St. Martin

174 The Playground of Europe

is supposed to have thrust his staff through one hill and marked the opposite slope by sitting down with extreme vigour. Some kind of lingering fetish worship is probably to be traced in these curious observances. Although the presence of this species is very annoying, I do not think myself justified in advocating any scheme for their extirpation, such as leaving arsenic about, as is done by some intelligent colonists in parallel cases, or by tempting them into dangerous parts of the mountains. I should be perfectly satisfied if they could be confined to a few penal settlements in the less beautiful valleys. Or, at least, let some few favoured places be set apart for a race who certainly are as disagreeable to other persons as others can be to them—I mean the genuine enthusiasts, or climbing monomaniacs.

Milder sentiments returned as my health improved.

CHAPTER VII

THE VIESCHER-JOCH

On the eighth day, July 29th, my leg was nearly well, and tying it up in a handkerchief, I resolved to get on to my feet once more, and make another pass across the Oberland. The same evening four of us (Hardy, Liveing, Morgan, and I), with the two Michels, Baumann, C. Bohren, and Inabnit, were the occupants of the Kastenstein, a kind of burrow under a big stone at the foot of the Strahleck Pass. A more glorious evening and a more lovely place for a bivouac I never saw. The long line of cliff from the Finsteraar-horn to the Eiger was in front of us. At their feet lay the vast reservoirs of snow, from which the huge Grindelwald glacier pours down right into the meadows and corn-fields below. Looking down the great ice-stream through the mighty gateway whose pillars are the Eiger and the Mcttelhorn, we had our one glimpse of vegetation and habitable regions. The faint reflection of the flashes of summer lightning showed us at intervals the clear outline of the snow-fields

176 The Playground of Europe

opposite, and one glimmering spark marked the resting-place of some friends who were to cross the Monch-Joch next day. Some discordant shrieks from our guides made the summer night hideous, but probably failed to reach the ears of our next neighbours at a distance of three or four miles. We certainly heard no response, and crept into our burrow, where I need only say that four of us were packed between a couple of nubbly rocks, some two feet apart, and reduced into that kind of mass which "moveth altogether if it move at all."

At 4.55 next morning, very much later than was either necessary or advisable, we were off. Crossing the crisp surface of level glacier beneath us, we arrived at the foot of a series of snow-slopes, which rise from the highest reach of the Grindelwald glacier to the eastern face of the Viescherhorn. Seen from this side, the lesser Viescherhorn (or Ochsenhorn) rises in a double-headed form; the peak towards the Finsteraar-horn being bounded by a rounded outline, and divided by a saddle from the sharper peak towards the north. Immediately below this saddle lies a comparatively level plain. Two or three ridges starting from it partition off the secondary glaciers, which descend steeply through deep gorges to the Grindelwald glacier. The most

obvious plan would perhaps be to ascend that glacier which starts from the actual col, south of the rounder point of the Viescherhorn and between it and the Finsteraarhorn. The lower part of this glacier is, however, torn by numerous crevasses, and its upper part divided from the col by long and very steep snow-slopes. We therefore preferred to ascend at once by the first glacier whose foot we reached, and which appears to form nearly a straight line from the sharper summit of the Viescherhorn to the Grin-delwald glacier. This glacier was itself torn by huge transverse crevasses in more than one place. We toiled slowly up it in a long line, dragging behind us a ladder, which our experience on the Jungfrau-Joch had induced us to lug along with us. The abominable machine acted rather like the log sometimes attached to a donkey's leg. It trailed heavily and deeply behind us. It of course abridged more or less our passage of some of the larger crevasses. But I am inclined to think that it was pressed upon us by the guides rather with a view to increased wages than to the actual exigencies of the case. Our glacier had a fine eastern aspect, and consequently, as the morning sun struck upon it, we sank deeper and deeper, and toiled more wearily up its apparently interminable

178 The Playground of Europe

slopes. The ladder made a deep trace along the snow, we floundered wearily on, and the Viescher-horn seemed to rise higher and higher with a monotonous but singularly steady motion. At last we struck into the path of an avalanche, which had come down not long before, and had effectually bridged some yawning crevasses. This helped us well, and at last, after about five hours of toil, we found ourselves on the little level I have mentioned. We struck across this, and circumventing a bergschrund by means of the ladder—the one time in the day when its absence would really have been inconvenient—we found ourselves, at 10.30, on a kind of snowy rib descending directly from the rounded dome which forms the southern hump of the Viescherhorn.

Up to this point the work had been simply a stiff pull against the collar, with no excitement, no variety, and very little pleasure. It was simply plodding up a very hot long, staircase, knee-deep in snow. From this point the labour was so far changed that we frequently had ice under our feet instead of snow; the guides had the additional amusement of cutting a good many steps, and there was a small amount of pleasurable excitement from the fact that there was a bare possibility of our coming down with a run. The surface of the ice was covered by

snow in that peculiar state in which it is sometimes found in these high regions. It consisted of a mass of granular lumps, like loose piles of hailstones. These poured into every footstep as it was cut, as so much sand might have done, and had to be cleared out by hand and foot before we could safely trust our weight to them. As it was, the rope once or twice tightened unpleasantly, and my next neighbour informed me that he was resting upon nothing in particular, and advised me to stand steady. I presume, too, that it is to this point of our journey that I am to refer an incident which Morgan has since related in thrilling terms, but which has mysteriously escaped my memory. I fear it was part of that queer incrustation of legend which gathers so rapidly round genuine historical narrative. He says that we were exhausted with our labour, parched with the reflected heat of the sun, and toiling knee-deep in snow up the steepest part of the slope. Guides and travellers were alike faint—frequently pausing for breath, and at times half inclined to give up their toilsome enterprise. A halt took place—we were undecided whether to advance or retire—the critical moment was come. Suddenly Morgan raised his voice, and dashed into one of the inspiring songs of his native land. As the notes

180 The Playground of Europe

struck our ears, fresh vigour seemed to come into our muscles. With a unanimous cry of "Forwards!" we rushed on, and in a fit of enthusiasm gained the top of the pass. I am content with stating as a fact that, somehow or other, we toiled up the dreary slopes, and at last found ourselves at the point where the snow-rib loses itself in the rounded knob of the Viescherhorn.

Just at this moment a cloud, which had been gathering along the ridge, became overcharged. A bright flash of lightning seemed to singe our beards, whilst a simultaneous roar of thunder crackled along the valley. A violent hailstorm rattled down, blinding and bewildering us. It was impossible to catch a glimpse of our route. We scooped some big holes in the snow with our axes, and cowered down in them to get some shelter. My hands were in that miserable condition when the more vehemently I nibbed them, the wetter and colder and more numbed they seemed to grow. The hail got in at the back of my neck; the cold wind froze my nose; the snow got into my boots and up my trousers, and filled my pockets. We helplessly waited for a change; and I have reason to suppose that my intellects were more than usually obscured. Certainly Mr. Ball has been compelled to state, in his admirable Guide, that he cannot

understand my description of the geography; and he charitably attributes my perplexity to the storm which here assailed us. I must admit that I do not quite understand the description myself; and now that eight years have elapsed since I saw T the scene of our adventure, the details have certainly not become clearer. The only comfort is that, as nobody has been foolish enough to follow our steps, no great harm can have been done. Storm-beaten, stupefied, and sulky, we crouched in the snow-drift till the storm lulled, and we jumped up to look round us. We might curve towards our left, or in a southerly direction, round the great knob of the Viescherhorn, so as to get on to the col. This would, as we saw afterwards, have been the right way. It involved, however, some more step-cutting. We therefore went round in the other direction, and at 2 p.m. got upon the saddle between the two points of the Viescherhorn. From this point it was obvious that we could descend upon the upper level of the Viescher glacier. Accordingly, without further investigation, we crept slowly down a steep but short slope of snow and rock to a point where we could easily surmount a threatening bergschrund, let ourselves down over it, and found ourselves on the upper level of the Viescher glacier. A tedious

182 The Playground of Europe

but not difficult series of manoeuvres placed us at the foot of the crevasses by which the upper part of the glacier is intersected, at about three o'clock. Our detour over the saddle of the Viescherhorn had cost us a considerable amount of unnecessary trouble. Our difficulties were, however, now all over. We had made a pass which, of all the passes I know, is certainly one of the most wearisome. A very long monotonous pull up a very steep slope of snow, with only the variation of sometimes having to cut steps and sometimes not, is apt to be stupid. The views were of course grand, and the black rocks of the Schreckhorn looked down upon us with a majestic assertion of their dignity. I cannot, however, describe the scenery of the Vieschergrat Pass as especially interesting. Perhaps I am biassed by our subsequent career.

We were now on known ground. Nothing but a level stretch of glacier intervened between us and the ordinary route to the Finsteraarhorn or Oberaar-Joch. The ^Eggischhorn inn began to paint itself distinctly to our imaginations. But I could not help remembering that we were hardly likely to reach the ^Eggischhorn before dark; and there are few Alpine travellers in whose minds darkness on the /Eggischhorn is not associated with weariness and vexation of

spirit. I therefore strongly objected to any unnecessary halts, and after taking a standing meal and contemptuously abandoning our ladder to the tender mercies of the glacier, we started at a rapid pace for our much-desired haven. We left the Grunhornlticke on our right, struck into the Oberaar-Joch route, passed the wilderness of boulders and mossy slopes, where a few wretched sheep pick up a mysterious existence above the Viescher glacier, descended the well-known waterfall, and after a rapid march found ourselves at 7.30 at the point where the stream from the Marjelen See descends beneath the ice close to a few isolated huts. We were all rather tired. We were disposed to look upon our day's work as done, and we hardly relished another climb. Still we were afraid to take the lower path to the ^Eggischhorn, and preferred ascending the stream to the Marjelen Alp, hoping to find natives there if it should be too dark to succeed in seeing the path to the inn. We climbed wearily and slowly upwards, halting to take an occasional pull at the stream and to imbibe certain remnants of brandy. Gradually it became dark. We were guided chiefly by the sound of the rushing water on our left. Every form of mountain and rock had become indistinct in the twilight, and then been 1 (lotted out in a

184 The Playground of Europe

drizzling mist. The stream seemed to be falling from an indefinite height out of absolute darkness, and the path refused obstinately to bend over into the little plain by the lake. We might be climbing right up to the top of the Grat, when at length we reached a small hummock of rock, on which was planted something like a wooden cross. We halted undecidedly and looked round. Nothing but a mixture of mist and night was to be seen. Some one raised a despairing jodel on the chance that we were near the chalets. No answer. Another louder yell, in which we all joined; silence again, and then, to our intense delight, something like a faint reply. A general yell now produced a singular phenomenon. A faint spark appeared at an indefinite distance, indistinctly glistening through the drizzle. The spark grew larger, began to move, and presently came rushing in a straight line towards us. On approaching, a boy was discovered attached to one end of a flaming piece of pine wood. He had come on our cries from the Marjelen Alp, and guided us back to it at 9 o'clock, a distance of two or three hundred yards. This piece of luck raised our spirits. We soon became valiant over warm milk and bread, and having thus unexpectedly changed our prospect of lodging in damp rhododendron beds for the certainty of

dry straw under a roof, began to think whether better things might not be done. Should we try to reach the /Eggischhorn ? The guides unanimously pooh-poohed the idea. Liveing, who had been rather unwell a day or two before, signified his opinion by taking off his boots and lying composedly down on the regulation mixture of hay and fleas. I was for giving in to the majority; but the strongest and most obstinate member of the party showed at once his courage and the uncompromising vigour of his appetite by insisting upon making a dash for supper at the ^Eggischhorn. A little diplomacy was therefore used. Certain hints at five francs produced an obvious willingness on the part of the small Will-o'-the-wisp to go in any direction we might please to mention. The guides grumbled emphatically. A variety of judicious appeals to their skill, and our extreme confidence in it, at last induced them to take a more favourable view of the case. The construction of a lantern out of an empty bottle and a candle removed one objection which had been strongly urged. The right plan, I may remark, is to strike out the bottom of the bottle and to insert the candle through the neck with the wick foremost. The glass of the bottle then forms a tolerably satisfactory screen. As an additional and (as it

186 The Playground of Europe

proved) more effective source of light, the boy constructed a torch by splitting one end of a large piece of wood with an axe, and inserting splinters of wood into the splits. These when lighted made a grand blaze, and we all started at 10 p.m. in high spirits for the inn. Liveing, animated by our example, sprang up and accompanied us.

For a time all went right enough. The torch led the van, and the lantern brought up the rear. We climbed the crest of the hill leading towards the ^Eggischhorn rapidly and successfully. "We shall have supper before n o'clock," said Hardy. Presently the torch went out. It was soon relighted, and we were off again. Soon, however, our progress, which had been straight forward, seemed to me to be rather wandering. "We have just missed the path," the boy explained, "but we shall have it again directly." It soon became rather doubtful, however, whether we were not looking for it in the wrong direction. Shortly afterwards a discussion arose whether the narrow gully which we were descending was not the very one we had come up ten minutes before. During the discussion the torch went out. In attempting to relight it we put the candle out. Then all the matches were wet through, and it was not till we had hunted to

the bottom of some one's knapsack that we found any that would work. At last we succeeded; and, to save trouble, I may say that this process of extinction of all our lights, followed by their laborious rekindling, went on at continually shorter intervals till we seemed to be sitting down longer than we were walking. Meanwhile the search for the missing path seemed every moment more hopeless. After scrambling up and down, and round and round for a long time, we found ourselves in a disconsolate and bewildered state of mind, standing on a damp ledge of grass at the foot of a big rock staring vacantly into blank darkness. Whether to go up or down, or right or left, we knew no more than if we had been suddenly dropped into the middle of the great Sahara. There was only one thing for it. We took our knapsacks and put on our remaining articles of dress, e.g., two pairs of socks, an extra pair of trousers, a flannel shirt, a waistcoat, and a dozen paper shirt-collars, and crouched down under the rock, hoping that the wind would keep in the right quarter, that the puddle in which we were sitting would be speedily absorbed, and that the sun would get up as early as possible. The guides made some very sarcastic remarks, in very broad patois, about gentlemen who would n't take advice, and I

refrained from allusions to supper. The boy who had attempted to guide us had meanwhile vanished mysteriously into the depths of the night. At this instant, just as I had drawn my second pair of trousers over my second flannel shirt, he suddenly emerged from the dark, exclaiming, "I've found a man!" It struck me as a bewildering and improbable circumstance that any other human being should be fool enough to be within reach of us; and I did not at first appreciate the fact that he was referring to a stone man or cairn, marking the route to the /Eggischhorn. It was just twelve as he made the announcement, and in a few seconds the whole party was under way again, not even halting to take off the extra apparel. A dreary and a dismal walk we had. In front was the boy with the torch. At short intervals halts had to be called, to coax the said torch by various means into renewed activity. In the intervals between these halts, I, being about fifth in the line, was only conscious of the torch as a kind of halo spreading out a very short way and very mistily on either side of certain black bodies, which oscillated strangely between me and it. From these black masses occasionally proceeded sounds expressive of revolutionary sentiments about hills and stones in general, and the yEggisch-

horn in particular. My radius of vision included about a yard of hill, inclining at a very steep angle to my left, scattered with mysterious objects, which generally turned out to be deep holes when I thought they were stones, and very unsteady and sharp-edged stones when I thought they were puddles. It is a well-known fact that the ^Eggischhorn consists of innumerable shoulders so arranged that you suppose even* successive one as you come to it to be the last, and find out when you have tinned it that it is only an insignificant unit in the multitude. I have often been made practically aware of this fact, but never was it so painfully impressed upon me as from 12 to 2.30 on the morning of July 30, 1862. Stumbling, groaning, slipping, and pulling up short over stones, puddles, slippery grass, and every variety of pitfall, including cows, we pushed wearily on, and about 2.30 became conscious that we were in a thing that called itself a path. A few minutes at a quicker pace, and the /Eggischhorn inn appeared. At 2.40 a.m. a wild yell from four weary, hungry, and thirsty travellers roused AT. Wcllig to a sense of his duties, and by 3 o'clock the said travellers were asleep, with two good bottles of champagne inside them.

CHAPTER VIII
THE COL DES HIRONDELLES

A queer sensation which sometimes comes over me on the sight of some familiar Alpine view may best be illustrated by a literary parallel. In reading some genuine old English dramatist, I have been tempted to exclaim, What does this fellow mean by imitating Lamb's John Woodvill, or Taylor's Philip Van Artevelde? Why does n't he see the absurdity of mimicking a man who was his junior by two centuries? His local colouring is the same, if it is not quite so obtrusive, as that of our modern Elizabethans. In the same way the view from the Wengern Alp, or the Gornergrat, or the Montanvert strikes me as little better than a plagiarism. Have we not seen the very same design used over and over again for the lids of carved boxes, and worked to death by the artists of those pictures with blue glaciers, and white peaks, and melodramatic chamois which stare at us from every shop-window in Interlaken or Chamouni? Why should the eternal Alps enter into rivalry with

such puerile performances? In no place have I been more frequently seduced into this whimsical inversion of logic than at the Montanvert. The Montanvert, in fact, is, with the possible exception of the Wengem Alp, the most cockney-rid den of all the well-known points of view. Within a few hundred yards of the inn lies a monument which strikingly illustrates this truth, and which, I fear, hardly receives from members of the Alpine Club the attention which it deserves. On the old moraine, just above the place where the solemn echoes of the mountains are waked for the sum of ten centimes, lies an ancient gre\'7d* stone, on which are carved the names of Pocock and Windham. Some Old Mortality of the district appears to have preserved this inscription which marks the bivouac of the first British tourists 130 years ago. Having surmounted the peril of the ascent to Chamouni, these primitive adventurers, whose memory should surely be dear to us, succeeded in scaling the Montanvert, and doubtless felt that they had well earned their night's rest beneath the now historical block. Perhaps the Alpine Club might do worse, in case of necessity, than apply a few francs towards the preservation of this memorial of their ancestors' heroism. Another inscription commemorative of tourist enthusiasm never

192 The Playground of Europe

aroused my conscious attention, often as my eyes must have rested upon it, until this summer. All who have made expeditions from the Montan-vert remember that queer little octagonal edifice opposite the door of the inn, which seems to be a compromise between a stable, a kitchen, and a sleeping-room for the guides. Here, I have sometimes fancied, were held the private sittings of the Everlasting Club commemorated in the Spectator. I have never, at least, looked in at any hour of day or night without seeing a guide seated by the fire—eating, drinking, or smoking with stolid persistency, and generally conspicuous for that air of extreme personal comfort which is only produced by the consciousness that you are keeping somebody waiting. The impatience which is naturally produced in the mind of an external observer had, I presume, hitherto prevented me from noticing that above the door are engraved the words, A la Nature. In fact, the building was erected by a prefect of some half-century ago, who indulged in the good old-fashioned sentimentalism of the Rousseau school, and devised this rather pagan edifice for the benefit of his fellow T -creatures. Then it was probably an almost solitary example of a building intended for the accommodation of Alpine sightseers. Since that day, two or three generations of tourists must have gazed from its doors up the ice-stream of the Mer de Glace, and admired the great block of the Geant and the Jorasses framed so symmetrically between the gigantic portals of the Charmoz and the Verte. The view has indeed become so familiar that almost every Alpine traveller, and many travellers who have never been to the Alps, could draw a recognisable outline of its main features with their eyes shut. The Alpine Club, I doubt not, is as familiar with its details as with a well-known passage beginning "Dearly beloved brethren"; and, as the statement that "the Scripture moveth us in sundry places" sometimes reaches their ears without exciting a very vivid emotion, so the eye glances along the well-known ridges without setting up any conscious train of reflection. To some such cause, at least, I must attribute the really curious fact, that up to the year 1873 nobody had yet attempted one of the most conspicuous passes in the whole range of the Alps. The grand block of the Jorasses is abruptly cut away, as we all know, at its northern end, and thence to the wild labyrinth of ridges which culminates in the Aiguille de Lechaud there stretches a level saddle, over which, as is obvious to the meanest capacity, there must lie a route to Courmayeur.

Indeed it would be the natural route for anybody intending to cross the Col du Geant by the light of nature. If you would make a bee-line from the Montanvert to the nearest points of the Italian valleys, your route would take you straight across this col, which is as obtrusive as the Theo-dule from Zermatt, or the Jungfrau-Joch from the Wengern Alp. The apparent steepness of the final barrier indeed was forbidding; but in an ascent of the Mt. Mallet, which I had made a couple of years previously, we had gone near enough to see that this appearance, as in so many other cases, promised to be illusory. M. Loppe was especially impressed by the view, and had frequently suggested to me the propriety of an assault when arranging the plans of coming campaigns. The discussion assumed fresh prominence during certain tobacco parliaments held in the beginning of July last in front of Couttct's inn at Chamouni. It took a practical turn on the arrival of Messrs. T. S. Kennedy and J. G. Marshall, who contemplated the same expedition, and brought two excellent guides, Johann Fischer of Meiringen, and Ulrich Aimer, son of the hero of Grindelwald. Kennedy and Marshall had already acquired useful information by examining the col from the other side, and were eager to add this to their previous conquests. Loppe

was naturally keen about the last pass of really first-rate excellence in the district which may fairly be called his own. For my part, I have long abandoned difficult and dangerous expeditions. Moreover, I was at Chamouni in the interesting character of invalid. I was suffering from a state of mind and body which wives and mothers generally attribute to overwork, and which one's masculine friends consider as a pronounced attack of idleness. Whatever the origin of my symptoms, I took a course which I can strongly commend to all my readers. I consulted a distinguished physician who to his great medical skill adds the special merit of being a member of the Alpine Club. He prescribed—less to my surprise than to my satisfaction—Alpine air and indolence. The last phrase I took to include moderate walking exercise, and, though abjuring anything bordering upon the performance of athletic feats, I felt myself at liberty to accompany my friends in the humble character of historiographer, with liberty to turn back if the danger or the fatigue should prove excessive.

And so it came to pass that once more I was sleeping at the Montanvert, on the night of Sunday, July 13th. The weather was so questionable that I had delayed my departure till the

last possible moment. Throughout the early summer we had a series of thunderstorms, the temperature, lowered by each storm, gradually becoming almost unbearably hot, till we were relieved by another explosion. On this occasion a storm had just passed, but as Loppe and I climbed the well-known Montanvert path in the late evening, the heavy pine branches were still dripping with moisture, and an occasional thunder-growl muttered amongst the distant ranges. I had therefore turned in with some doubts as to the next day's weather. A happy faculty of sleeping soon produced utter oblivion, though my couch was little softer than Pocock and Windham's stone. What passed for a mattress seemed rather to be a cylindrical bolster of abnormal hardness, and reminded me of that dummy which Jack the Giant-killer placed in his bed in one of his adventures; as it would have been only too well calculated to withstand the most vicious blows of an infuriated Blunderbore. I see that I am inevitably falling into the old groove. I am treating my readers to the thousand and first description of the discomforts of bad beds. My only excuse is, that the grievance is as lasting as the grumbling. The Montanvert inn is a disgrace to the district. The commune of Chamouni receives, I am told, a rent of some

500/. a year for this dirty, tumbledown, old hovel, which has received no improvement or addition since it was first erected. The number of visitors must have multiplied tenfold, but the accommodation is strictly stationary, and the prices steadily advancing. This phenomenon is quite in accordance with the laws of political economy. Monopoly, whether of railways or innkeepers, is fatal to the comforts of travellers. To complain is probably mere waste of ink; and yet one would fain hope that the good people of Cha-mouni may be impressed in the course of a generation or two with the conviction that better accommodation on so celebrated a point of view would provide an excellent investment for some of their spare capital. In Switzerland the Mon-tanvert would have been rebuilt and enlarged a dozen times over; and the example of their enterprising neighbours should be set before these good stolid Chamouniards as vigorously as possible. Meanwhile, in spite of dirt, discomfort, a squalid bedroom, and a close atmosphere, I was sleeping peacefully on the early morning of the 14th, lapped in some dim consciousness that I had still an hour and a half before the inevitable hour of starting, when a stentorian voice resounded through the house— "Ohe! la-bas! Aufstehen! Garcon! get up!" were

some of the fragmentary utterances which rang like a trumpet through my dreams; and led me to realise the fact that my young friend Marshall, boiling over with the impetuosity of youth, was resolved to avoid any danger of oversleeping by premature vociferation. Some wretched tourists, it was true, were beginning to fortify themselves by a few hours' repose for the toils of an expedition to the Jardin. They must take the consequences of venturing into the haunts of the enthusiastic climbers, and speedily they had a lively accompaniment to the vocal music played on the planks by a pair of sturdy hobnailed boots. Lulled by this music, I endeavoured to compose myself once more to rest by carefully extending myself along that granite column which played the part of mattress. Alas! my efforts were in vain. The voice became more emphatic.

Still it cried "Sleep no more!" to all the house; Marshall hath murdered sleep; and therefore Loppe" Shall sleep no more; Stephen shall sleep no more.

Nay, if I am not mistaken, a personal application was given to some of the more energetic remonstrances; and, finally, I found myself dozing over the usual fragments of dry bread and tepid coffee, and endeavouring, according to a principle

which I observe with uncleviating punctuality, to shirk all responsibility in the matter of ordering provisions or otherwise arranging for a start. Still drowsy and dull, I turned out about three o'clock into the drowsy night. The prospect was equivocal. Torn fragments of vapour floated aimlessly above the valleys and clustered in long streamers upon the mountain sides. The pyramid of the Aiguille Verte was nearly hidden; on the opposite side, the Aiguille de Charmoz appeared, as it were, in a ragged dressing-gown, resembling the costume of Mr. Pickwick's companions in the Fleet Prison. A maudlin kind of monster it seemed, apparently reeling homewards from some debauch in a general state of intellectual haziness. One huge finger — well known to all buyers of photographs and coloured drawings for the last fifty years— was held up, pointing, with a muddled significance, towards the heavens. Doubtless some sort of meaning might lurk in that intoxicated gesture; but I am no diviner of omens. Whether the old Charmoz intended an encouragement or a warning was to me an impenetrable secret. Perhaps, too, my language is rather profane. The mountain, gleaming in the dim moonlight through the veil of mist, and revealing that strange pinnacle of rock which, as I have seen

it from a nearer point, is one of the most daring of mountain spires, should have excited awe rather than unseemly familiarity. I do not profess, however, to have my emotions at command ; solemn objects sometimes fail to create in me that "great disposition to cry" which is the becoming mode of testifying sensibility to natural beauty. Moreover, I have a spite against the Charmoz. I tried to climb him a few weeks afterwards, and his scarped cliffs foiled our best efforts; and, therefore, I take the liberty, not unprecedented under such circumstances, of attacking the character of a mountain which has shown itself too hard for me. We had soon turned our backs on the Charmoz, and, as we advanced, two facts became evident: the sunrise was healthy, giving promise at least of a tolerable clay; and the pace speedily threatened to be tremendous. Our party was of heterogeneous composition. Experience was represented by the elder travellers and youthful precipitance by our friend Marshall. Youth accordingly set out, in spite of sage warnings, at a brisk rate, and was soon leaping crevasses in a playful spirit far ahead of creeping age. Had we been united we might have succeeded in suppressing this undignified impetuosity; but the guides, as well as their employers, were divided. Loppe

and I had engaged Henri Devouassoud, a younger brother of the well-known Francois. Now, Henri—and I am glad to make the remark in view of some recent criticisms upon Chamouni guides—is a strong, willing, and pleasant fellow, though not, as I judge, more than second-rate as a leader of a party. He caught the contagion from Marshall, and was willing to show his Ober-land companions that a Chamouni guide could make the running. Accordingly, we crossed the glacier at a pace which brought us to the foot of the final bergschrund in little over three hours. It is, I am aware, contrary to all rules of Alpine writing to reach a bergschrund so early in the narrative of the expedition. But I have a sufficient apology. It is as easy to get to this bergschrund as to reach the Jardin—as easy as another process which I need not particularly mention, and the facility of which needs no demonstration to an audience of travellers by profession. There is simply a gently sloping snow-plain to cross, where the few crevasses could be turned by trifling deviations from our route; and thus our only mentionable adventure was the inevitable quarrel with the porter from the Montanvert, who asked more for going part of the way to the Jardin from the inn than he would have received, according

to the tariff, for going the whole way from Cha-mouni and back. Moreover, I am not going to let my readers off too easily. For here I must insert a brief digression whilst we are eating our breakfast and speculating upon the best line of assault. A day or two before, we had committed the usual folly of an exploring expedition. It had the normal fate of such performances. We had climbed to nearly our present position and had thence watched a noble bank of boiling cloud, which effectually screened from sight every detail of our proposed route. One incident, however, deserves fuller commemoration. As we began to climb the snow-slopes we observed at a little distance ahead certain mysterious objects arranged with curious symmetry in a circle upon the glacier. Some twenty black spots lay absolutely motionless before us; and as we approached we became aware of their nature and not, as I will venture to add, without a certain feeling of sadness. In fact, we had before us a proof of the terrible power with which tempests sometimes rage in these upper regions. The twenty objects were corpses— not human corpses, which, indeed, would in some sense have been less surprising. As a melancholy accident lias lately shown, man may easily be done to death by the icy winds which

have such terrible power in these exposed wastes of snow. But the poor little bodies which lay before us were the mortal remains of swallows. How it came to pass that the little company had been struck down so suddenly as their position seemed to indicate gave matter for reflection. Ten minutes' flight with those strong winds would have brought them to the shelter of the Chamouni forests, or have taken them across the mountain wall to the congenial climate of Italy. Whether the birds had gathered together for warmth, or been stupefied so suddenly by the blasts as to be slain at once in a body, there they were, united in death, and looking, I confess, strangely pathetic in the midst of the snowy wilderness. I mention it here, not merely because none of us had met with such an incident before, but also for another purpose. We proposed at the time to give to our pass the name of the Col des Hirondelles, which may be justified by the precedent of the Adler-Joch at Zermatt. First discoverers have, I believe, a right to christen their passes; but, unluckily or otherwise, it is one of those rights which are not very valuable, because they cannot be enforced. If future travellers choose to call the pass the Col des Jorasses, or the Col de Lechaud, we cannot exact any penalty from them. So far, however, as our

authority is recognised, I beg to state that we in all due form passed a resolution declaring that henceforth the col which I am about to describe should be known to all whom it concerns by the sole style and title of the Col des Hiron-delles. And having thus done my duty to the swallows, and given satisfaction, as I hope, to such souls as Mr. Darwin and the Thirty-nine Articles may allow them to possess, I will return to the narrative of our adventures.

As I have already said, a precipitous wall stretches northward from the foot of the Jorasses. On the French side it consists chiefly of rock; on the Italian it is covered by the wild Glacier de Freboutzie, As we approached it we recognised various routes each of which appeared at times to be easy, and then again put on an appearance of inaccessibility from some different point of view. Close to the Jorasses there descends a broad couloir of ice, crowned by a wall of serac, as to which it is still a matter of controversy whether it ever does or does not discharge avalanches. I cannot decide the point, not having made the necessary observations; but I may briefly say that any one who likes to risk these possibly non-existent avalanches might probably shorten his route to the summit. It would, perhaps, be possible, moreover, to reach

the top of the col by climbing the lower rocks of the Jorasses, and so keeping entirely to the right, or south, of the great couloir. To the left, or north, there is a long rocky wall, seamed by deep narrow couloirs of much smaller dimensions, occasionally varied by steep snow-slopes, by scarped surfaces of rock, and by huge ribs which descend steeply from the summit and are more or less cut off at their lower extremities. More than one route might, perhaps, be discovered amongst them. Our attention, however, was fixed upon the ridge which bounded the great couloir immediately to the north, and upon a very deep and narrow couloir, which again lies immediately to the north of the ridge. This last couloir was filled with snow at the time of our passage, and, as seen from the Montanvert, appeared to us like a bright white thread. The snow, however, frequently disappears, and the whole wall then seems to be little more than a mass of rock. To be clear, I shall call this narrow couloir the chimney, and I may proceed to describe our assault.

The chimney opens out at its lower end, and is lost in the main slope above the bergschrund. At 6.45 we attacked this natural fosse with the usual gymnastics. They involved no particular difficulty, and I only had to complain of a decided propensity of the rope to get itself entangled in

my hat. The said hat, having shrunk, was easily knocked off my head, and the fact that I was constantly struggling to preserve it against the skilful assaults of the rope may show that the line of ascent was tolerably steep. For a time, however, the climb was perfectly easy. Digging our feet into soft but tenacious snow T , we speedily reached the chimney and found it in good condition. The snow-bed which lined it enabled us to climb hand over hand without a check for some considerable distance. But by degrees, Fischer, who was leading, became nervous. He has a prejudice, in which I admit that I share, against stones bigger and harder than the human head, and subject entirely to the force of gravitation. Lopp6, who is always loudly proclaiming his own extreme prudence— it is his pet virtue, and the only one upon which he prides himself—is a sceptic in the matter of stones. Whether he has confidence in the strength of his skull, or a faith in his capacity for being missed, I cannot say. However, he assured us emphatically that stones would not fall, or if they did fall, would not hurt us. Deaf to these arguments—I call them arguments for want of a better word—Fischer insisted upon leaving the chimney and climbing the rib between ourselves and the great couloir. And hence arose

a division of the party, and a certain amount of emulation, though no want of cordiality. Whilst Loppe and Devouassoud as representatives of Chamouni stuck to the chimney like men, we effected a flanking movement on to the rib. Now, as all climbers know, these transverse performances which, if I may say it, take a mountain across the grain, are apt to lead to difficulties. For about fifty yards we had, what seemed to me, a really nasty bit of climbing. The rocks were powdered with a layer of snow, sufficiently deep to aggravate seriously the difficulties due to their rottenness and irregularity. I will not presume to say that the consequence of this was any real difficulty. Objectively speaking the rocks may have been easy; subjectively considered I heartily condemned them. A different word has been used in some translations from the Greek. At any rate, I was reduced to a state of mind of which many travellers have never been conscious; that is to say, I got so far as the incipient stage of a resolution never to trust my precious neck (the word precious, again, is used in a subjective sense) in discovering new Alpine passes. One or two positions, distinctly imprinted upon my memory, could be easily represented by Mr. Whymper's pencil, but are not so easily translatable into

language. Nor, indeed, is it worth while to tell the old story over again. The discontent incident to precarious scrambling was aggravated by the sight of Loppe and Devouassoud climbing their chimney with great ease and rapidity and greatly gaining upon us in height. Soon, however, the tables were turned. Once on the backbone of the ridge we had the best of it. In fact all difficulty was over, and we moved at breathless speed towards the top. Fischer was excited, and felt that his reputation was more or less at stake. We were bound to be first on the top, lest those verriickte Franzosen —the name, I deeply regret to say, which he applied to our excellent friends in the chimney—should laugh at our beards. We saw, indeed, and the sight was balm to our souls, that they had left the chimney on the opposite side, and were pressing, with some difficulty, up a steep snow-slope which led them to a point considerably to the north of that at which we were aiming. It brought them, however, to the other side of a great knob which here crowns the ridge, and we were therefore invisible to each other during the last few hundred feet. All the more we strained every nerve to reach the top; and a new cause increased our anxiety. I had pointed out to Kennedy the beauty of certain light clouds which were drifting over the col from Italy, and tinged by prismatic colours as they came above our heads. Unluckily they came thicker and deeper. As we reached the snow-mound on the summit-ridge we were enveloped in a light vapour which effectually hid from us the grand precipices of the Jorasses, and, for a time, concealed all but the snows in our immediate neighbourhood. We raised a shout, partly of self-applause and partly as a challenge to our rivals. Had we reached the top first? I have an opinion upon that subject, and it is one which I think I could support by sufficiently conclusive facts. I will add, however, that no persuasion, short of absolute physical torture, shall induce me to reveal it even to the Alpine Club, which has the first right to my confidence. Far be it from me to give the slightest sanction, direct or indirect, to any spirit of rivalry between climbers. Racing in the Alps is an utter abomination, and I have never been guilty of such a crime; except, indeed, once in an ascent of Mont Blanc, and again, I fear, in a dash up the ^Eggischhorn, and yet once or twice more on some of the Oberland peaks, and perhaps on a few other occasions which I decline to mention more particularly at the present moment. But my principles are good if my conduct is occasionally inconsistent.

And therefore, without throwing any light upon the question, I will merely remark that our party reached the summit about nine; having thus occupied a little over two hours in climbing the last rocks. I should guess their height very roughly at some 1200 feet; and, as the process involved some step-cutting, and the passage of the bergschrund, it will be seen that no serious difficulties were encountered. I will add further, that though our col was the point which would naturally be selected from the French side, the descent upon the Italian side was probably easier from Loppe's. The difference, however, is trifling.

To lie on the summit of a new and first-rate pass is a pleasure which, in the nature of things, can be but rarely enjoyed. Our spirits were naturally exuberant. What was it to us that imagination instead of bodily eyesight had to picture the butt-end of the lion-like mass of the Jorasses, the wild sea of unfrequented peaks towards the Lechaud and Triolet, the long vista down which the Mer de Glace flows to the Cha-mouni Valley, and the purple hills towards the St. Bernard? If to us it makes little difference, it clearly makes less to my readers, except that it saves them a passage of description which they can imagine for themselves quite as easily as

we imagined the view. They may take it for granted, too, that we were hilarious, excited, full of fellow-feeling, and very much inclined to such skylarking as can be indulged upon a glacier. And I may add that the skylarking was of a very superior order. A momentary rent in the clouds had revealed the green valley floor of the Val Ferret some 7000 feet below us, and showed, too, the right way to reach it. From our feet the grand glacier, strongly resembling the upper part of the Viescher-Firn below the Monch-Joch, hurled itself madly downwards from the mighty cirque of cliffs. It was a glacier of a rollicking spirit, given to plunging in broad curves over hidden ridges of rock; playing all kinds of practical jokes with grotesque masses of serae; sometimes allowing us to indulge in a glissade where we had expected to be cut off by an ice-cliff, and sometimes playfully opening a large crevasse beneath our feet, and forcing us to take a flying leap which was decidedly more convenient from above than it would have been from below. It was a grand sight to see the heavy-weights of the party hesitating for a few moments above some such chasm, and then come flying through the air with the swoop of an eagle and the grace of a coal-sack. It was delicious to go head over heels in a huge bank

of knee-deep snow, and feel that the farther you fell the more trouble you saved. Without a single serious check we rushed at the pas gymnast ique from the foot of the first snow-slope, which was a little too steep to be trifled with, to the point where we had to leave the glacier. And it is only necessary to say, for a rule to our followers, that they will not go far wrong if they keep as much to the left as possible during the descent. The knowledge acquired by Kennedy's party on their former expedition was of material service to us in discovering the precise route to be followed. The Glacier de Freboutzie itself falls over cliffs through which it is impossible to find a way. But, by crossing the ice which descends from the Aiguille de Lechaud, just above the point where the torrent bursts forth in a waterfall, a lofty patch of grass is reached on the northern side of the lateral valley. Thence to the floor of the Val Ferret there is a rather troublesome walk. It is necessary to find a passage through some slippery rocks, and when at their base to cross a region covered with huge loose stones, which appear to be the ruins of a gigantic moraine. For half an hour, I should think, we were risking sprained ankles across this detestable wilderness; but safety and luxury were at the other end. It was a delicious walk

that afternoon clown to Courmayeur. Delicious was the milk which an old woman brought from a chalet in return for a franc, volunteering a benevolent blessing into the bargain. Delicious, too, was the rest under a clump of fragrant pines, rendered still more fragrant by our fumigation, on the edge of the flooded meadows. And most delicious was the view of the soft Val d'Aosta which opened upon us as we rounded the Mont Saxe, and saw the group of inferior mountains round Courmayeur, whose graceful forms and rich hues announce their Italian character. With all my love for the sterner scenery of the hither side of the Alps, and my dread of demoralisation in the lazy atmosphere of the South, I cannot deny that Courmayeur is one of the very most exquisite of all Alpine scenes. I felt friendly towards the good-natured Italian bathing guests, who stared at their uncouth visitors from the ice-world as their classical ancestors might have stared at a newly-caught Briton. Even that noble creature who rejoiced in the costume of our operatic bandit by way of tribute to the general spirit of the place, was pleasant in my eyes; for was not his presence suggestive of good inns, where we might luxuriate in some comfort, and with less interruption from cock-neydom than at Chamouni? The next day was spent as the day after a grand expedition should always be spent—in chewing the cud of our recollections whilst lounging about- the lovely Courmayeur meadows. We lay in the sun in company with basking lizards, alternately watching the idiotic pranks of the grasshoppers, who are always taking the most violent and purposeless exercise in the middle of the day, and speculating on the possibility of making a direct escalade of Mont Blanc by the southern buttress. That feat still waits for a performer. Loppe and I returned next day to Chamouni by the Col du Geant, arriving at about the same time with the telegram which we had despatched on our arrival at Courmayeur.

And now it only remains for me to give an impartial estimate of the merits of our pass. Its height is not marked upon the French map, and I can only conjecture that it is approximately the same as that of the Col du Geant. Comparing it *~ 'ch that king of passes, I may say, in the first place, that it would probably occupy a rather longer time on an average. Six hours brought us from Montanvert to the summit, and six more took us to the inn at Courmayeur. The first six might have to be indefinitely extended in unfavourable conditions of the snow. I do not think, with some of our party, that we were

exceptionally lucky in this respect. I am rather inclined to the opinion that the new snow bothered us on the rocks more than it helped us in the chimney. This is a matter on which subsequent experience must decide. The climb, however, of the last ridge will always present greater difficulties than any part of the Col du Geant route, unless, indeed, it should happen that the passage through the seracs of the Geant, now so easy, should again become troublesome. On the Italian side, again, the Col des Hirondelles, though not exceptionally bad, lies over a very contorted glacier, and may at times be toilsome, especially in the ascent. It, of course, will require more labour than the delightful walk over the Mont Frety to the Col du Geant. On the whole, therefore, our pass will probably be the more laborious of the two. Comparing them in regard to scenery, I fear that there can be but one reply. The Col du Geant is and must always remain one of the first two or three, if not actually the first, in beauty of all Alpine passes. The partiality of new discoverers has set up rivals to it at one time or another; but its grandeur and variety are always fresh, and nowhere, in my knowledge, to be fairly equalled. The view towards Italy, the magnificent view of Mont Blanc, the grand basin of the upper glacier, the icefall, still noble

in its decay, may be separately equalled elsewhere ; but I do not think that any pass, even in the Oberland or at Zermatt, presents so marvellous a combination. The Col des Hirondelles, shut in by the Jorasses, must have but a limited prospect, if any, of the great peaks. To my mind, its great charm is in the wild Glacier de Freboutzie, which is the perfection of savage seclusion. I always love these recesses of the great chasm, where the spirits that haunt solitudes have not yet been finally exorcised. Centuries will elapse at our present rate of progress before the Freboutzie will become a sightseer's glacier, and perhaps by that time it will be a glacier no more. All that I can fairly claim, however, for our new pass is that it may afford a useful alternative to the Col du Geant; but it is eminently beautiful, though decidedly inferior to its superlatively beautiful rival. Moreover, no true Alpine traveller can look at it from the Montan-vert without wishing to cross it. If he does, it is my last warning to him that the descent towards Italy, easy enough when the right way is known, requires some local knowledge or careful steering. May our successors have as good fortune as fell to our lot in this as in all other respects! If so, I have no fear that they will be ungrateful to the fortunate discoverers of this, amongst the most familiar of all great Alpine passes as part of a view, though the last to be recognised as a practicable route.

CHAPTER IX

THE BATHS OF SANTA CATARINA

On a bright day in the autumn of 1869, I was standing on the balcony of a well-known inn near the baths of St. Aloritz. A little procession of ladies and gentlemen issued from the hotel and descended the slopes towards the banks of the lake. I immediately became aware— I know not whether from positive information or from some instinctive sense of reverence— that for the first time in my life I was standing in presence of a genuine king. An emperor I have seen before, and I have more than once taken off my hat to the queen of these islands. But a king is now a rarity, and I was proportionately delighted with the opportunity of discharging in my own person the functions of a Court Circular. His majesty, I might say on my own authority, accompanied by his royal consort, and attended by the lords and ladies in waiting, took the recreation of a walk on the banks of the Lake of St. Moritz. Yet a certain drop of bitterness mingled in my cup, and it

was intensified by an incident which took place that evening. I was confronted at supper by a person belonging to a class unfortunately not so rare as that of royal personages. The genuine British cockney in all his terrors was before me. The windows of the dining-room opened upon all the soft beauty of a quiet Alpine valley in a summer evening. Far above us the snow-clad range of the Palii and Bernina still glowed with the last rays of the setting sun. But the cockney was not softened by its influence, and he talked in full perfection the language of his native streets. He elaborately discussed the badness of the liquors provided for us. He tasted some of the bottle which I had ordered, and was peacefully consuming, and condescended to inform me that it was "devilish bad." He went into the merits of all the inns which had had the benefit of his patronage, discriminated with great clearness between the qualities of the Cognac which they provided; and showed his superiority as a Briton by condemning them all with various degrees of severity, with the exception of one whose landlord had been waiter at a great London hotel, and had thereby attained a comparative degree of civilisation. He thought it proper to add a few remarks upon the scenery of the country-, extracted with more or less fidelity

from Murray or Baedeker; and I know not whether his aesthetical or his practical remarks were the more significant of delicate sensibility. Anyhow, two hours of his conversation were enough for my nerves, and I retired to meditate on things in general and the beauty of the evening. One conclusion became abundantly clear to me. Kings and cockneys, I thought, may be excellent people in their way. I love cockneys because they are my neighbours, and the love of our neighbour is a Christian duty. I revere kings because I was taught to do so at school, to say nothing of the sermons and church services in which the same duty was impressed. But they have in common the property of being very objectionable neighbours at an hotel. They raise prices and destroy solitude, and make an Alpine valley pretty nearly as noisy and irritating to the nerves as St. James's. Was it worth while to travel some hundred miles to find one's self still in the very thick of civilisation? Kings, I know, have to travel (sometimes against their will), and so must cockneys, if it be right, which I admit to be an open question, that either class should continue to exist; and certainly so long as they exist, I have no right to demand their expulsion from the Engadine. Indeed, on second thoughts, it is perhaps as well that they should

go there. The gregarious instinct has doubtless been implanted in the breast of the commonplace traveller for a wise purpose. It is true that it leads migratory herds to spoil and trample under foot some of the loveliest of Alpine regions, such as Chamouni or Interlaken. But, on the other hand, it draws them together into a limited number of districts, and leaves vast regions untrodden and unspoilt on either side of the beaten tracks. St. Moritz acts like one of those flytraps to be seen in old-fashioned inns, which do not indeed diminish the swarm of intrusive insects, but profess at least to confine them to one spot. And if any district were to be selected into which the cockneyism of the surrounding Alps might be drained as into a reservoir, certainly no better selection could be made than St. Moritz. The upper valley of the Inn is one of the very few Alpine districts which may almost be called ugly. The high bleak level tract, with monotonous ranges of pine forests at a uniform slope, has as little of the picturesque as can well be contrived in the mountains. Even in the great peaks there is a singular want of those daring and graceful forms, those spires, and domes, and pinnacles, which give variety and beauty to the other groat mountain masses. I should rejoice if it could be made into Norfolk Island of the Alps, and

222 The Playground of Europe

all kings, cockneys, persons travelling with couriers, Americans doing Europe against time, Cook's tourists and their like, commercial travellers, and especially that variety of English clergyman which travels in dazzling white ties and forces church services upon you by violence in remote country inns, could be confined within it to amuse or annoy one another. Meanwhile, though this policy has not been carried out, it is gratifying that a spontaneous process of natural selection has done something of the kind. Like flies to like; the cockney element accumulates like the precious metal in the lodes of rich mines; and some magnificent nuggets may be found in and about St. Moritz; but luckily at no great distance may be found regions as bare of cockneys as a certain Wheal something or other of my (too close) acquaintance appears to be of copper. A day's journey, I knew, would take us into regions still in all the freshness of their primitive innocence; regions where the Times is never seen, where English is heard as rarely as Sanskrit, and where the native herdsman who offers milk to the weary traveller refuses to take coin in exchange for it. As I thought of these things I rejoiced that we could leave St. Moritz behind us, and fly to a certain haven of refuge. I almost hesitate to reveal the name of the hiding-place

The Baths of Santa Catarina 223

to which we retreated. Shall I not in some degree be accessory to the intrusion of some detachment from that army of British travellers which is forcing its relentless way into every hole and corner of the country? Will not some future wanderer take up his parable against me and denounce this paper as amongst the first trifling hints which raised the sluices and let the outside world into this little paradise? My reluctance, however, is overpowered by certain weighty reasons. As, first, I cannot hope that my voice will attract the notice of any great number of persons; secondly, my readers, though few, will of course be amongst the select, whose presence will be a blessing rather than a curse to the inhabitants; thirdly, the inhabitants would, I am sure, be grateful for an advertisement, and I should be glad to do them a trifling service, even though, in my judgment, of doubtful value; fourthly, if any appreciable number of Britons should take the hint, they will at least bring with them one benefit, which cannot be reckoned as inconsiderable, namely, a freer use of the tub and scrubbing-brush; and, considering that the insinuation conveyed in the last sentence would in itself be sufficient to hold many persons at a distance, I will take courage and avow that the place of which 1 have been speaking is Santa

224 The Playground of Europe

Catarina, near Bormio. Thither, in two clays' easy travelling from St. Moritz, we conveyed ourselves and our baggage, and to it I propose to devote a few pages of rather desultory remark. I cannot do all that would be required from the compiler of a handbook; I know little of the waters consumed by the guests, except that they have a nasty taste at their first outbreak, but are good to drink with indifferent wine; nor am I great at orographical or geological or botanical disquisitions; but are not these things written in the admirable guide-book of Mr. Ball? and, finally, if one person should be induced by the perusal—but the formula is something musty.

I must beg my readers to imagine an Alpine meadow, a mile or two in diameter, level as a cricket field, covered with the velvet turf of a mountain pasturage, and looking exquisitely soft and tender to eyes wearied with the long dusty valley which stretches from the Lake of Como to the foot of the Stelvio. Let him place a few chalets, upon whose timbers age has conferred a rich brown hue, at picturesque intervals, and then enclose the whole with mighty mountain walls to keep the profane vulgar at a distance. On two sides purple forests of pine rise steeply from the meadow floor and meet a little way

The Baths of Santa Catarina 225

below the inn to form the steep gorge through which the glacier torrent foams downwards to join the Adda at Bormio. In front the glen is closed by a steeper mountain, whose lower slopes are too rough and broken to admit of continuous forest. Above them rise bare and precipitous rocks, and from the platform thus formed there soars into the air one of the most graceful of snow-peaks, called the Tresero. It resembles strongly the still nobler pyramid of the Weiss-horn, as seen from the Rillel at Zermatt. It is certainly not comparable in majesty with that most majestic of mountains; as indeed it falls short of it in height by some three or four thousand feet. One advantage it may perhaps claim even above so redoubtable a rival: the Weisshorn only reveals its full beauties to those who have climbed to a considerable height above the ordinary limits of habitation, whereas the Tresero condescends to exhibit itself even to the least adventurous of tourists. It is, indeed, like all other great mountains, more lovely when contemplated from something like a level with itself. Lofty Alps, like lofty characters, require for their due appreciation some elevation in the spectator. One of the most perfect moments in which I have ever caught a share of the true

mountain spirit was when looking at the Tresero

226 The Playground of Europe

from a high shelf on the opposite range. The immediate foreground was formed by a little tarn, covered in great part with the white tufts of the cotton grass, dancing as merrily in the evening breeze as Wordsworth's notorious daffodils. Two massive ribs of rock descending on each side, like Catchedicam and the "huge nameless peak" embracing the Red Tarn on Helvellyn, formed a kind of framework to the picture. In front, the whole intervening space was filled by the towering cone of the Tresero, with torn glaciers streaming from its sides, and glowing with the indescribable colours of sunset on eternal snow. The perfect calmness of an Alpine evening, with not a sound but the tinkling of cattle-bells below, gave a certain harmony to the picture, and breathed the very essence ot repose. The domestic quiet of English fields in an autumn evening is impressive and soothing; but there is something far more impressive to my mind in the repose of one of these great Alps, which shows in every rock and contorted glacier that clings to its sides the severity of its habitual struggle with the elements. It is the repose of a soldier resting in the midst of a battle, not that of a stolid farmer smoking his evening pipe after a supper of fat bacon. Seen, however, from any point of view, and under any circumstances, whether under a clear sky or when a thunderstorm is gathering under the lee of its grand cliffs, the Tresero is a lovely object. At Santa Catarina it naturally forms the centre of every view, or serves as a charming background to the more diminutive but hardly less exquisite pictures which a traveller may discover in every nook and corner of the Alps.

To complete the portrait of Santa Catarina, I must add one, and, it must be admitted, a very important element in the view. We are constantly assured in an advertisement which has lately been appearing that the finest scenery in the world is improved by a good hotel in the foreground. There is some truth in the aphorism; and I shall certainly not seek to dispute its application in the present case. I must therefore ask the reader to place on the edge of a flat meadow a long low building of rough stone, resembling a barrack more than an hotel. Outside there is nothing very attractive; and within there are certain difficulties to be overcome by a fastidious taste. The establishment has a certain dishevelled and perplexed aspect, not exactly in harmony with English notions of order. There is an unorganised crowd of persons, male and female, who appear more or less to discharge the duty of waiters and chamber-

maids. One is occasionally tripped up by a stumbling-block on the stairs composed of an overwearied woman who has fallen asleep whilst accidentally blacking a miscellaneous boot. The scrubbing of floors seems to be trusted to the occasional zeal of volunteers, and the zeal requires some prompting from surreptitious bribes. A garment entrusted to the washerwoman has to be recovered a week afterwards by a journey of discovery through certain mysterious subterraneous passages. If you want a dish, the best plan is to go into the kitchen, where amongst a crowd of smokers and idlers you may be able to enter into conversation with the cook. The landlord as a general rule is round the corner with a cigar in his mouth talking to a friend. Were it not that the head waiter is a man of genius, the whole management of the business would be in danger of collapse. Moreover, to hint at a delicate point, you may probably be seated at dinner opposite to a lady or gentleman of primitive costume, whose ideas on the respective uses of knives, fingers, and forks are totally opposed to all the usages current in the polite society of London. Neither, I am bound to confess, is Santa Catarina a complete exception to a highly general rule" that the visitors to baths are not amongst the most congenial of companions.

Yet the remark reminds me of one great compensation. Neither guests nor inhabitants are English. If they were they would nearly be intolerable. Xor does this proposition, when rightly understood, imply any want of proper patriotism. An Englishman is, of course, the first of created beings; and he owes this preeminence in great degree to his remarkable powers of self-assertion. As an Italian visitor informed me, the great motto of the English race is "Selelf" a mysterious word, which, after some investigation, I discovered to be the Italian version of the title of Mr. Smiles's book Self-Help. Now "selelf" means the power and the will of treading on any toes that are in your way. As a corollary from this it follows that an English snob is the most offensive of snobs, English dirt the most obtrusive of dirt, and, in short, even-thing bad that is English, about the most objectionable of its kind to be found in Europe. Had those knifophagous persons who sat opposite me at dinner been of English extraction they would have been actively as well as passively offensive. Indeed I think it highly probable that they would have gone so far as to speak to me. An inn with floors as ignorant of the broom as those in Santa Catarina would in England have implied a defiance of all decency. The house would have resembled one described in a late lawsuit in London where a witness swore to having met five bugs calmly walking downstairs abreast—I had almost said arm in arm—and where, if I remember rightly, the fleas sat on the chairs and barked at you. The food in such a case would have been calculated to try the digestion of an ostrich; and the landlord would have been a cross between a prizefighter and a thimblerigger. But Italian dirt, though unpleasant, is not of that uncompromising character. It is the product, not of a brutal revolt against decency, but of an easy-going indolence. It is, as Heine somewhere says, " grossartiger Schmutz." The squalor of an Italian town surrounds monuments of incomparable beaut\'7d", and somehow does not seem altogether out of harmony with them. It is of a different order from the hopeless filth which agrees only too well with the unspeakable ugliness of a back slum in London. Like the dirt which obscures some masterpiece in painting, one fears to see it removed, lest soap and water too energetically used should remove something more than the superfluous coating of matter out of place, and reveal a raw glaring surface, untouched by the mellowing influence of time, and fit rather for some mushroom city in America than for an

ancient building smelling—only too literally— of history. And thus the dirt of Santa Catarina is not incompatible with many excellencies. The food, for example, which issues from that singular kitchen, with its crowds of unoccupied loungers, is of unimpeachable quality. The servants are externally grubby, but have always a pleasant answer to demands which to them must appear unreasonable, and are willing to do their best to satisfy the "selelf"-ful Englishman. And mixed with guests of strangely uncouth appearance are many of whose refinement and kindliness we shall always retain a grateful recollection.

Here, indeed, occurs a problem which, I fear, must be abandoned as insoluble. No philosophical account has yet been given of national differences of character, and it is hard to pronounce positively upon the rival merits of types so different as the English and Italian. The Briton drops in upon the guests at such an establishment and looks upon them with wondering contempt. He is not improbably a member of the Alpine Club. His patron saints are Saussure and Balmat. His delight is to wander all day amidst rocks and snow; to come as near breaking his neck as his conscience will allow, and after consuming a Homeric meal, to smoke his evening pipe and

retire for a short sleep before another start. The Italian appears to pass his day in elaborate indolence. He walks half a mile, till the hill begins to rise, and then sits down and basks through the sunny day. His most vigorous exercise is a short game of bowls after dinner, and he passes his evening dancing, or getting up lotteries, or listening to an impromptu concert, or, for to such a height did the revels rise on one occasion, in playing blindman's buff. He is a sociable being, and does not glower at his fellows with the proper British air, which means, to all appearance, You may go to any place in this world or the next sooner than I will touch you with a pair of tongs. Which is the best type of mankind? Personally I confess, that though I would fain be cosmopolitan, I prefer my fellow-countrymen. After the most vigorous efforts to be properly cynical as to muscular Christianity, or the more common disease of muscularity, pure and simple, I have a sneaking but ineradicable belief in the virtues of the scrambling Briton. He shares some of that quality which, in consequence of some strange theological notions, we generally describe as "devil." That it should be complimentary to a man in common parlance to say that he has plenty of the Evil One in his disposition is a curious circumstance, and shows, it may be, how easily we come to the old heathen substratum by scratching the modern surface. Perhaps our opinion of the devil is rather better than might be gathered from sermons. We sympathise with the true hero of Para-disc Lost, and think that he would make a very useful ally, if he could be persuaded to desert his party. He was certainly not wanting in the spirit of "selelf." But, at any rate, I confess to a liking for my restless and unreasonable compatriots, whatever be the proper name of the quality to which their vigour is owing. I admit, however, that much is to be said on the other side; and I should despair of impressing my opinions upon minds of a different cast. Not far from Santa Catarina is an object which impressed upon me, in a far wider sense, the width of the gulf which intervenes between our own and certain foreign modes of thought. It is a pleasant practice in those regions to collect the bones of the dead to afford an edifying spectacle to posterity. But I have never seen, nor do I wish to see, anything comparable to the ossuary in the neighbouring village of St. Antonio. There is the usual pile of bones and grinning skulls outside of the parish church. In the midst of them stand two inexpressibly ghastly skeletons with the remnants of flesh still clinging to the

234 The Playground of Europe

bones——-a sight to turn one sick at the time and to revisit one in dreams. It appears to be a superstition that the bodies of those who die on Christmas Day never decompose; and the loathsome objects which confront the villagers of St. Antonio are intended, it seems, as practical exemplifications of this truth. I can only say that it is too obvious, either that the legend is mistaken, or that the persons exhibited died on some other day. He would be a bold man who should propose to a British vestry to erect a couple of bodies of defunct parishioners by the side of a church door. Yet it would be easy to make out some kind of argument for the practice. Our nerves, it might be said, are unduly delicate, and our tastes too squeamish. We don't want to see dead bodies opposite St. James's Church in Piccadilly, but that is because modern life is devoid of seriousness. How could one more forcibly impress upon the mind of the beefy shopkeeper or plethoric farmer the truths that all flesh is grass, that in the midst of life we arc in death, and other well-worn platitudes, than by exhibiting in all its horrors the loathsome spectacle of a slowly wasting mummy? We may preach for hours the solemn truths, as we are pleased to call them, of human liability to decay, but five minutes opposite a mouldering

The Baths of Santa Catarina 235

dead body every morning would enable us to pierce thick hides impenetrable by the shafts of our rhetoric. Is not the power of contemplating such objects, "between the wind and our nobility," connected with the fact that religion seems to mean something much more living in an Alpine valley than it does in the English lowlands? The little chapel at Santa Catarina was seldom without a devout worshipper, telling his or her beads with immense earnestness, and apparently believing that it would really do some kind of good; perhaps make the cows produce more milk, or bring down more rain in spite of a rising barometer. The British farmer, as we know, goes to church as he pays his rates, and when he has heard the parson " bumming away like a buzzard-clock over his head," thinks he has said "what he owt to a' said," and comes away not appreciably the better or the worse. Might not a body or a skull or two do him a little good, and wring from him some meditations after the fashion of Hamlet on Yorick? We have become so philosophical and refined that our national religion has rather lost its savour. A ranter may touch the hearts of his audience by a plentiful use of hell-fire; but how is the well-dressed parson, who aspires to have a taste, who reads the Saturday Review, and knows that

236 The Playground of Europe

hell-fire is a metaphorical expression, to provide food highly spiced enough for such robust digestions ? Would not some good material images —pictures of souls writhing in purgatory, bloodstained crucifixes, and actual bones and bodies— do something to point his periods? Sluggish imaginations require strong stimulants; and if the one object be to tickle an insensitive palate, I don't know that the prescription employed at St. Antonio may not be a very good one. Sceptics, indeed, may doubt how far such religious observances help to elevate the understanding or to refine the imagination; whether prayers addressed under such influences are much better than a charm, or the worship of the Virgin a very great improvement upon that of the old tutelary deity of the valley. Religion gives birth not to ennobling art but to ghastly images of a morbid asceticism; but the Church has probably a firmer hold on the minds of believers still in the intellectual stage which cherishes such ideas, and, of course, they had better remain in it as long as may be.

When staying as tourists in such a district, we realise the vast interval by which we are removed from the minds of the people. We talk to them as we might talk for half an hour to some mediaeval ghost—just long enough to discover that

we are, as it were, non-conducting mediums to each other. The thought which should be conveyed from one mind across the electric chain of conversation is transformed by something more than actual defects of language. In a sense we might make acquaintance with some of the natives; we might know how many cows they kept, at what time they rose and went to bed, and what they had for dinner. But to know anything of them—to see the world through their eyes and understand what it looks like when considered as centring in an Italian valley with a bathing establishment, two or three churches, and a certain number of bodies and crucifixes, as the main objects of interest— was of course impossible. We are all two-legged creatures capable of consuming beefsteak or polenta, and, as we are generally told, possessing a certain common element of human nature; but between varieties of the same species indistinguishable to the scientific eye, there may be an invisible wall of separation sufficient to intercept any real exchange of sympathy. Now that we are separated by hundreds of miles from the Santa Catarinians, it is hard to think of the mountains as possessing more reality than the scenes of a theatre, or of the peasants as anything but the supernumeraries who were

hired to put on appropriate costumes for the occasion. Perhaps they have now changed their dresses and are meeting us as cabmen, beggars, or first, second, and third citizens in London streets. At any rate they played their parts well, and acted like Arcadians of genuine kindliness and simplicity. The practice of heaving half a brick at the head of a stranger would be considered as decided rudeness, instead of an obvious mode of extracting amusement from their visitors. One would rather wonder at the natural courtesy which they displayed, were it not that it is only in certain British districts that the obvious reply to "Good day" is, "You be damned."

I have perhaps strayed rather widely from Santa Catarina, but the nature of the population amongst which we are living is, after all, a matter of some interest even to the most superficial and cursory of tourists—amongst whom I reckon myself. In Switzerland the gulf between you and your fellow-men w r as not so wide originally and has been more nearly filled up. The Swiss, unlike their neighbours, are living in the nineteenth century. They have travelled on railways, they understand addition and subtraction, and can make out bills to perfection. They have some notion of the use of a tub, and many

of them dimly perceive that the ultimate end of a man is to climb snow-peaks. Moreover, a kind of human amalgam has been formed by the steady infiltration of British tourists; there are guides, innkeepers, and other parasitical growths, which, it must be admitted, discharge many useful functions. It is pleasant, for a change, to be amongst a more primitive race and to be able to introduce into the background of a sketch a genuine crucifix, or a peasant with some remains of a national costume. The very contrast of national characteristics makes such surroundings agreeable for a time, and our Italian companions were agreeable, from the rough shepherds, who had brought their flocks of lop-eared Roman-nosed sheep from distant valleys, up to the intelligent and cultivated gentleman who studied Mr. Smiles's works, and quoted Byron with surprising fluency. To him, indeed, the dead bodies would probably have been as amazing phenomena as to ourselves, but though the higher classes approach each other in all civilised countries, his ideas were yet sufficiently different from our own to make a contrast pleasant, at least to us.

There was, indeed, one point on which we could all agree. It was desirable to see something of the beauties of the exquisite scenery around us,

but of how much to see, and how to see it, different views might be taken. Travellers, like plants, may be divided according to the zones which they reach. In the highest region, the English climber—an animal whose instincts and peculiarities are pretty well known—is by far the most abundant genus. Lower down comes a region where he is mixed with a crowd of industrious Germans, and a few sporadic examples of adventurous ladies and determined sightseers. Below this is the luxuriant growth of the domestic tourist in all his amazing and intricate varieties. Each of them may flourish at Santa Catarina, though perhaps it is best adapted for the middle class. It would afford ample illustrations to the treatise which ought to be written on the true mode of enjoying the Alps. One amusement should be common to all; every one should have days devoted to mere objectless and indolent loafing. To the more adventurous, such days offer that happiness which Dr. Johnson's friend discovered, when he wished to be a Jew in order to combine the pleasure of eating pork with the excitement of sinning. It is delightful to lie on one's back on a glorious day, to watch the gleaming snow-line against the cloudless sky, and to say, If I were doing my duty, I should be toiling up a slippery ice staircase on that tremendous

slope. To be doing nothing when every muscle in your body ought to be at its utmost strain, is to enjoy a most delightful sensation. On such occasions, the traveller may climb the little glen through which two streams descend from the Confinale to join the Frodolfo just opposite the Stabilimento. At a height of some two or three hundred feet may be found delicious resting-places, beneath the lowest stragglers from the pine forests above. The sweet smell of new-mown hay comes to you from the surrounding meadow, and you may watch the peasants toiling from morn till night shaving the Alp as close as the face of a British parson in the diocese of Rochester, and bearing down huge burdens on their shoulders. Or you may go to the industrious ant, who, it is true, is rather too abundant on these slopes, and give thanks that you, for the time being, are a butterfly——not indeed that the butterfly is a satisfactory emblem, for he is much too fussy an insect to enjoy himself properly, and is quite incapable of lying on his back in the sunshine. The Alpine pig which roots contentedly round the chalets, whilst the goats and cattle are climbing the steep stony ridges, sets a better example; or, if a more poetical symbol be required, there is much to be said for the lizard, who creeps out of his cranny to bask in

the sun, and retires to his domestic comforts when the light disappears. Resting in sublime indolence you may admire the beauty of Alpine foregrounds. What, for example, is more perfect than one of those great boulders, that have descended into quiet valley life from their unpleasant elevation on exposed and lofty ridges? Every ledge is enamelled by some harmonious lichen. The miniature caves are spread with soft beds of moss, and delicate ferns look out from unexpected crannies. Brilliant flowers (the names of every one of which are entirely unknown to me) supply points of glowing colour along the ridges and salient angles, and some graceful tree manages to find sufficient nourishment for its roots, and rises like the crest of a helmet above the crag. One may spend a lazy hour in tracing out the beauties of the diminutive terraces and slopes of these charming gardens, and at intervals cast one's eyes upwards to the great peaks that look down upon one through the forest branches. Rash painters who try to grapple with the Alps generally make an impossible sketch of some imaginary crag, whose architecture they misunderstand, and whose colours they grossly exaggerate, and then put a mist and an imaginary precipice in the foreground to exaggerate the apparent height of their

chimerical monsters. If they would be kind enough for once to paint truly some of the lovely little dells which travellers pass with eyes glued to their guide-books, and merely throw in a mountain as a subordinate object, they would attempt a task more on a level with human powers, they would give a truer idea of some of the greatest charms of the scenery, and we should hear less of the want of the picturesque in Alpine scenery. If the traveller feels slightly more energetic, he may climb the slopes behind the house, and hunt for strawberries in the open glades of the pine forest, or a little higher, where the natives have ruthlessly extirpated the trees and left their decaying stumps to form admirable beds for the most delicious of fruits. Or he may wander through lovely woods and meadows to the glen where a stream from the Sovretta glacier forms a waterfall too humble to be an object for tourists, but singularly picturesque when it comes as a sudden surprise. Or he may follow the beautiful gorge which gradually rises from the level of Santa Catarina, to the foot of the Forno glacier, the path through which shows as charming a variety of valley scenery as is to be found in any similar walk in Switzerland. Or, he may confine himself to the ordinary postprandial constitutional of the bath guests along

the road to Bormio. Even there, every turn of the valley shows a new beauty, and we paused many an evening to admire the purple shades of the distant mountains against the evening sky, or to watch for the strange afterglow which comes out on the Tresero when the sunlight seems to have died away, and all the lower region is already in deep starlight. Wherever he wanders, that graceful summit looks down upon him and seems to be the presiding influence of the district; and it is hard to say at what hour it is most graceful—whether it is best relieved against a group of chalets, or a slope of Alpine meadow, or the dark shadows of the pine forest.

But these are humble pleasures, and to be enjoyed in their measure in almost every district where the everlasting snows are visible from the lower country. Let us rise a little higher, and in the first place say a few words on that inevitable sight, without which no gentleman's visit can be complete. I have, I must confess, always admired the courage which enables its possessor to set the established code of sightseers at defiance—to go to America without seeing the falls of Niagara, or to Rome without seeing St. Peter's, or to Jerusalem without seeing the Holy Sepulchre. The number of persons who have the necessary independence of character

is rare indeed; but such, and only such persons, might visit Santa Catarina without ascending the Monte Confinale. When I speak of "persons," I at present exclude not only the female sex, in defiance of Mr. Mill, but most foreigners and all Englishmen with less than two legs. When Santa Catarina, however, is a little more known, the proposition will be true though a wider sense be given to the word. There are at present none of the conveniences which would make the ascent as easy as any of the recognised centres of Alpine panorama; yet without such helps, an Italian lady (of, it must be admitted, unusual pedestrian powers) made one of a party which I accompanied, and the path lies over gently sloping Alps, succeeded near the top by a short slope of snow, and then some rocks, easier than those of the Piz Languard. With that upstart peak it may boldly compare itself. True it is that the Languard has presumptuously compared itself of late years with the Rigi, the Paulhorn, the /Eggischhorn, and the Gornergrat. It is high time that such audacity should be nth-rebuked. Its one claim upon public favour is founded on the fact that a large number of peaks may be counted from its summit; but it is just as rational to decide on the beauty of a view bv the number of visible mountains as on the

246 The Playground of Europe

merits of a candidate by the number of votes he receives under household suffrage. It raises a certain presumption that the mountain or the candidate can make a noise in the world, but whether he be of genuine merit or a mere charlatan is an open question. Now the Languard, in my opinion, would very likely catch the suffrages of the Tower Hamlets, but would scarcely be fitted to represent an intelligent constituency. It is deficient in the essential quality of a grand foreground; the mountains seen from it are not well grouped; and though I admit that there is something striking in a wilderness of peaks, countless as "the leaves in Vallombrosa," there is throughout a want of cohesion and concentration. In this respect, the Confinale is a striking contrast, and is a good example of a rare class of views. It stands approximately at the centre of a gigantic horseshoe of snow-clad mountains, from which it is divided by a deep trench, except at the point where a low isthmus connects it with one of the loftiest summits (the Konigspitz), and divides the waters of the two streams at its base. Had I been consulted as a landscape gardener on the laying out of this district, I should certainly have recommended the complete omission of the Confinale, and substituted for it a level plain or perhaps a lake. Its site would

The Baths of Santa Catarina 247

then have formed, as it were, the pit of a mighty-theatre some five and twenty miles in circumference; the huge mountain crescent occupying the place of the boxes and galleries. As, for obvious reasons, my advice was not asked, the visitor must be contented with the present arrangement, and imagine himself elevated on a lofty rostrum in the centre of the pit, but still far below the galleries. On his left hand a long wall of tremendous black cliffs (strongly resembling those of the Gasternthal near the Gemmi) sinks into the wild valley of the Zebru, inhabited only in the summer months by a few herdsmen. Above this wall, at some distance, towers the massive block of the Ortler Spitz, cleaving the air with its sharp final crest. About the centre of the crescent, in front of the spectator, the ridge culminates in the noble Konig-spitz, falling on this side in a sheer cliff towards the valley. The mighty precipices of this segment of the crescent, through which one or two huge glaciers have hewn deep trenches towards the valley, are well contrasted with the graceful undulations of the long snow-slopes and streaming glaciers which clothe the ridges to the right. The ever beautiful Tresero marks an interruption to the wall, where a lateral valley comes in from the south, but it is continued in the lonir swell

248 The Playground of Europe

of the Sovretta. This half of the semicircle is divided from the Confinale by the green valley of the Frodolfo, into which the eye plunges for some thousand feet, though not quite far enough to catch sight of the baths which nestle at the bottom of the gorge. There are nobler mountains, steeper cliffs, and vaster glaciers elsewhere, but it would be hard to find any point from which the sternness and sweetness of the High Alps are more skilfully contrasted and combined. From the top of yonder parapets, not forty, but (say) forty thousand ages look down upon you; and the scarred and crumbling parapets seem well placed to guard the quiet pasturages above which they tower. It may remind one of the inaccessible ridge that surrounded the mythical Abyssinian valley of Rasselas; and involuntarily I used to quote a fragment from Mr. Kingsley's ballad describing old Athanaric's sensations on looking.at the walls of Constantinople:

Quoth the Bait, Who would leap that garden wall King Sivrid's boots must own!

The Alpine Club have perhaps found King Sivrid's boots, and Rasselas would be able to leave his valley by the excellent road of the Stelvio; but to enjoy an Alpine view properly, one should at times be dreamy and sentimental, and believe

The Baths of Santa Catarina 249

in the inaccessible. Of one half of the view I have yet said nothing; and it will be enough to say that, turning round and looking between the horns of the crescent, there appears a tumbled sea of mountains and valleys, in which the Bernina chain is conspicuous. I do not attempt to say what is or is not in sight, for three reasons: first, I don't care; secondly, I am sure the reader doesn't care; and thirdly, I don't know. But if the spectator is lucky enough not to have a clear day, he may enjoy some such view as that at which I wondered. Vast snowstorms were sweeping across the sky, casting many square leagues at a time into profound shadow, with broad intervening stretches of sunshine. The solid mountains, under the varying effects of light and shade, seemed to melt, and form, and melt again; and it was impossible to recognise particular points without minute local knowledge. At every instant some new ridge seemed to start into existence, and then to be blotted out or sink into a plain. It is a strange sight to see mountains resemble the changing sea-waves: and yet, if geologists speak truth, it is only what we should sec, if we could live a little slower, and consider a million years or so as a single day. Meanwhile it is just as well for us that these freaks are nothing but the effects of

fancy, and that the Confinale is, for practical purposes, as firm as the Monument—or, indeed, rather firmer. Yet I have still a faint wish that it could be levelled, and the interior of that mighty crescent be converted into a level park. There would really be nothing like it in Europe, and there would be some admirable locations for monster hotels and casinos. Perhaps the Americans will set about it, when these effete countries are annexed to the United States.

Once more, and only once more, I must invite my reader to yet a further effort. I confess— for it would be useless to conceal—that I am a fanatic. I believe that the ascent of mountains forms an essential chapter in the complete duty of man, and that it is wrong to leave any district without setting foot on its highest peak. In this chapter I will endeavour for once to keep clear of snow-slopes and step-cutting, of ropes and crevasses, and even of the inevitable description of an Alpine meal. But I cannot, in common decency, leave Santa Catarina before paying my respects to the monarch of the district, the noble Konigspitz. Long had that peak haunted my dreams, and beckoned to me whenever I had climbed above the lower slopes of the valley. I head treated the complaint homceo-pathically, by an ascent of the Tresero; but

my appetite was whetted instead of satiated. I had distracted my attention by various long, solitary rambles up some of the minor peaks. There is this great advantage about walking without guides-—namely, that it is easy to get into real difficulties on places where it would be apparently impossible to do so on the ordinary system. Thus, for example, on the Sovretta there is only one cliff on the mountain where anything like a scramble is conceivable, and that cliff is perfectly easy to cross except after a fresh fall of snow. It is entirely out of the way of any sensible route to anywhere. But by abstaining from guides I succeeded in placing myself on the face of this cliff the morning after a heavy snowfall, and had two hours of keen excitement in a climb which was ultimately successful. By pursuing this system courageously, a traveller may discover difficulties and dangers on the Rigi or the Brevcnt; and, if he be careless and inexperienced, may even manage a serious accident in either of those places. I felt, however, that though a pleasant substitute, this was not quite the real thing. I was too much like the sportsman reduced by adverse circumstances from tiger-hunting to rabbit-shooting; and when the Konigspitz renewed its invitation, one lovely afternoon, I could not find it in mv

heart to refuse, and made an appointment for the next morning at 2 a.m. And here, in accordance with the pledge just given, I omit a thrilling description. The reader may fancy precipices covered with treacherous rock, giddy slopes of ice, yawning crevasses, or any combination of terrors taken at random from Peaks, Passes, and Glaciers, or the year-books of

Alpine Clubs. It is enough to say, that with the help of a good guide (one Pietro Compagnoni, whom I hereby commend to Alpine climbers), I found myself, about half-past nine, enjoying a strangely impressive view. It is easy enough to describe what I saw; but the mischief is that I was chiefly impressed by what I did not see; and herein lies one great difficulty of the descriptive traveller. He can draw some rough outline of the picture photographed on his mind's eye, but how is he to reproduce the terrors of the unseen, which were probably the most potent elements in the total effect produced? Here, for example, I was standing on the highest point of the Konig-spitz; a few yards of tolerably level snow-ridge were distinctly visible; I could easily picture to myself the steep icy staircase by which I had climbed to it from the top of a lower precipice; but, looking upwards, or in any direction horizontally, nothing met the eye but a blank wall

of mist. On cither side 1 could sec slopes of snow or rock descending with apparent frightful steepness for a few feet, and then, once more, that blank misty wall. I knew not what gulfs might have been revealed if the mists had suddenly lifted, or what grand form of cliff or mountain spire might have shaped itself out of the background. In short, I saw little more than might be observed in a thick mist on a snowy day on the top of Snowdon or Helvellyn; and yet I count that the mountain tops which I have visited under such circumstances have not been the least impressive of my acquaintance. It is a secret of good art to leave something to the imagination; and I had quite enough materials to work with. I knew how steep and slippery was the path which had led to this mid-aerial perch; and the precipices which I saw on every side plunging furiously downwards must be far steeper than those by which I had ascended. Suppose I had suddenly cut the rope, and pushed Compagnoni over the edge—I could realise only too vividly the plunge which he would take into the lower regions, the terrible acceleration of his pace, and the fearful blows, at increasing intervals, against the icy ribs of the mountain. It is an amusing and instructive experiment, if you have a weak-nerved com-

panion, to throw down a large stone under such circumstances; and if by any ingenious manoeuvre you can give him the impression that it is one of the party, the effect is considerably heightened. The hollow sound of the blows coming up, fainter and fainter, from the invisible chasm beneath naturally enables one to realise the course which one's own body would follow, and renders the cliff, as it were, audible instead of visible. By such dallying with danger, one learns to appreciate the real majesty of an Alpine cliff. There are various delusions of perspective which on a bright day sometimes diminish the apparent height of a precipice; but when it is robed in mysterious darkness, and only some such dim intimations as the sound of a falling stone come up to stimulate your curiosity, it is your own fault if you do not make it the most terrible of cliffs that ever tried the steadiness of a mountaineer's head. I confess, indeed, that the Konigspitz was too thickly shrouded on the day of which I speak; it would have been still more majestic had its robes been parted at intervals, so as to give artistic revelations of its massive proportions. Yet it is worth remarking that nothing helps more to give a certain mysterious charm to the mountains than an occasional ramble through their recesses in bad

weather; it is only a half-hearted lover of their scenery who would pray for a constant succession of unclouded skies. Could such a prayer be granted, the mountain which was its victim would be as tiresome as a thoroughly good-tempered man—that is, it would be on the highroad to become a bore.

We left Santa Catarina by the Stelvio, and halted for a day or two at the charming little village of Trafoi. Trafoi is undoubtedly more lovely than Santa Catarina, and indeed may rank with the most perfect of Alpine centres. Accordingly, certain sceptical doubts beset me for a time as to the charms of the district I have endeavoured to describe. Had we really been comfortable or well-fed? Was our admiration genuine, or more or less due to affectation? The first discoverers of a new district are always unduly eulogistic, because praising it is indirectly praising themselves. Might we not have been giving way in some degree to that common weakness? These unpleasant doubts have gradually given way to a settled faith. I am far from declaring that a belief in the inimitable glories of Santa Catarina is an essential part of the true mountaineer's creed. Still more should I shrink from condemning to everlasting exclusion from that little paradise any one: who

might take a lower view of its merits than I do. He would be wrong, but I doubt whether his error w T ould be of so deep a dye as to be necessarily criminal. I would speak to him if I met him in the streets, especially in London. Indeed, heresy in Alpine matters is not always so unpardonable as appears at first sight. No one can appreciate good scenery when his digestion is out of order; few people can appreciate it with blisters on their feet, and not every one who is bitten of fleas. Therefore, if a person who has visited any Alpine district under such disadvantages ventures to differ from me, I am frequently inclined to forgive him. One of the evils I have mentioned is, I fear, for the present, almost inseparable from Santa Catarina, and so far heretics may put forward a plea of some value; but if any one provided with a good bottle of insecticide, and otherwise in health and spirits, should deny the charms of Santa Catarina, I consider him as beyond the pale of the true faith, and liable to the consequences of such a position, whatever they may be. The only piece of advice I shall give him is, to stay away, that there may be the more room for orthodox believers.

CHAPTER X

THE PEAKS OF PRIMIERO

At some distant period, when the Alpine Club is half forgotten, and its early records are obscured amongst the mist of legends and popular traditions, there is one great puzzle in store for the critical inquirer. As he tries to disentangle truth from fiction, and to ascertain what is the small nucleus of fact round which so many incredible stories have gathered, he will be specially perplexed by the constant recurrence of one name. In the heroic cycle of Alpine adventure, the irrepressible Tuckett will occupy a place similar to that of the wandering Ulysses in Greek fable, or the invulnerable Sivrid in the lay of the Niebelungs. In every part of the Alps, from Monte Viso and Dauphine to the wilds of Carinthia and Styria, the exploits of this mighty traveller will linger in the popular imagination. In one valley the peasant will point to some vast breach in the everlasting rocks, hewn, as his fancy will declare, by the sweep of the mighty ice-axe of the hero. In another, the sharp conical summit, known as the Tuckettspitz, will be

regarded as a monument raised by the eponymous giant, or possibly as the tombstone piled above his athletic remains. In a third the broken masses of a descending glacier will fairly represent the staircase which he built in order to scale a previously inaccessible height. That a person so ubiquitous, and distinguished everywhere by such romantic exploits, should have been a mere creature of flesh and blood will, of course, be rejected as an absurd hypothesis. Critics will rather be disposed to trace in him one more example of that universal myth whose recurrence in divers forms proves, amongst other things, the unity of the great Aryan race. Tuckett, it will be announced, is no other than the sun, which appears at earliest dawn above the tops of the loftiest mountains, gilds the summits of the most inaccessible peaks, penetrates the remotest valleys, and passes in an incredibly short space of time from one extremity of the Alpine chain to the other.

Fortunately, the Alpine Club well knows that Air. Tuckett is a flesh and blood reality— no empty phantom of the imagination, but a being capable of consuming even Alpine food and being consumed by Alpine insects. Possibly, like Sivrid or Achilles, he may have one vulnerable point, though I am pretty sure that it is not his heel; but if it exists, it has not yet been betrayed to his followers. When,

therefore, I read in that great collection of tacts and stories founded, it is to be hoped, on facts— Mr. Ball's Guide to the Alps — that the mighty Tuckett himself, and the equally mighty Melchior Anderegg, had pronounced the peaks of Primiero to be inaccessible, there came to me something of the thrill felt by

Some watcher of the skies When a new planet swims into his ken, Or like stout Cortes, when with eagle eyes He stared at the Pacific, and all his men Looked at each other with a wild surmise, Silent upon a peak in Darien.

I stood silent before the peaks of Primiero, and saw in them a new land, still untouched by the foot of the tourist, and opening vast possibilities of daring adventure and deathless fame for some hero of the future. To me, alas! those possibilities were closed. I was alone (at 6.45 a. m. on a brilliant morning of August, 1869) in the quiet street of the lovely little town of Primiero. I was prepared indeed for a day's mountaineering, but a day how unlike to those when, with alpenstock in hand and knapsack on back, with a little corps of faithful guides and tried companions, I had moved out to the attack of some hitherto un-conquered peak! Ik-fore me, indeed, lay mountains most exciting to the imagination. Above the

260 The Playground of Europe

meadows of the Primiero valley there rises a long slope, first of forest and then of Alp, to the foot of the mighty peaks which spring at one bound to a height of some ten thousand feet. The two conspicuous summits in front are called the Sas Maor, and resemble, if I may be pardoned so vulgar a comparison, the raised ringer and thumb of a more than gigantic hand. Behind them, I knew, lay a wilderness of partially explored summits, with sides as steep as those of a cathedral, and surrounded by daring spires and pinnacles, writhing into every conceivable shape, and almost too fantastical to be beautiful. Mr. Tuckett had made two passes through their intricate valleys and ridges; yet even Mr. Tuckett had shrunk, as I have said, from an attempt to reach their loftiest points. The Dolomites are the fairyland of the Alps. All visitors to Botzen know the strange rocky walls that guard the Rose garden of the goblin King Laurin; and the dominion of the same monarch probably extends throughout these most interesting valleys. The Primiero peaks seem to have a double measure of enchantment; some strange magic had held the Alpine Club at a distance, and, what was more provoking, had cast a profound drowsiness over the dwellers at their feet, and almost prevented them from raising their eyes to these wild summits, or be-

stowing names upon them. Yet I could not flatter myself that I should be the first to break the charm or to plant my feet on those daring peaks which had remained undisturbed since they first rose, by some strangely mysterious process, to break the softer scenery around them. I had a Spanish wine-bottle slung round me, a crust of bread in my pocket, and an axe in my hand; but alone, and determined to come back in one piece, I could only hope to open a path for more daring adventurers, and, like a church spire, to point to Paradise without attempting to lead the way. The present chapter, therefore, must be prefaced with a warning to true mountaineers that they must expect from it no records of thrilling adventure, and that I shall not even assert (for the perhaps insufficient reason that it is not true) that at any given point a false step might have broken my neck.

My way led at first along a good road, to the foot of the Castle of La Pietra. I cannot imagine a more enviable dwelling-place for a baron of a few centuries back. From his rocky fortress he looked down upon the little village lying at his feet, and, having the power of life and death over its inhabitants, was doubtless regarded with universal respect. The most practicable road into this secluded country lay immediately beneath his

walls, and must have enabled him conveniently to raise such duties as were compatible with the commercial theories of the epoch; that is, he could take whatever he liked. The rock is so precipitous that a few landslips have rendered it literally inaccessible without the use of ladders. But the most eligible part of the estate (to use the dialect of auctioneers) must have been the lovely little side valley, the entrance to the col, which was covered by the castle. This valley, called the Val di Canale, stretches north-eastward into the heart of the mountains. The stream which waters it, sparkling with the incomparable brilliancy characteristic of the Dolomite regions, flows through a level plain of the greenest turf dotted with occasional clumps and groves of pines that have strayed downwards from the bounding slopes. In the comparison between mountainous and lowland countries, it is an obvious advantage to the former—though I do not remember to have seen it noticed—that it is only amongst the mountains that you can properly appreciate a plain. Such a meadow as that I was crossing would have been simply a commonplace pasturage in Leicestershire. Contrasting it with the mighty cliffs that enclosed it on every side, it was a piece of embodied poetry. Nature had been a most effective landscape gardener,

and had even laid out for the benefit of the lords of the Castle of La Pietra a kind of glorified park. I apologise for the expression. I have, indeed, heard true British lips declare that one of the loveliest bits of Alpine scenery was really parklike, and serenely condescend to flatter the mountains by comparing them to the deadly dulness of the grounds that surround a first-class family mansion in our respectable island. Here, however, there was undoubtedly a faint resemblance; only it was such a park as we may hope to meet in the Elysian fields; a park as much like its British representative as an angel is like a country gentleman. The difference la)'principally in the system of fences adopted in the two cases. Here it was formed by one of those gigantic walls which almost oppress the imagination by their stupendous massiveness. I was evidently contemplating one of the great scenic effects of the Alps, not, to my taste, rivalling Grindelwald, Macugnaga, or Courmayeur, but yet in its own style almost unique. The huge barrier before me was the defence of that fairyland into which 1 was seeking entrance. The cliffs rose abruptly and with tremendous steepness, though their bases were joined to the valley by long slopes of debris that had accumulated in countless ages. It is impossible to paint such scenery in words, or to give any notion of the

force with which the bare rocks, a deadly grey in some places, and tinged in others with the ruddy hue common in the Dolomites, contrasted with the rich Italian vegetation at their feet. The only comparison I can think of is somewhat derogatory to their dignity. However, one can hardly be called responsible for the strange freaks played in one's mind by queer associations of ideas. For reasons which would be too long to explain, I can never look at crevasses of a certain character without being reminded of the meal called five o'clock tea; and it was certainly a closer analogy which on this occasion suggested to me the picture of a gigantic raised pie, such as sometimes completes the circuit of a table before any audacious guest makes an inroad into its contents. At last appetite gets the better of modesty: a sacrilegious hand is raised, and a few bold gashes with the knife make terrible rents into its solid sides, and heap piles of ruined paste in the dish below. Even so had some mysterious agent sliced and hacked the great Dolomite wall, and though the barrier still rose as proudly as ever along a great part of the line, there were deep trenches and gullies hewn through it at various places, masses had evidently given way at some distant period, and others were apparently threatening to follow them. I was still in utter darkness

as to the geography of the district, but on reflection I thought it best to enter the broadest and most accessible of these gashes, which lay immediately behind the Sas Maor, and is known as the Val di Pravitali. It was what would be called a ghyll in the English lakes, that is, a steep lateral gorge enclosed by precipitous rocks on each side, and it appeared to terminate at a distinctly marked col, from which there would probably be a descent to the other fork of the Primiero valley. By following this route I should at least pass through the very heart of the mountains.

My climb was interesting from the strangeness of the scenery, but not in any sense difficult. The Dolomite rocks have this disadvantage, that the debris is generally formed of small hard pebbles of dazzling whiteness, from which the water drains off rapidly, and which have therefore little power of cohesion. The foot rests on a bed of loose stones, which in other formations would give firm hold, but which here crumbles away, to the imminent risk of your equilibrium. Not a drop of water is to be had; the sun strikes down with tremendous force, and its rays are reflected with almost unabated power from the blinding stones. In the gully which I was speedily climbing there was not a breath of air. 1 was in good training, but without the stimulating effect of company.

266 The Playground of Europe

Great as is the charm of solitary walks on due occasion, they produce a severe strain on the moral energies. Why, it has been asked by certain assailants of utilitarian heresies, should a man do right when there is no chance of his being found out? Why should not the true Benthamite pick pockets, or knock his friend on the head, if the penitentiary and the gallows are out of the question? Most victoriously had I refuted that sneer, or so I fancied, when living in London with a policeman round the corner. But now, in the deep solitude of the Alps, it recurred to me with great force, and I felt inclined to accept the other horn of the dilemma. Why not break the mountaineer's code of commandments? Why not sit down in the first bit of shade, to smoke my pipe and admire the beauties of nature? The tempter did not reveal himself to me in bodily form as in that charming story told in the notes to Guy Mannering, but I developed a fearful skill in sophistical argumentation, which supplied the place of any external deceiver, and for a moment was in danger of lapsing into the fearful heresies in things Alpine which are popular amongst the fat and the lazy. I struggled, however, against the meshes of false reasoning which seemed to be winding themselves tangibly round my legs, and 1 oiled slowly upwards. I raised my feet slowly

and sleepily; I groaned at the round, smooth, slippery pebbles, and lamented the absence of water. At length I reached a little patch of snow, and managed to slake my parched lips and once more to toil more actively upwards. A huge boulder, in colour and form resembling a gigantic snow-ball, filled up the gully, and gave me a little amusement in surmounting it. A few minutes more and I entered a very remarkable grassy plain, of which I shall again have occasion to speak, and after about five hours' walk from Primiero, sat down on the col I have mentioned to determine my future course. Here I was in the position of that celebrated gentleman who could not see the town on account of the houses. I was fairly perplexed and bewildered. On every side there were gigantic cliffs, soaring pinnacles, and precipitous ravines. They rose so abruptly, and apparently in such wild confusion, all perspective was so hopelessly distorted, that I was totally unable to get my bearings. The fantastic Dolomite mountains towered all around me in shapes more like dreams than sober realities; they recall quaint Eastern architecture, whose daring pinnacles derive their charm from a studied defiance of the sober principles of stability. The Chamouni aiguilles, as I have said, inevitably remind one of Gothic cathedrals; but in their most daring moments they

appear to be massive, immovable, and eternal. The Dolomites are strange adventurous experiments, which one can scarcely believe to be formed of ordinary rock. They would have been a fit background for the garden of Kubla Khan; there are strange romantic chasms where "Alph the sacred river" might plunge into "caverns measureless to man"; while at times I found myself looking out instinctively for the strange valley where Sinbad collected his heaps of diamonds. Indeed, I am half inclined to think that I found it, as shall be presently told; at any rate, as I looked upwards at the strange walls around me, I was thoroughly bewildered with their intricacies, and by the singular change wrought in them by the new perspective.

I was at the foot of the promised peaks—nay, I might be halfway up them, but I could not even guess which was the right line of assault, and in which direction the main summits lay. I might descend the ravine which I saw plunging rapidly downwards amongst the roots of the mountains on the other side of the col, but by such a course I should see no more than I had hitherto observed. After some reflection and hesitation it became obvious that the single fact on which I could confidently rely was that the great mass of rock to the south, on my left hand, must intervene between

me and the valley of Primiero. If it were possible to climb it, I should get a more distinct view of the mountains to the north, and might possibly find a short cut home across the ridge. With this plan I commenced operations by climbing a long snow-slope which was luckily in fair order. I ascended rapidly, cutting a step or two in one place, and, on reaching the head of the snow, I took to the ridge of rocks at a point where a very remarkable pinnacle of great height rises into a shape which a fanciful traveller may compare to a bayonet with the point bent over to one side. The rocks, though apparently difficult at a distance, turned out on closer approach to be excellently adapted to my purpose. I topped the ridge, and bearing to my left forced my way along it in spite of one or two gaps which for a moment threatened my advance. It was growing late, and I had reason to suppose that my absence, if much prolonged, might cause some anxiety to those I had left at Primiero. I resolved that I would turn back under any circumstances at 2.30, but I made strenuous efforts to be as far advanced as possible at the fatal hour. My energy was rewarded. With still a minute or two to spare, I stood upon the top of the mountain—of what mountain I could not possibly say. Had I been an artist, I should have instantly sat down, in spite of my hurry, to

make some sort of outline of the view which presented itself. As it was, I drained the last drops of my wine-flask, ate my last crust of bread, and endeavoured to make a mental photograph of the scene before me as rapidly as possible. To the north rose the great mass of peaks at whose feet I had been clambering for hours. In every direction they presented fearfully steep cliffs, and, with the exception of a single glacier of trifling dimensions, scarcely one patch of snow. The summit upon which I was standing was part of the great ridge from which rise the singular peaks of the Sas Maor. I was divided from them by a deep cleft, and, so far as I could judge, was at a point about intermediate in height between those astonishing twins. More singular towers of rock are scarcely to be found in the Alps. At the time, I compared the ridge before me to some monstrous reef stretching out to seaward, with a singularly daring lighthouse erected on a distant point, or rather, if such a thing could be imagined, growing spontaneously out of the rock and bending over as it rose. Or perhaps a more perfect likeness might be found to the head of some great monster extended at full length, and armed with a couple of curved horns like those of the double-horned rhinoceros. The monster was covered with all manner of singular excrescences, spines

and knobs growing out of his stony hide; amidst which these two singular elevations towered in daring disregard of the laws of equilibrium. One could hardly believe that rock would shape itself into such strange forms, and that there was not some kind of muscular fibre to weave them into comparative firmness. 1 looked at them with a strong sense of wonder, though, to confess the truth, with a belief that somebody might possibly discover a route to the loftier of the two from the deep trench which divided them from me.

And here, more than anywhere else, the spells of King Laurin, or the mysterious monarch, whatever may be his name, who rules these enchanted districts, seemed to become almost tangible. The absolute solitude was doubtless favourable to their effectual working. Bentley, in one of his slashing corrections of Milton, proposed to substitute the "sacred" for the "secret top of Horeb or of Sinai," for the reason that the top of a mountain is of all places the least "secret" or private. De Quincey remarks upon this that "no secrecy is so complete and so undisturbed by sound or gaze from below as that of a mountain-top, such as Helvellyn, Great Gavel, or Blen-cathra." The truth lies in the combination of these views. The mountain solitude is so intense because the mountains are, in one sense, so far

from secret. You may be as solitary in the centre of a wood or a plain, but you cannot realise your isolation so distinctly. It is because the meadows and inhabited places are apparently within the cast of a pebble, that the great gulf between you and them becomes emphatic. You know that you might fall, for example, from the summit of a cliff, upon which a hundred sightseers are gazing at the time, and yet they would be unaware that a tragedy was being performed before their eyes. Solitude in a crowd is supposed to be the worst kind of solitude; but perhaps the most impressive is the solitude on a point visible and familiar to half a nation. The ordinary accompaniments of such a scene, the gossip of guides and the noisy triumph of a successful party, are apt to break the charm; and indeed I remember, with something like a sense of shame, how on one of the loftiest peaks of Switzerland I spent the precious moments in having my trousers mended by a guide, who happened to be also a tailor. Romance was of course out of the question under such circumstances. Here, on this strange desolate crag, I was exposed without interruption to the magic of the scenery. Far along the horizon rose the mysterious peaks—not arranged, like mountains of mere ordinary flesh and blood, along a respectable watershed, with glaciers symmetrically ar-

ranged upon their flanks, and some regard for geographical propriety—but dispersed in picturesque confusion like the spires of a mediaeval town. The Dolomite country appears to me to be properly speaking a hill, rather than a mountain, district—a region of green meadows and sparkling waters. These great masses of bare discoloured rock have somehow been intruded by diabolical art—I mean no offence by the epithet, for the devil, if we may judge by his dykes and punch-bowls even in England, has had great success as a landscape gardener—and, in short, seem to be mountains bewitched rather than mountains due to the ordinary forces of upheaval and erosion.

The strangest part of all the scenery around me was the valley to which I have already referred as accessible through the Val di Pravitali, and which was now some 2000 or 3000 feet beneath me. It is well worth a visit from Primiero and may be easily reached in four or five hours' walking. Imagine a vast cauldron, bounded by cliffs some 3000 feet in height. To the north, indeed, there is a gradual ascent to a wild and extensive plateau, whence a small glacier trickles into the desolate valley. On the east towers the tremendous wall of the Palledi S. Martino, vertical to all appearance if not to the eye of a geologist. It is scarred and

gashed by some of the characteristic gullies of the Dolomite mountains. Some of them might be climbed for a distance, or a path may even lie through their hidden depths to the summit of the mountain, but they appear at any rate to be closed by the most forbidding of rocky walls. Opposite to the Palle is a precisely similar wall formed by a nameless outlier of the Fradusta. To the south rise the more varied but equally precipitous pinnacles and rock towers of the Sas Maor. A single narrow gap leaves room for the escape of the torrent of the Val di Pravitali. When I passed, however, the torrent was dry; and, indeed, the utter absence of water is one of the characteristic peculiarities of these mountains. The ordinary music of the streams, which relieves some of the wildest Alpine gorges, was absolutely mute. Not a sound was to be heard, and I felt almost too superstitious to try to raise an echo with my voice, lest I should receive a ghostly answer in return. The valley floor is nearly level, except where it is concealed by heaps of debris from the neighbouring peaks, and its surface is very dry and barren, except in one place where the melting snows must occasionally form a lake. A more savage piece of rock scenery is nowhere to be seen. No undulating snow-field or bounding torrent of i/lacier breaks the tremendous monotonv. In

The Peaks of Primicro

/b

every direction blank walls or daring spires of rock close yon in as it were in a gigantic dungeon. Philosophers may explain how such places are made; but doubtless it was in some distant period the keep of the old goblin king. He was, if I am not mistaken, a potentate of bad character, and kept up intimate relations with the personage whose taste in matters of scenery has just been noticed. His residence has the appearance of having been blasted by a supernatural curse which marks the former abode of witches and evil spirits. The poor old women who had dealings with the evil one in Germany had to content themselves with a hillock like the Brocken; but that part of the female population of Primiero which still takes an occasional ride on a broomstick—and I am convinced from appearances that there are a good number of them— gathers in all probability in this wild amphitheatre where the walls are gleaming in the moonlight or curtained by strange wreaths of curling mist. Another fancy came into my head, as I have already hinted, though I admit that there are some geographical objections. Nothing could be more like the wonderful valley in which Sinbad found the diamonds and where he had to be carried by the eagles. True, there arc now neither serpents nor diamonds. But it is hard to doubt that the old

dragon brood inhabited one of the ghastly chasms in the rocks before the cave died out, and Sinbad may well have been speaking of them. As for the diamonds, I have always thought that part of the story too good to be true. One other suspicious circumstance about these mountains impressed me forcibly. Never did I see hills change their shapes so rapidly, in all varieties of weather. The beauty of the Sas Maor induced me—though no artist—to try to make an outline of their singular forms. I lay under a chestnut-tree in a lovely meadow at Primiero through a hot summer afternoon, and watched the strange transformation of the cliffs. They would not remain steady for five minutes together. What looked like a chasm suddenly changed into a ridge; plain surfaces of rock suddenly shaped themselves into towering pinnacles; and then the pinnacles melted away and left a ravine or a cavern. The singular shifting phantasmagoria reminded me of the mystical castle in the Vale of St. John; and it required a heartless scepticism to believe that the only witchcraft at work was that of the sun, as it threw varying lights and shadows over the intricate labyrinths of the rocks.

Whatever goblin haunts these cliffs and bewilders the judgment of the traveller I must do him the justice to say that he is tolerably pro-

pitious to the climber. The rocks shoot out unexpected knobs and projections to help one at a pinch. Even where they were most apparently threatening, a nearer inspection revealed abundant crannies and cracks where it was easy to obtain very good hold for hands and feet. If I had limited my reflections to the question of ascending the Sas Maor, I should have simply returned by the way I came. Another plan, however, occurred to me with irresistible force. The rocks were so good that I inferred the possibility of descending straight to the Primiero valley, i.e., by the opposite ridge of the mountain to that which I had climbed. All my life I have suffered from an invincible love of short cuts. Short cuts to learning, as moralists tell us, end in general ignorance; short cuts to wealth, in Pentonville Penitentiary; short cuts to political glory, in Leicester Square; and short cuts in mountain districts to a destiny not less disagreeable than any of these — namely, to the nearest churchyard. However, I yielded to the overpowering impulse. Prom my lofty perch I could see the Primiero valley in its whole length, lying almost at my feet. If the ridge which descended straight towards it proved, as I thought the rocks indicated, to be easily practicable, I might reach the valley in a very short time, and save the trouble of descending the tiresome Val

278 The Playground of Europe

di Pravitali. Time was limited, and after one final glance, I committed myself to the ridge. This ridge, I must explain, lies between two deep trenches; that which I have already noticed as dividing me from the Sas Maor looked the more promising, if I could but effect a descent into it; and, after a short climb, the sight of a few sheep which had evidently strayed up toward the ridge from the valley satisfied me that there must be a practicable route. Unluckily my impatience led me to violate that useful canon of mountaineering science which prescribes the duty of keeping to the backbone of a difficult ridge rather than descending by the ribs. Tempted by an apparently easy route, I made a diversion towards the valley, and, after some complicated scramblings, found myself at the edge of some tremendous cliffs, invisible from above, but, so far as I could see, impassable. There is a pleasure in these accidental discoveries which is some reward to the guideless traveller for his unnecessary wanderings. I was probably the first person who ever reached a place which is totally out of the proper route from any given point to any other, and it is probable enough that my performance may never be repeated. I might therefore flatter myself that I alone of the human race can enjoy the memory of one particular view—not, it is true,

more striking in itself than many other views, but having the incalculable merit of being in a sense my own personal property. At such places, too, one feels the true mountain charm of solitude. If my grasp had suddenly given way as I was craning over those ghastly crags, I should have been consigned to a grave far wilder than that "in the arms of Helvellyn," and which might as likely as not remain undiscovered till there was little left to reward the discoverer. A skeleton, a few rags, the tattered relics of certain more coherent rags which just passed themselves off for clothes at Primiero, and perhaps the mangled remains of a watch and an ice-axe, would hardly be worth the trouble of a prolonged search. These cheerful reflections passed through my mind, and added considerably to the influence of the strangely wild scenery. They also helped to recall me to the propriety of finding my way home, with a skeleton still decently apparelled in flesh and blood —to say nothing of Mr. Carter's boots. Before long I had returned to my ridge, and was fighting my way downwards. It was an amusing bit of climbing until, just above the point which I had marked as offering an easy descent to the valley, I was interrupted by a sudden wall of rock. It is an unpleasant peculiarity of the Dolomite mountains that such vertical walls of

rock, which of course are invisible from above, frequently run for great distances around the base of the peaks. I had the unpleasant prospect of being forced to return once more to the summit of the mountain, as the only known line of retreat; in which case I must probably have spent the night upon the rocks. As certain persons then at Primiero took a lively interest in my safety, and would probably put the worst interpretation on my absence, I looked round eagerly for a mode of escape. I managed at one point to creep so far downwards that if mattresses had been spread at the foot of the cliff, I could have dropped without fear; but the rocks were hard as iron, and moreover, while I was not quite certain that the point thus attainable was really beyond the cliff, I was quite certain that I could not climb back. To be imprisoned on such a ledge would be no joke. A more circuitous route gave me a better chance, but required some gymnastics. At one point, as I was letting myself carefully down, a pointed angle of rock made a vicious clutch at the seat of my trousers, and, fatally interfering with my equilibrium, caused me to grasp a projecting knob with my right hand and let my ice-axe fall. With a single bound it sprang down the cliff, but to my pleasure lodged in a rocky chasm some hundred and fifty feet below me. In

regaining it I had some real difficulty. I was forced to wriggle along a steep slope of rock where my whole weight rested on the end joints of my fingers inserted into certain pock-marks characteristic of this variety of rock, and, to be candid, partly upon my stomach. This last support gives very efficient aid on such occasions. Just beyond this place I had to perform the novel manoeuvre of passing through the rock. A natural tunnel gave me a sudden means of escape from what appeared to be really a difficult place. But, alas! what is the use of such descriptions? How can I hope to persuade anybody that I encountered any real difficulties?—the next traveller who climbs these rocks will laugh at the imbecile middle-aged gentleman who managed to get into trouble amongst them, and, to say the truth, the troubles were of no great account. With an active guide to hold out a hand above, and another to supply a prop below, I might have skipped over these difficulties like the proverbial chamois. As it was, I reflected that whatever modes of progression I adopted, there would be no one to criticise; and, taking good care to adopt the safest, I speedily rejoined my ice-axe, and stood at a kind of depression in the ridge, from which, as I had anticipated, there would be an easy descent to the pastures below. I was in

fact at the point where I had already seen the sheep; and it would be unworthy of an Alpine traveller to describe a route already traversed by such unadventurous animals. All that I need say for the benefit of my successors is this. The valley by which I ultimately effected my descent is that which descends from the col between the Sas Maor and the peak (to the north-west) which I had just climbed. The only difficulty in finding a route lies in the circumstance that the valley is broken by certain walls of rock which divide it into terraces at different elevations. It is rather difficult for one coming from above to discover the proper line. I wasted some precious time by following sheep-tracks, under the impression that they led downwards instead of upwards. The route, however, will easily be struck out by reaching the valley as near its head as possible, and then keeping downwards by the left bank of the stream, or rather watercourse. I ultimately reached Primiero soon after dark, having had an interesting twelve hours' walk.

Primiero is situated, geographically speaking, on the head waters of the Cismone, a tributary of the Brenta. It lies, however, to be more precise, at a distance of some thousand miles, more or less, and two or three centuries from railways and civilisation. I fear that both in time and

3

space it is rapidly making up its leeway. Though many of the inhabitants told us that they had never ventured beyond their valley, others have pushed their audacity so far as to pay a visit to Botzen. Nay, reform has progressed to the pitch indicated by the possession of a bit of carriage-road. Two or three ardent leaders of the party of progress go so far as recklessly to advocate the connection of this road with others already constructed upon the opposite side of the mountains. The conservatives who cling to patriarchal modes of life dread the opening which would thus be made for the corrupt influences of civilisation. The innkeeper, in other respects a most deserving man, has, I fear, prepared for the anticipated influx of travellers by raising his scale of prices. It will be long, however, before the more solid inhabitants will yield to the spirit of innovation. The fat old shopkeeper will continue, it may be hoped, to sit intensely in the door of his shop smoking those tough cigars that can only be kept alight for a few seconds by energetic action of the lungs; he will read his queer little printed news-sheet of a month or two back, and will resent the intrusion of customers who would disturb his profound repose; the peasants will gather on Sundays to strike a huge ball about the streets anrl into the windows of the loftiest houses;

284 The Playground of Europe

the women will kneel reverently on the pavement outside the church, and keep an eye on the passing stranger, whilst they diligently tell their beads; and in the winter evenings there will be friendly gatherings to spin the long-grown fleeces of the queer lop-eared sheep. There is something about these animals that has an inexpressible attraction for me. As a rule, I prefer the more lively goat; and surely the prettiest of all Alpine scenes is the return of the little herd to the village when the evening bells are ringing, and each goat, after a few inquisitive excursions into odd corners, to see whether any change has taken place in its absence, betakes itself with a few dogmatic wags of its beard to the bosom of its family. Primiero, however, was just then filled with flocks of sheep returning from the high pasturages. They looked so tired and sleepy, and were evidently on such friendly terms with the ragged shepherds who led them, that it was impossible not to regard them as setting the tone of the country. I had many talks with them on the hills, and they explained to me with much sense the proper mode of enjoying the scenery. To lounge about in the rich pasturages when the weather is fresh, to climb the rocks when the sun is hot and creep into cool shadowy ledges, and to gather for a pleasant chat in the evenings is

The Peaks of Primiero

-°5

their mode of passing the long vacation. They disapprove of the restless goats, who are fitter for the bracing air of the northern Alps, and Primiero seems to agree with them. There was, indeed, a certain amount of activity perceptible, especially amongst the women, who were incessantly mangling hemp (I don't know whether that is the proper term) in the village street. But the male population is distinctly of a placid temperament. They don't excite themselves about news. The story of the siege of Paris would probably be fresh to them when the first tourists arrived in the following summer. They care little, as may be supposed, even for their own mountains, and the doings of the few climbers who had disturbed their repose seemed to have excited no interest. Nobody knew or cared anything about my little expedition, and I began to fancy that there was something almost profane about troubling these placid regions with mv scrambling propensities. Luckily I was

roused by a very pleasant meeting with the most omniscient of mountaineers. Mr. Ball joined us at Primiero, and I laid certain geographical perplexities before him, as the best possible authority. What, in the first place, could be the name of the pcrik I had climbed? Even Mr. Ball did not know, and the cause of his

ignorance was speedily explained by an intelligent native. The fact was that the peak had no name at all. But as our friend explained, Herr Suda, who, if I mistake not, held an official position in some way connected with the Government survey, had proposed to the editor of the map to bestow a name upon it; and that name, as I heard with great satisfaction, was the Cima di Ball. I sincerely hope that the name will be adopted. Yet I cannot say that it is in all respects appropriate. The mountain, it is true, has many merits, and amongst them the rather questionable merit of a retiring modesty. Of no mountain that I have ever seen of the same importance in a range is it so difficult to obtain a view. When it appears, it has a vexatious habit of looking lower than it is, and, still more provokingly, of passing itself off as the mere hanger-on of some peak of really inferior merits. Moreover, like the conversation of some of my acquaintance, it is totally deficient in point, and meanders carelessly away until it may be said rather to leave off than to culminate. Its top is a rambling plateau, which cannot quite make up its mind to act like the summit of a respectable mountain, and nobody had even erected a cairn upon it previous to my arrival, when I threw up a hasty heap of stones. Yet it is distinctly a

summit, cut off by deep and wide depressions from all its rivals, and, moreover, it has one merit which may make it less unworthy to be called after Mr. Ball. By its assistance, as by that of its godfather, 1 was aide to gain a considerable insight into the geography of the district; and though I decline to enter into this rather dreary subject, I may say shortly that I was prompted by his remarks to one further expedition.

On this occasion it was determined by the higher powers that I should not be trusted alone. A guide was to be entrusted with the duty of keeping me to safe places, and repressing any tendency to short cuts. The person designated for this duty by universal consent was one Colesel Rosso. Colesel is very poor and very deserving; he is willing, exceedingly cheerful, full of con-versation—which I regret to say was imperfectly intelligible to his companion,—a good walker, and a mighty bearer of weights. In short, he has every virtue that a guide can have consistently with a total and profound ignorance of the whole theory and practice of mountain climbing. When I first saw him, 1 confess that, in spite of previous warning, I was struck with amazement. It was little that his height was not above 4 feet 6 inches, and that his general appearance might suggest that I was taking with me an animated scare-

crow to frighten the eagles of the crags. His small stature and wizened face had a strong resemblance to the features of good-humoured goblins, though he was little enough at home in the ranges haunted by his fellows. Colesel, I suspect, had been assigned to me out of charity, on the ground that he was one of the poorest men in a district where the people generally seem to enjoy a fair degree of comfort. Although this principle is scarcely compatible with sound views of political economy, I was glad enough to give my companion a good turn. But I was rather more startled by observing that he held in his hand a shillalah in place of an ice-axe, thereby increasing his general resemblance to a good-tempered Paddy rather more than usually out at elbows; and that he regarded my rope and axe with undissembled wonder. It has so rarely happened to me to walk with any Alpine peasant who could not easily beat me at every kind of climbing, that I still felt some faith in Colesel, and put my best foot forwards during the first part of my expedition, with the view of impressing him with a respect for my powers. The proceeding was quite unnecessary; my guide never showed the least propensity to give any opinion as to my best route, but followed me with great cheerfulness until I reached the glacier. Then, having

no nails in his shoes, he was unable to make much progress; and he finally broke down when I came to a climb about equal in difficulty to the last rocks of the Brevent. So much 1 feel bound to say for the benefit of future travellers; but I repeat that I have good grounds for supposing Colesel to be an excellent porter. Any one, however, meditating an assault on the Primiero peaks must either go alone or bring guides from more satisfactory districts.

Of my further adventures it is enough to say that I once more ascended the Val di Pravitali, turned to the right through the haunted valley, climbed the Fradusta, and thence crossing the wild elevated plateau from which some of the highest peaks take their rise, descended by the Passo delle Cornelle and S. Martino di Castrozza, and so returned to Primiero. The walk deserves notice, because it is perfectly easy, and gives a complete view of all the strange peaks 1 have endeavoured to describe. I hoped at the time that some of them might turn out to be inaccessible. Nay, I foolishly ventured to express that hope to the Alpine Club. Straightway a gentleman, against whom 1 have no other complaint, destroyed mv vision by climbing the wildest of all, the Cimon della Pala, and lias pronounced the Palle di vS. Martino to be accessible, and, what is worse, 19

to be accessible by a route which I had condemned. Far be it from me to contradict him! but if the evil day must come, I will have no more guilt upon my conscience. I refrain, therefore, from throwing out the slightest hint to future travellers of the aspiring kind. So far as I am concerned, the last peaks of Primiero may remain unsealed as long as the British constitution flourishes, or the Alpine Club continues to exist. Yet when all the peaks are climbed, Primiero will be scarcely less attractive than of old. Every now and then it suddenly comes back to me in a vague dream, when I am more than usually struck with the absurdities of English life, and my soul is vexed with paying bills, wearing black hats, and attending evening parties. The little town, with its background of peaks, shapes itself out of a tobacco-cloud at dead of night, when the organ-grinders are dumb, and the drowsy rolling of the distant omnibus just penetrates the silence of my study. Then I say to myself, I will retire in my old age to Primiero; there will I take the airs of a British milord; I will get leave to occupy the old castle of Pietra, and extend dignified hospitality to a few select friends. But I will certainly be a prop of the strictest conservative party; I will oppose carriage - roads tooth and nail; no newspapers shall be admitted within six months of their

publication; if possible, the post-office shall be put down; all imports shall be forbidden, except, indeed, a little foreign tobacco; and the Primierians shall eat their own mutton and be clothed with their own fleeces. Freethinking of all kinds shall be suppressed; I will set an admirable example by regular attendance upon early mass—But somewhere about this point the vision becomes unsubstantial; the peaks resolve themselves once more into commonplace tobacco-smoke, and I magnanimously consent, like Savage and Johnson, to stand by my native country. London shall not be deprived of one member of the Alpine Club.

CHAPTER XI

SUNSET ON MONT BLANC

I profess myself to be a loyal adherent of the ancient Monarch of Mountains, and, as such, I hold as a primary article of faith the doctrine that no Alpine summit is, as a whole, comparable in sublimity and beauty to Mont Blanc. With all his faults and weaknesses, and in spite of a crowd of upstart rivals, he still deserves to reign in solitary supremacy. Such an opinion seems to some mountaineers as great an anachronism as the creed of a French Legitimist. The coarse flattery of guide-books has done much to surround him with vulgarising associations; even the homage of poets and painters has deprived his charms of their early freshness, and climbers have ceased to regard his conquest as a glorious, or, indeed, as anything but a most commonplace exploit. And yet Mont Blanc has merits which no unintelligent worship can obscure, and which bind with growing fascination the unprejudiced lover of scenery. Tried by a low, but not quite

a meaningless standard, the old monarch can still

ASCENDING MONT BLANC Fr'JtTi .i pliot'iur.iph liy S.:hpje<ler A Cii\, I.

extort respect. He can show a longer list of killed and wounded than any other mountain in the Alps, or almost than all other mountains put together. In his milder moods he may be approached with tolerable safety even by the inexperienced; but in angry moments, when he puts on his robe of clouds and mutters with his voice of thunder, no mountain is so terrible. Even the light snow-wreaths that eddy gracefully across his brow in fine weather sometimes testify to an icy storm that pierces the flesh and freezes the very marrow of the bones. But we should hardly estimate the majesty of men or mountains by the length of their butcher's bill. Mont Blanc has other and less questionable claims on our respect. He is the most solitary of all mountains, rising, Saul-like, a head and shoulders above the crowd of attendant peaks, and yet within that single mass there is greater prodigality of the sublimest scenery than in whole mountain districts of inferior elevation. The sternest and most massive of cliffs, the wildest spires of distorted rock, bounding torrents of shattered ice, snow-fields polished and even as a sea-shell, are combined into a whole of infinite variety and yet of artistic unity. One might wander for days, were such wandering made possible- by other conditions, amongst his crowning snows, and

every day would present new combinations of unsuspected grandeur.

Why, indeed, some critics will ask, should we love a ruler of such questionable attributes? Scientifically speaking, the so-called monarch is but so many tons of bleak granite determining a certain quantity of aqueous precipitation. And if for literary purposes it be permissible to personify a monstrous rock, the worship of such a Moloch has in it something unnatural. In the mouth of the poet who first invested him with royal honours, the language was at least in keeping. Byron's misanthropy, real or affected, might identify love of nature with hatred of mankind: and a savage, shapeless, and lifeless idol was a fitting centre for his enthusiasm. But we have ceased to believe in the Childe Harolds and the Manfreds. Become a hermit—denounce your species, and shrink from their contact, and you may consistently love the peaks where human life exists on sufferance, and whose message to the valleys is conveyed in wasting torrents or crushing avalanches. Men of saner mind who repudiate this anti-social creed should love the fertile valleys and grass-clad ranges better than these symbols of the sternest desolation. All the enthusiasm for the wilder scenery, when it is not simple affectation, is the product of a temporary phase of

sentiment, of which the justification has now ceased to exist. To all which the zealot may perhaps reply most judiciously, Be it as you please. Prefer, if you see fit, a Leicestershire meadow or even a Lincolnshire fen to the cliff and glacier, and exalt the view from the Crystal Palace above the widest of Alpine panoramas. Natural scenery, like a great work of art, scorns to be tied down to any cut-and-dried moral. To each spectator it suggests a different train of thought and emotion, varying as widely as the idiosyncrasy of the mind affected. If Mont Blanc produces in you nothing but a sense of hopeless savagery, well and good; confess it honestly to yourself and to the world, and do not help to swell the chorus of insincere ecstasy. But neither should you quarrel with those in whom the same sight produces emotions of a very different kind. That man is the happiest and wisest who can draw delight from the most varied objects: from the quiet bandbox scenery of cultivated England, or from the boundless prairies of the West; from the Thames or the Amazon, Malvern or Mont Blanc, the Virginia Water or the Atlantic Ocean. If the reaction which made men escape with sudden ecstasy from trim gardens to rough mountain sides was somewhat exeessiw, yet there was in it a core of sound feeling. Dors not science teach us more

and more emphatically that nothing which is natural can be alien to us who are part of nature? Where does Mont Blanc end, and where do I begin? That is the question which no metaphysician has hitherto succeeded in answering. But at least the connection is close and intimate, lie is a part of the great machinery in which my physical frame is inextricably involved, and not the less interesting because a part which I am unable to subdue to my purposes. The whole universe, from the stars and the planets to the mountains and the insects which creep about their roots, is but a network of forces eternally acting and reacting upon each other. The mind of man is a musical instrument upon which all external objects are beating out infinitely complex harmonies and discords. Too often, indeed, it becomes a mere barrel-organ, mechanically repeating the tunes which have once been impressed upon it. But in proportion as it is more vigorous or delicate, it should retain its sensibility to all the impulses which may be conveyed to it from the most distant sources. And certainly a healthy organisation should not be deaf to those more solemn and melancholy voices which speak through the wildest aspects of nature. "Our sweetest songs," as Shelley says in his best mood, "are those which tell of saddest thought." No

poetry or art is of the highest order in which there is not blended some strain of melancholy, even to sternness. Shakespeare would not be Shakespeare if it were not for that]profound sense of the transitory in all human affairs which appears in the finest sonnets and in his deepest dramatic utterances. When he tells us of the unsubstantial fabric of the great globe itself, or the glorious morning which "flatters the mountain tops with sovereign, eye," only to be hidden by the "basest clouds," or, anticipating modern geologists, observes

The hungry ocean gain Advantage on the kingdom of the shore,

he is merely putting into words the thoughts obscurely present to the mind of every watcher of the eternal mountains which have outlasted so many generations, and are yet, like all other things, hastening to decay. The mountains represent the indomitable force of nature to which we are forced to adapt ourselves; they speak to man of his littleness and his ephemeral existence; they rouse us from the placid content in which we may be lapped when contemplating the fat fields which we have conquered and the rivers which we have forced to run according to our notions of convenience. And, therefore, they

298 The Playground of Europe

should suggest not sheer misanthropy, as they did to Byron, or an outburst of revolutionary passion, as they did to his teacher Rousseau, but that sense of awestruck humility which befits such petty creatures as ourselves.

It is true, indeed, that Mont Blanc sometimes is too savage for poetry. He can speak in downright tragic earnestness; and any one who has been caught in a storm on some of his higher icefields, who has trembled at the deadly swoop of the gale, or at the ominous sound which heralds an avalanche, or at the remorseless settling down of the blinding snow, will agree that at times he passes the limits of the terrible which comes fairly within the range of art. There are times, however, at which one may expect to find precisely the right blending of the sweet and the stern. And in particular, there are those exquisite moments when the sunset is breathing over his calm snowfields its "ardours of rest and love." Watched from beneath, the Alpine glow, as everybody knows, is of exquisite beauty; but unfortunately the spectacle has become a little too popular. The very sunset seems to smell of "Baedeker's Guide." The flesh is weak; and the most sympathetic of human beings is apt to feel a slight sense of revulsion when the French guests at a table d 1 hotc are exclaiming in chorus, "Mag-

nifique, superbc!" and the Germans chiming in with "Wunderschon!" and the British tourist patting the old mountain on the back, and the American protesting that he has shinier sunsets at home. Not being of a specially sympathetic-nature, I had frequently wondered how that glorious spectacle would look from the solitary top of the monarch himself. This summer 1 was fortunate enough, owing to the judicious arrangements of one of his most famous courtiers—my old friend and comrade M. Gabriel Loppe,—to be able to give an answer founded on personal experience. The result was to me so interesting that I shall venture—rash as the attempt may be to give some account of a phenomenon of extraordinary beauty which has hitherto been witnessed by not more than some half dozen human beings.

It was in the early morning of August 6, 1873, that I left Chamouni for the purpose. The sun rose on one of those fresh dewy dawns unknown except in the mountains, when the buoyant air seems as it were to penetrate every pore in one's body. I could almost say with Sir Galahad- -

This mortal armour that I wear, This weight and size, this heart and eyes, Are touch"! and turn'd V> finest air.

The heavy, sodden framework of flesh and blood

300 The Playground of Europe

which I languidly dragged along London streets has undergone a strange transformation, and it is with scarcely a conscious effort that I breast the monstrous hill which towers above me. The pine-woods give out their aromatic scent, and the little glades are deep in ferns, wild-flowers, and strawberries. Even here, the latent terrors of the mountains are kept in mind by the huge boulders which, at some distant day, have crashed like cannon-balls through the forest. But the great mountain is not now indulging in one of his ponderous games at bowls, and the soft carpeting of tender vegetation suggests rather luxurious indolence, and, maybe, recalls lazy picnics rather than any more strenuous memories. Before long, however, we emerged from the forest, and soon the bells of a jolly little company of goats bade us farewell on the limits of the civilised world, as we stepped upon the still frozen glacier and found ourselves fairly in the presence. We were alone with the mighty dome, dazzling our eyes in the brilliant sunshine, and guarded by its sleeping avalanches. Luckily there was no temptation to commit the abomination of walking "against time" or racing any rival caravan of climbers. The whole day was before us, for it would have been undesirable to reach the chilly summit too earlv; and we could afford the unusual luxury of

lounging up Mont Blanc. We took, I hope, full advantage of our opportunities. We could peer into the blue depths of crevasses, so beautiful that one might long for such a grave, were it not for the awkward prospect of having one's bones put under a glass ease by the next generation of scientific travellers. We could record in our memories the strange forms of the shattered seracs, those grotesque ice-masses which seem to suggest that the monarch himself has a certain clumsy sense of humour. We lingered longest on the summit of the Dome du Gouter, itself a most majestic mountain were it not overawed by its gigantic neighbour. There, on the few ledges of rock which are left exposed in summer, the thunder has left its scars. The lightning's strokes have covered numbers of stones with little glasslike heads, showing that this must be one of its favourite haunts. But on this glorious summer day the lightnings were at rest; and we could peacefully count over the vast wilderness of peaks which already stretched far and wide beneath our feet. The lower mountain ranges appeared to be drawn up in parallel ranks like the sea waves heaved in calm weather by a monotonous ground-swell. Each ridge was blended into a uniform hue by the intervening atmosphere, sharply defined along the summit line, and yet

302 The Playground of Europe

only distinguished from its predecessor and successor by a delicate gradation of tone. Such a view produces the powerful but shadowy impression which one expects from an opium dream. The vast perspective drags itself out to an horizon so distant as to blend imperceptibty with the lower sky. It has a vague suggestion of rhythmical motion, strangely combined with eternal calm. Drop a pebble into a perfectly still sheet of water; imagine that each ripple is supplanted by a lofty mountain range, of which all detail is lost in purple haze, and that the farthest undulations melt into the mysterious infinite. One gazes with a sense of soothing melancholy as one listens to plaintive modulations of some air of "linked sweetness long drawn out." Far away among the hills we could see long reaches of the peaceful Lake of Geneva, just gleaming through the varying purple; but at our backs the icy crest of the great mountain still rose proudly above us, to remind us that our task was not yet finished. Fortunately for us, scarcely a cloud was to be seen under the enormous concave of the dark blue heavens; a few light streamers of cirrus were moving gently over our heads in those remote abysses from which they never condescend even to the loftiest of Alpine summits. Faint and evanescent as they might be, they possibly had an

ominous meaning for the future, but the present was our own; the little puffs of wind that whispered round some lofty ledges were keen enough in quality to remind us of possible frost-bites, but they had scarcely force enough to extinguish a lucifer match.

Carefully calculating our time, we advanced along the "dromedary's hump" and stepped upon the culminating ridge of the mountain about an hour before sunset. We had time to collect ourselves, to awake our powers of observation, and to prepare for the grand spectacle, for which preparations were already being made. There had been rehearsals enough in all conscience to secure a perfect performance. For millions of ages the lamps had been lighted and the transparencies had been shown with no human eye to observe or hand to applaud. Twice, I believe only twice, before, an audience had taken its place in this lofty gallery; but on one of those occasions, at least, the observers had been too unwell to do justice to the spectacle. The other party, of which the chief member was a French man of science, Dr. Martens, had been obliged to retreat hastily before the lights were extinguished; but their fragmentary account had excited our curiosity, and we had the pleasure of verifying the most striking phenomenon which

they described. And now we waited eagerly for the performance to commence; the cold was sufficient to freeze the wine in our bottles, but in still air the cold is but little felt, and by walking briskly up and down and adopting the gymnastic exercise in which the London cabman delights in cold weather, we were able to keep up a sufficient degree of circulation. I say "we," but I am libelling the most enthusiastic member of the party. Loppe sat resolutely on the snow, at the risk, as we might have thought, of following the example of Lot's wife. Superior, as it appeared, to all the frailties which beset the human frame suddenly plunged into a temperature I know not how many degrees below freezing-point, he worked with ever-increasing fury in a desperate attempt to fix upon canvas some of the magic beauties of the scene. Glancing from earth to heaven and from north to south, sketching with breathless rapidity the appearance of the eastern ranges, and then wheeling round like a weathercock to make hasty notes of the western clouds, breaking out at times into uncontrollable exclamations of delight, or reproving his thoughtless companions when their opaque bodies eclipsed a whole quarter of the heavens, he enjoyed, I should fancy, an hour of as keen delight as not often occurs to an enthusiastic lover of the sublime in nature. We

laughed, envied, and admired, and he escaped frost-bites. 1 wish that 1 could substitute his canvas—though, to say the truth, 1 fear it would exhibit a slight confusion of the points of the compass—for my words; but, as that is impossible, I must endeavour briefly to indicate the most impressive features of the scenery. My readers must kindly set their imaginations to work in aid of feeble language; for even the most eloquent language is but a poor substitute for a painter's brush, and a painter's brush lags far behind these grandest aspects of nature. The easiest way of obtaining the impression is to follow in my steps; for in watching a sunset from Mont Blanc one feels that one is passing one of those rare moments of life at which all the surrounding scenery is instantaneously and indelibly photographed on the mental retina by a process which no secondhand operation can even dimly transfer to others. To explain its nature requires a word or two of preface.

The ordinary view from Mont Blanc is not specially picturesque—and for a sufficient reason. The architect has concentrated his whole energies in producing a single impression. Everything has been so arranged as to intensify the sense of vast height and an illimitable horizon. In a good old guide-book I have read, on the authority

(I think) of Pliny, that the highest mountain in the world is 300,000 feet above the sea; and one is apt to fancy, on ascending Mont Blanc, that the guess is not so far out. The effect is perfectly unique in the Alps; but it is produced at a certain sacrifice. All dangerous rivals have been removed to such a distance as to become apparently insignificant. No grand mass can be admitted into the foreground; for the sense of vast size is gradually forced upon you by the infinite multiplicity of detail. Mont Blanc must be like an Asiatic despot, alone and supreme, with all inferior peaks reverently couched at his feet. If a man, previously as ignorant of geography as a boy who has just left a public school, could be transported for a moment to the summit, his impression would be that the Alps resembled a village of a hundred hovels grouped round a stupendous cathedral. Fully to appreciate this effect requires a certain familiarity with Alpine scenery, for otherwise the effect produced is a dwarfing of the inferior mountains into pettiness instead of an exaltation of Mont Blanc into almost portentous magnificence. Grouped around you at unequal distances lie innumerable white patches, looking like the tented encampments of scattered army corps. Hold up a glove at arm's length, and it will cover the whole of such a group. On the

boundless plain beneath (1 say "plain," for the greatest mountain system of Europe appears to have subsided into a rather uneven plain), it is a mere spot, a trifling dent upon the huge shield on whose central boss you are placed. But you know, though at first you can hardly realise the knowledge, that that insignificant discoloration represents a whole mountain district. One spot, for example, represents the clustered peaks of the Bernese Oberland; a block, as big as a pebble, is the soaring Jungfrau, the terrible mother of avalanches; a barely distinguishable wrinkle is the reverse of those snowy wastes of the Blumlis Alp, which seem to be suspended above the terrace of Berne, thirty miles away; and that little whitish streak represents the greatest ice-stream of the Alps, the huge Aletsch glacier, whose monstrous proportions have been impressed upon you by hours of laborious plodding. One patch contains the main sources from which the Rhine descends to the German Ocean, two or three more overlook the Italian plains and encircle the basin of the Po; from a more distant group flows the Danube, and from your feet the snows melt to supply the Rhone. You feel that you are in some sense looking down upon Europe from Rotterdam to Venice and from Varna to Marseilles. The vividness of the impression depends entirely upon the degree to which

you can realise the immense size of all these immeasurable details. Now, in the morning, the usual time for an ascent, the details are necessarily vague, because the noblest part of the view lies between the sun and the spectator. But in the evening light each ridge, and peak, and glacier stands out with startling distinctness, and each, therefore, is laden with its weight of old association. There, for example, was the grim Matter-horn: its angular dimensions were of infinitesimal minuteness; it would puzzle a mathematician to say how small a space its image would occupy on his retina; but, within that small space, its form was defined with exquisite accuracy; and we could recognise the precise configuration of the wild labyrinth of rocky ridges up which the earlier adventurers forced their way from the Italian side. And thus we not only knew, but felt that at our feet was lying a vast slice of the map of Europe. The effect was to exaggerate the apparent height, till the view had about it something portentous and unnatural: it seemed to be such a view as could be granted not even to mountaineers of earthly mould, but rather to some genie from the Arabian Nights, flying high above a world tinted with the magical colouring of old romance. Thus distinctly drawn, though upon so minute a scale, every rock and slope preserved its true

value, and the impression of stupendous height became almost oppressive as it was forced upon the imagination that a whole world of mountains, each of them a mighty mass in itself, lay couched far beneath our feet, reaching across the whole diameter of the vast panorama. And now, whilst occupied in drinking in that strange sensation, and allowing our minds to recover their equilibrium from the first staggering shock of astonishment, began the strange spectacle of which we were the sole witnesses. One long delicate cloud, suspended in mid-air just below the sun, was gradually adorning itself with prismatic colouring. Round the limitless horizon ran a faint fog-bank, unfortunately not quite thick enough to produce that depth of colouring which sometimes makes an Alpine sunset inexpressibly gorgeous. The weather—it was the only complaint we had to make—erred on the side of fineness. But the colouring was brilliant enough to prevent any thoughts of serious disappointment. The long series of western ranges melted into a uniform hue as the sun declined in their rear. Amidst their folds the Lake of Geneva became suddenly lighted up in a faint yellow gleam. To the east a blue gauze seemed to cover valley by valley as they sank into night and the intervening ridges rose with increasing distinctness, or rather it seemed

that some fluid of exquisite delicacy of colour and substance was flooding all the lower country beneath the great mountains. Peak by peak the high snow-fields caught the rosy glow and shone like signal-fires across the dim breadths of delicate twilight. Like Xerxes, we looked over the countless host sinking into rest, but with the rather different reflection, that a hundred years hence they would probably be doing much the same thing, whilst we should long have ceased to take any interest in the performance. And suddenly began a more startling phenomenon. A vast cone, with its apex pointing away from us, seemed to be suddenly cut out from the world beneath; night was within its borders and the twilight still all round; the blue mists were quenched where it fell, and for the instant we could scarcely tell what was the origin of this strange appearance. Some unexpected change seemed to have taken place in the programme; as though a great fold in the curtain had suddenly given way, and dropped on to part of the scenery. Of course a moment's reflection explained the meaning of this uncanny intruder; it was the giant shadow of Mont Blanc, testifying to his supremacy over all meaner eminences. It is difficult to say how sharply marked was the outline, and how startling was the contrast between this pyramid of darkness

and the faintly-lighted spaces beyond its influence; a huge inky blot seemed to have suddenly fallen upon the landscape. As we gazed we could see it move. It swallowed up ridge by ridge, and its sharp point crept steadily from one landmark to another down the broad Valley of Aosta. We were standing, in fact, on the point of the gnomon of a gigantic sundial, the face of which was formed by thousands of square miles of mountain and valley. So clear was the outline that, if figures had been scrawled upon glaciers and ridges, we could have told the time to a second; indeed, we were half-inclined to look for our own shadows at a distance so great that whole villages would be represented by a scarcely distinguishable speck of colouring. The huge shadow, looking ever more strange and magical, struck the distant Becca di Nona, and then climbed into the dark region where the broader shadow of the world was rising into the eastern sky. By some singular effect of perspective, rays of darkness seemed to be converging from above our heads to a point immediately above the apex of the shadowy cone. For a time it seemed that there was a kind of anti-sun in the east, pouring out not light, but deep shadow as it rose. The apex soon reached the horizon, and then to our surprise began climbing the distant sky. Would it never stop, and

was Mont Blanc capable of overshadowing not only the earth but the sky? For a minute or two I fancied, in a bewildered way, that this unearthly object would fairly rise from the ground and climb upwards to the zenith. But rapidly the lights went out upon the great army of mountains; the snow all round took the livid hue which immediately succeeds an Alpine sunset, and almost at a blow the shadow of Mont Blanc was swallowed up in the general shade of night.

The display had ceased suddenly at its culminating point, and it was highly expedient for the spectators to retire. We had no time to lose if we would get off the summit before the grip of the frost should harden the snows into an ice-crust; and in a minute we were running and sliding downwards at our best pace towards the familiar Corridor. Yet as we went the sombre magnificence of the scenery seemed for a time to increase. We were between the day and the night. The western heavens were of the most brilliant blue with spaces of transparent green, whilst a few scattered cloudlets glowed as if with internal fire. To the east the night rushed up furiously, and it was difficult to imagine that the dark purple sky was really cloudless and not blackened by the rising of some portentous storm. That it was, in fact, cloudless, appeared from the unbroken disc of the full moon,

Sunset on Mont Blancom

which, if I may venture to say so, had a kind of silly expression, as though it were a bad imitation of the sun, totally unable to keep the darkness in

order.

With how sad steps, O moon, thou climb'st the sky, How silently and with how wan a face!

as Sidney exclaims. And truly, set in that strange gloom, the moon looked wan and miserable enough; the lingering sunlight showed by contrast that she was but a feeble source of illumination; and, but for her half-comic look of helplessness, we might have sympathised with the astronomers who tell us that she is nothing but a vast perambulating tombstone, proclaiming to all mankind in the words of the familar epitaph, "As I am now, you soon shall be!" To speak after the fashion of early mythologies, one might fancy that some supernatural cuttlefish was shedding his ink through the heavens to distract her, and that the poor moon had but a bad chance of escaping his clutches. Hurrying downwards with occasional glances at the sky, we had soon reached the Grand Plateau, whence our further retreat was secure, and from that wildest of mountain fastnesses we saw the last striking spectacle of the evening. In some sense it was perhaps the most impressive of all. As all Alpine travellers know, the Grand

314 The Playground of Europe

Plateau is a level space of evil omen, embraced by a vast semicircle of icy slopes. The avalanches which occasionally descend across it, and which have caused more than one catastrophe, give it a bad reputation; and at night the icy jaws of the great mountain seem to be enclosing you in a fatal embrace. At this moment there was something half grotesque in its sternness. Light and shade were contrasted in a manner so bold as to be almost bizarre. One half of the cirque was of a pallid white against the night, which was rushing up still blacker and thicker, except that a few daring stars shone out like fiery sparks against a pitchy canopy; the other half, reflecting the black night, was relieved against the last gleams of daylight; in front a vivid band of blood-red light burnt along the horizon, beneath which seemed to lie an abyss of mysterious darkness. It was the last struggle between night and day, and the night seemed to assume a more ghastly ferocity as the day sank, pale and cold, before its antagonist. The Grand Plateau, indeed, is a fit scene for such contrasts; for there in mid-day you may feel the reflection of the blinding snows like the blast of a furnace, where a few hours before you were realising the keenest pangs of frost-bite. The cold and the night were now the conquerors, and the angry sunset glow seemed to grudge the victory.

The light rapidly faded, and the darkness, no longer seen in the strange contrast, subsided to its ordinary tones. The magic was gone; and it was in a commonplace though lovely summer night that we reached our resting-place at the Grands Millets. We felt that we had learnt some new secrets as to the beauty of mountain scenery, but the secrets were of that kind which not even the initiated can reveal. A great poet might interpret the sentiment of the mountains into song; but no poet could pack into any definite proposition or series of propositions the strange thoughts that rise in different spectators of such a scene. All that I at last can say is that some indefinable mixture of exhilaration and melancholy pervades one's mind; one feels like a kind of cheerful Tithonus "at the quiet limit of the world," looking down from a magic elevation upon the "dim fields about the homes"

Of happy men that have the power to die.

One is still of the earth, earthy; for freezing toes and snow-parched noses are lively reminders that (me has not become an immortal. Even on the top of Mont Blanc one may be a very long way from heaven. And yet the mere physical elevation of a league above the sea level seems to raise one by moments into a sphere above the petty

interests of everyday life. Why that should be so, and by what strange threads of association the reds and blues of a gorgeous sunset, the fantastic shapes of clouds and shadows at that dizzy height, and the dramatic changes that sweep over the boundless region beneath your feet, should stir you like mysterious music, or, indeed, wdiy music itself should have such power, I leave to philosophers to explain. This only I know, that even the memory of that summer evening on the top of Mont Blanc has power to plunge me into strange reveries not to be analysed by any-capacity, and still less capable of expression by the help of a few black remarks on white paper.

One word must be added. The expedition I have described is perfectly safe and easy, if, but only if, two or three conditions be scrupulously observed. The weather, of course, must be faultless; the snow must be in perfect order or a retreat may be difficult; and, to guard against unforeseen contingencies which are so common in high mountains, there should be a sufficient force of guides more trustworthy than the gentry who hang about Chamouni drinking-places. If these precautions were neglected, serious accidents would be easy, and at any rate there would be a very fair chance that the enthusiastic lover of scenery would leave his toes behind him.

THE ALPS IN WINTER

Men of science have recently called our attention to the phenomena of dual consciousness. To the unscientific mind it often seems that consciousness in its normal state must be rather multiple than dual. We lead, habitually, many lives at once, which are blended and intercalated in strangely complex fashion. Particular moods join most naturally, not with those which are contiguous in time, but with those which owe a spontaneous affinity to their identity of composition. When in my study, for example, it often seems as if that part alone of the past possessed reality which had elapsed within the same walls. All else—the noisy life outside, nay, even the life, sometimes rather noisy too, in the next room, becomes dreamlike. I can fancy that my most intimate self has never existed elsewhere, and that all other experiences recorded by memory have occurred to other selves in parallel but not continuous currents of life. And so, after a holiday, the day on

which we resume harness joins on to the day on

which we dropped it, and the interval fades into a mere hallucination.

There are times when this power (or weakness) has a singular charm. We can take up dropped threads of life, and cancel the weary monotony of daily drudgery; though we cannot go back to the well-beloved past, we can place ourselves in immediate relation with it, and break the barriers which close in so remorselessly to hide it from longing eyes. To some of us the charm is worked instantaneously by the sight of an Alpine peak. The dome of Mont Blanc or the crags of the Wetter-horn are spells that disperse the gathering mists of time. We can gaze upon them till we "beget the golden time again." And there is this peculiar fascination about the eternal mountains. They never recall the trifling or the vulgarising association of old days. There are times when the bare sight of a letter, a ring, or an old house, overpowers some people with the rush of early memories. I am not so happily constituted. Relics of the conventional kind have a perverse trick of reviving those petty incidents which one would rather forget. They recall the old follies that still make one blush, or the hasty word which one would buy back with a year of the life that is left. Our English fields and rivers have the same malignant freakishness. Nature in our little island is

too much dominated by the petty needs of humanity to have an affinity for the simpler and deeper emotions. With the Alps it is otherwise. There, as after a hot summer day the rocks radiate back their stores of heat, every peak and forest seems to be still redolent with the most fragrant perfume of memory. The trifling and vexatious incidents cannot adhere to such weighty monuments of bygone ages. They retain whatever of high and tender and pure emotion may have once been associated with them. If I were to invent a new idolatry (rather a needless task) I should prostrate myself, not before beast, or ocean, or sun, but before one of those gigantic masses to which, in spite of all reason, it is impossible not to attribute some shadowy personality. Their voice is mystic and has found discordant interpreters; but to me at least it speaks in tones at once more tender and more awe-inspiring than that of any mortal teacher. The loftiest and sweetest strains of Milton or Wordsworth may be more articulate, but do not lay so forcible a grasp upon my imagination.

In the summer there are distractions. The business of eating, drinking, and moving is carried on by too cumbrous and clanking a machinery. But 1 had often fancied that in the winter, when the whole region becomes part of dreamland, the

voice would be more audible and more continuous. Access might be attained to those lofty reveries in which the true mystic imagines time to be annihilated, and rises into beatific visions untroubled by the accidental and the temporary. Pure undefined emotion, indifferent to any logical embodiment, undisturbed by external perception, seems to belong to the sphere of the transcendental. Few people have the power to rise often to such regions or remain in them long. The indulgence, when habitual, is perilously enervating. But most people are amply secured from the danger by incapacity for the enjoyment. The temptation assails very exceptional natures. We the positive and matter-of-fact part of the world——need be no more afraid of dreaming too much than the London rough need be warned against an excessive devotion to the Fine Arts. Our danger is the reverse. Let us, in such brief moments as may be propitious, draw the curtains which may exclude the outside world, and abandon ourselves to the passing luxury of abstract meditation; or rather, for the word meditation suggests too near an approach to ordinary thought, of passive surrender to an emotional current.

The winter Alps provide some such curtain. The very daylight has an unreal glow. The noisy summer life is suspended. A scarce audible hush

seems to be whispered throughout the region. The first glacier stream that you meet strikes the . keynote of the prevailing melody. In summer the torrent comes down like a charge of cavalry—all rush and roar and foam and fury—turbid with the dust ground from the mountain's flanks by the ice-share, and spluttering and writhing in its bed like a creature in the agonies of strangulation. In winter it is transformed into the likeness of one of the gentle brooks that creep round the roots of Scawfell, or even one of those sparkling trout-streams that slide through a water-meadow beneath Stonehenge. It is perfectly transparent. It babbles round rocks instead of clearing them at a bound. It can at most fret away the edges of the huge white pillows of snow that cap the boulders. High up it can only show itself at intervals between smothering snow-beds which form continuous bridges. Even the thundering fall of the Handeck becomes a gentle thread of pure water creeping behind a broad sheet of ice, more delicately carved and moulded than a lady's veil, and so diminished in volume that one wonders how it has managed to festoon the broad rock faces with so vast a mass of pendent icicles. The pulse of the mountains is beating low; the huge arteries through which the life-blood courses so furiously in summer have become a world too wide

for this trickle of pellucid water. If one is still forced to attribute personality to the peaks, they are clearly in a state of suspended animation. They are spellbound, dreaming of dim abysses of past time or of the summer that is to recall them to life. They are in a trance like that of the Ancient Mariner when he heard strange spirit voices conversing overhead in mysterious murmurs.

This dreamlike impression is everywhere pervading and dominant. It is in proportion to the contrary impression of stupendous, if latent, energy which the Alps make upon one in summer. Then when an avalanche is discharged down the gorges of the Jungfrau, one fancies it the signal gun of a volley of artillery. It seems to betoken the presence of some huge animal, crouching in suspense but in perpetual vigilance, and ready at any moment to spring into portentous activity. In the winter the sound recalls the uneasy movement of the same monster, now lapped in sevenfold dreams. It is the rare interruption to a silence which may be felt—a single indication of the continued existence of forces which are for the time lulled into absolute repose. A quiet sea or a moonlit forest on the plains may give an impression of slumber in some sense even deeper. But the impression is not so vivid because less

permanent and less forcibly contrasted. The lowland forest will soon return to such life as it possesses, which is after all little more than a kind of entomological buzzing. The ocean is the only rival of the mountains. But the six months' paralysis which locks up the energies of the Alps has a greater dignity than the uncertain repose of the sea. It is as proper to talk of a sea of mountains as of a mountain wave; but the comparison always seems to me derogatory to the scenery which has the greatest appearance of organic unity. The sea is all very well in its way; but it is a fidgety, uncomfortable kind of element; you can see but a little bit of it at a time; and it is capable of being horribly monotonous. All poetry to the contrary notwithstanding, I hold that even the Atlantic is often little better than a bore. Its sleep chiefly suggests absence of the most undignified of all ailments; and it never approaches the grandeur of the strange mountain trance.

There are dreams and dreams. The special merit of the mountain structure is in the harmonious blending of certain strains of emotion not elsewhere to be enjoyed together. The winter Alps are melancholy, as everything sublime is more or less melancholy. The melancholy is the spontaneous recognition by human nature of its own pettiness when brought into immediate

contact with what we please to regard as eternal and infinite. It is the starting into vivid consciousness of that sentiment which poets and preachers have tried, with varying success, to crystallise into definite figures and formulae; which is necessarily more familiar to a man's mind, as he is more habitually conversant with the vastest objects of thought; and which is stimulated in the mountains in proportion as they are less dominated by the petty and temporary activities of daily life. In death, it is often said, the family likeness comes out which is obscured by individual peculiarities during active life. So in this living death or cataleptic trance of the mountains, they carry the imagination more easily to their permanent relations with epochs indefinitely remote.

The melancholy, however, which is shared with all that is sublime or lovely has here its peculiar stamp. It is at once exquisitely tender and yet wholesome and stimulating. The Atlantic in a December gale produces a melancholy tempered by the invigorating influence of the human life that struggles against its fury; but there is no touch of tenderness in its behaviour; it is a monster which would take a cruel pleasure in mangling and disfiguring its victim. A boundless plain is often at once melancholy and tender, especially

when shrouded in snow; but it is depressing as the vapours which hang like palls over a dreary morass. The Alps alone possess the merit of at once soothing and stimulating. The tender halftones, due to the vaporous air, the marvellous delicacy of light and shade on the snow-piled ranges, and the subtlety of line, which suggests that some sensitive agent has been moulding the snow-covering to every gentle contour of the surface, act like the media which allow the light-giving rays to pass, whilst quenching the rays of heat; they transmit the soothing and resist the depressing influences of nature. The snow on a half-buried chalet suggests a kind hand laid softly on a sick man's brows. And yet the nerves are not relaxed. The air is bright and bracing as the purest breeze on the seashore, without the slightest trace of languor. It has the inspiring quality of the notorious "wild North-Easter," without its preposterous bluster. Even in summer the same delicious atmosphere may be breathed amongst the higher snow-fields in fine weather. In winter it descends to the valleys, and the nerves are strung as firmly as those of a race-horse in training, without being over-excited. The effect is heightened by the intensity of character which redeems every detail of a mountain region from the commonplace. The first sight of a pine-tree, bearing

so gallantly—with something, one may almost say, of military jauntiness—its load of snow-crystals, destroyed to me for ever the charm of one of Heine's most frequently-quoted poems. It became once for all impossible to conceive of that least morbid of trees indulging in melancholy longings for a southern palm. It may show something of the sadness of a hard struggle for life; but never in the wildest of storms could it condescend to sentimentalism.

But it is time to descend to detail. The Alps in winter belong, I have said, to dreamland. From the moment when the traveller catches sight, from the terraces of the Jura, of the long encampment of peaks, from Mont Blanc to the Wetterhorn, to the time when he has penetrated to the innermost recesses of the chain, he is passing through a series of dreams within dreams. Each vision is a portal to one beyond and within, still more unsubstantial and solemn. One passes, by slow gradations, to the more and more shadowy regions, where the stream of life runs lower and the enchantment binds the senses with a more powerful opiate. Starting, for example, from the loveliest of all conceivable lakes, where the Blumlis Alp, the Jungfrau, and Sehreekhorn form a marvellous background to the old towers of Thun, one comes under 1 he dominion of the charm. The lake waters, no longer clouded by turbid torrents, are mere liquid turquoise. They are of the colour of which Shelley was thinking when he described the blue Mediterranean awakened from his summer dreams "beside a pumice-isle in Baise's Bay." Between the lake and the snow-clad hills lie the withered forests, the delicate reds and browns of the deciduous foliage giving just the touch of warmth required to contrast the coolness of the surrounding scenery. And higher up, the pine-forests still display their broad zones of purple, not quite in that uncompromising spirit which reduces them in the intensity of summer shadow to mere patches of pitchy blackness, but mellowed by the misty air, and with their foliage judiciously softened with snow-dust like the powdered hair of a last-century beauty. There is no longer the fierce glare which gives a look of parched monotony to the stretches of lofty pasture under an August sun. The perpetual greens, denounced by painters, have disappeared, and in their place are ranges of novel hue and texture which painters may possibly dislike- for I am not familiar with their secrets—but which they may certainly despair of adequately rendering. The ranges are apparently formed of a delicate material of creamy whiteness, unlike the dazzling splendours of the eternal snows, at once so pure and so mellow

that it suggests rather frozen milk than ordinary snow. If not so ethereal, it is softer and more tender than its rival on the loftier peaks. It is moulded into the same magic combination of softness and delicacy by shadows so pure in colour that they seem to be woven out of the bluest sky itself. Lake and forest and mountain are lighted by the low sun, casting strange misty shadows to portentous heights, to fade in the vast depths of the sky, or to lose themselves imperceptibly on the mountain flanks. As the steamboat runs into the shadow of the hills, a group of pine-trees on the sky-line comes near the sun, and is suddenly transformed into molten silver; or some snow-ridge, pale as death on the nearest side, is lighted up along its summit with a series of points glowing with intense brilliancy, as though the peaks were being kindled by a stupendous burning-glass. The great snow-mountains behind stand glaring in spectral calm, the cliffs hoary with frost, but scarcely changed in outline or detail from their summer aspect. When the sun sinks, and the broad glow of gorgeous colouring fades into darkness, or is absorbed by a wide expanse of phosphoric moonlight, one feels fairly in the outer court of dreamland.

Scenery, even the wildest which is really enjoyable, derives half its charm from the occult sense

of the human life and social forms moulded upon it. A bare fragment of rock is ugly till enamelled by lichens, and the Alps would be unbearably stern but for the picturesque society preserved among their folds. In summer the true life of the people is obscured by the rank overgrowth of parasitic population. In winter the stream of existence shows itself in more of its primitive form, like the rivulets which represent the glacier torrents. As one penetrates farther into the valleys, and the bagman clement-—the only representative of the superincumbent summer population-—disappears, one finds the genuine peasant, neither the parasite which sucks the blood of summer tourists nor the melodramatic humbug of operas and picture-books. He is the rough, athletic labourer, wrestling with nature for his immediate wants, reducing industrial life to its simplest forms, and with a certain capacity-—not to be quite overlooked-—for the absorption of schnapps. Even Sir Wilfrid Lawson would admit the force of the temptation after watching a day's labour in the snow-smothered forests. The village is empty of its male inhabitants in the day, and towards evening one hears distant shouts and the train of sleighs emerges from the skirts of the forest, laden with masses of winter fodder, or with the mangled trunks of "patrician trees," which strain to the utmost the muscles of their drawers. As the edge of an open slope is reached, a tumultuous glissade takes place to the more level regions. Each sleigh puts out a couple of legs in advance, like an insect's feelers, which agitate themselves in strange contortions, resulting by some unintelligible process in steering the freight past apparently insuperable obstacles. One may take a seat upon one of these descending thunderbolts as one may shoot the rapids of the St. Lawrence; but the process is slightly alarming to untrained nerves.

As the sun sinks, the lights begin to twinkle out across the snow from the scattered cottages, more picturesque than ever under their winter covering. There is something pathetic, I hardly know why, in this humble illumination which lights up the snowy waste and suggests a number of little isolated foci of domestic life. One imagines the family gathered in the low close room, its old stained timbers barely visible by the glimmer of the primitive lamp, and the huge beams in the ceiling enclosing mysterious islands of gloom, and remembers Macaulay's lonely cottage where

The oldest cask is opened And the largest lamp is lit.

The goodman is probably carving lop-sided

chamois instead of "trimming his helmet's plume"; but it may be said with literal truth that

The good\vife's shuttle merrily Goes flashing through the loom,

and the spinning-wheel has not yet become a thing of the past. Though more primitive in its arrangements, the village is in some ways more civilised than its British rival. A member of a School Board might rejoice to see the energy with which the children are making up arrears of education interrupted by the summer labours. Olive branches are plentiful in these parts, and they seem to thrive amazingly in the winter. The game of sliding in miniature sleighs seems to be inexpressibly attractive for children of all ages, and may possibly produce occasional truancy. But the sleighs also carry the children to school from the higher clusters of houses, and they are to be seen making daily pilgrimages long enough to imply a considerable tax upon their pedestrian powers. A little picture comes back to me as I write of a string of red-nosed urchins plodding vigorously up the deep tracks which lead from the lower valley to a remote hamlet in a subsidiary glen. The day was gloomy, the light was fading, and the grey hill-ranges melted indislinguishably into the grey sky. The forms of the narrow glen,

of the level bottom in which a few cottages clustered near the smothered stream, of the sweeps of pine-forests rising steeply to the steeper slopes of alp, and of the ranges of precipitous rock above were just indicated by a few broad sweeps of dim shadow distinct enough to suggest, whilst scarcely defining, the main features of the valley and its walls. Lights and shadows intermingled so faint and delicate that each seemed other; the ground was a form of twilight; and certainly it looked as though the children had no very cheerful prospect before them. But, luckily, the mental colouring bestowed by the childish mind upon familiar objects does not come from without nor lepend upon the associations which are indissoluble for the older observer.

There is no want, indeed, of natural symbols of melancholy feeling, of impressive bits of embodied sadness, recalling in sentiment some of Bewick's little vignettes of storm-beaten crag and desolate churchyard. Any place out of season has a certain charm for my mind in its suggestions of dreamful indolence. But the Alpine melancholy deepens at times to pathos and even to passionate regret. The deserted aspect of these familiar regions is often delicious in its way, especially to jaded faculties. But it is needless to explain at length why some familiar spots should now be haunted, why silence should sometimes echo with a bitter pang the voices of the past, or the snow seem to be resting on the grave of dead happiness. The less said on such things the better; though the sentiment makes itself felt too emphatically to be quite ignored. The sadder strains blend more audibly with the music of the scenery as one passes upwards through grim gorges towards the central chain and the last throbs of animation begin to die away. In the calmest summer day the higher Aar valley is stern and savage enough. Of all congenial scenes for the brutalities of a battlefield, none could be more appropriate than the dark basin of the Grimsel, with nothing above but the bleakest of rock and the most desolate of snow-fields, and the sullen lake below, equally ready to receive French or Austrian corpses. The winter aspect of the valley seems to vary between two poles. It can look ghastly as death when the middle air is thick with falling snow, just revealing at intervals the black bosses of smoothed cliff that glare fantastically downwards from apparently impassable heights, whilst below the great gash of the torrent-bed looks all the more savage from the cakes of thick ice on the boulders at the bottom. It presents an aspect which by comparison may be called gentle when the winter moonlight shows every swell in the continuous snow-fields

that have gagged the torrent and smoothed the ruggedness of the rocks. But the gorge is scarcely cheerful at the best of times, nor can one say that the hospice to which it leads is a lively place of residence for the winter. Buried almost to the eaves in snow, it looks like an eccentric grey rock with green shutters. A couple of servants spend their time in the kitchen with a dog or two for company and have the consolations of literature in the shape of a well-thumbed almanac. Doubtless its assurance that time docs not actually stand still must often be welcome. The little dribble of commerce, which never quite ceases, is represented by a few peasants, who may occasionally be weatherbound long enough to make serious inroads on the dry bread and frozen ham. Pigs, for some unknown reason, seem to be the chief article of exchange, and they squeal emphatic disapproval of their enforced journey. At such a point one is hanging on to the extremest verge of civilisation. It is the last outpost held by man in the dreary regions of frost. One must generally reach it by floundering knee-deep, with an occasional plunge into deeper drifts, through hours of severe labour. Here one has got almost to the last term. The dream is almost a nightmare. One's soul is sinking

The Alps in Winter

00

into that sleep

Where the dreamer seems to be Weltering through eternity.

There is but a fragile link between ourself and the outer world. Taking a plunge into deep water, the diver has sometimes an uncomfortable, feeling, as though an insuperable distance intervened between himself and the surface. Here one is engulfed in abysses of wintry silence. One is overwhelmed and drenched with the sense of mountain solitude. And yet it is desirable to pass yet farther, and to feel that this flicker of life, feeble as it may be, ma\'7d- yet be a place of refuge as the one remaining bond between yourself and society. One is but playing at danger; but for the moment one can sympathise with the xVrctic adventurer pushing towards the pole, and feeling that the ship which he has left behind is the sole basis of his operations. Above the Grimsel rises the Galenstock, which, though not one of the mightiest giants, is a grand enough peak, and stands almost at the central nucleus of the Alps. The head waters of the Rhone and the Rhine flow from its base, and it looks defiantly across a waste of glaciers to its great brethren of the Oberland. It recalls Milton's magnificent phrase, "The great vision of the guarded Mount," but looks over a

nobler prospect than St. Michael's. Five hours' walk will reach it in summer, and it seemed that its winter panorama must be one of the most characteristic in the region. The accident which frustrated our attempt gave a taste of that savage nature which seems ready to leap to life in the winter mountains. The ferocious element of the scenery raged for a few minutes, which might easily have been terrible.

We had climbed high towards the giant backbone of the mountain, and a few minutes would have placed us on the top. We were in that dim upper stratum, pierced by the nobler peaks alone, and our next neighbour in one direction was the group of Monte Rosa, some sixty miles away, but softly and clearly denned in every detail as an Alpine distance alone can be. Suddenly, without a warning or an apparent cause, the weather changed. The thin white flakes which had been wandering high above our heads changed suddenly into a broad black veil of vapour, dimming square leagues of snow with its shadows. A few salmon-coloured wreaths that had been lingering near the farthest ranges had vanished between two glances at the distance, and in their place long trailers of cloud spread themselves like a network of black cobwebs from the bayonet-point of the Weisshorn to the sreat bastion of the Monte

Rosa, and seemed to be shooting out mysterious fibres, as the spider projects its nets of gossamer. Though no formed mass of cloud had showed itself, the atmosphere bathing the Oberland peaks rapidly lost its transparency, and changed into a huge blur of indefinite gloom. A wind, cold and icy enough, had all day been sucked down the broad funnel of the Rhone glacier, from the limiting ridges; and the light powdery snow along the final parapet of the Galenstock had been blowing off in regular puffs, suggestive of the steady roll of rifle smoke from the file-firing of a battalion in line. Now the wind grew louder and shriller; miniature whirlwinds began to rollick down the steep gullies, and when one turned towards the wind, it seemed as if an ice-cold hand was administering a sharp blow to the cheek. In our solitude, beyond all possible communication with permanent habitation, distant by some hours of walk even from our base at the Grimsel, there was something almost terrible in this sudden and ominous awakening of the storm spirit. We had ventured into the monster's fastness and he was rousing himself. We depended upon the coming moon for our homeward route, and the moon would not have much power in the thick snowstorm that was apparently about to envelop us. Retreat was evidently prudent, and when the

dim light began to fade we were still climbing that broad-backed miscellaneous ridge or congeries of ridges which divides the Grimsel from the Rhone glacier. In summer it is a wilderness of rocky hummocks and boulders, affording shelter to the most ambitious stragglers of the Alpine rose, and visited by an occasional chamois—a kind of neutral ground between the kingdom of perpetual snow and the highest pastures—one of those chaotic misshapen regions which suggest that the world has not been quite finished. In winter, a few black rocks alone peep through the snowy blanket; the hollows become covered pitfalls; and some care is required in steering through its intricacies, and crossing gullies steep enough to suggest a possibility of avalanches. Night and storm might make the work severe, though there was no danger for men of average capacity, and with first-rate guides. But, suddenly and perversely, the heaviest and strongest man of the party declared himself to be ill. His legs began to totter, and he expressed a decided approbation of sitting in the abstract. Then, I must confess, an uncomfortable vision flitted for a moment through my brain. I did not think of the spirited description of the shepherd, in Thomson, lost in the snow-drifts, when, foul and fierce, All winter drives along the darkened air.

But I did recall a dozen uncomfortable legends— only too authentic—of travellers lost, far nearer to hospitable refuges, in Alpine storms; of that disgusting museum of corpses, which the monks are not ashamed to keep for the edification of travellers across the St. Bernard; of the English tourists frozen almost within reach of safety on the Col du Bonhomme; of that poor unknown wanderer, who was found a year or two ago in one of the highest chalets of the Val de Bagne, having just been able to struggle thither, in the winter, with strength enough to write a few words on a bit of paper, for the instruction of those who would find his body when the spring brought back the nomadic inhabitants. Some shadowy anticipation suggested itself of a possible newspaper paragraph, describing the zeal with which we had argued against our friend's drowsiness, of our brandy giving out, and pinches, blows, and kicks gradually succeeding to verbal remonstrance. Have not such sad little dramas been described in numberless books of travel? But the foreboding was thrown away. Our friend's distress yielded to the simplest of all conceivable remedies. A few hunches of bread and cheese restored him to a vigour quite excluding even the most remote consideration of the propriety of applying physical force. lie was, 1 believe, the freshest of the party

when we came once more, as the moonlight made its last rally against the gathering storm, in sight of the slumbering hospice. It certainly was as grim as ever—solitary and gloomy as the hut of an Esquimau, representing an almost presumptuous attempt of man to struggle against the intentions of nature, which would have bound the whole region in the rigidity of tenfold torpor. To us, fresh from still sterner regions, where our dreams had begun to be haunted by fierce phantoms resentful of our intrusion, it seemed an embodiment of comfort. It is only fair to add that the temporary hermit of the place welcomed us as heartily as might be to his ascetic fare, and did not even regard us as appropriate victims of speculation.

After this vision of the savageness of winter, I would willingly venture one more description; but I have been already too daring, and beyond certain limits I admit the folly of describing the indescribable. There are sights and scenes, in presence of which the describer, who must feel himself to be, at best, a very poor creature, begins to be sensible that he is not only impertinent but profane. I could, of course, give a rough catalogue of the beauties of the Wengern Alp in winter; a statement of the number of hours wading in snow across its slopes; a rhapsody about the loveliness of peaks

seen between the loaded pine-branches, or the marvellous variety of sublimity and tender beauty enjoyed in perfect calm of bright weather on the dividing ridge. But I refrain. To me the Wen-gern Alp is a sacred place—the holy of holies in the mountain sanctuary, and the emotions produced when no desecrating influence is present and old memories rise up, softened by the sweet sadness of the scenery, belong to that innermost region of feeling which I would not, if I could, lay bare. Byron's exploitation of the scenery becomes a mere impertinence; Scott's simplicity would not have been exalted enough; Wordsworth would have seen this much of his own image; and Shelley, though he could have caught some of the finer sentiments, would have half spoilt it by some metaphysical rant. The best modern describers cannot shake off their moralising or their scientific speculations or their desire to be humorous sufficiently to do justice to such beauties. A follower in their steps will do well to pass by with a simple confession of wonder and awe.

The last glorious vision showed itself as we descended from Lauterbrunnen, in the evening, regretting the neglect of nature to provide men with eyes in their backs. The moonlight, reflected from the all-enveloping shroud of snow, slept on the lower ridges before us, and gave a mysterious beauty to the deep gorge of the white Lutschine; but behind us it turned the magnificent pyramid of the Jungfrau from base to summit into one glowing mass of magical light. It was not a single mass—a flat continuous surface, as it often appears in the more emphatic lights and shades of daytime—but a whole wilderness of peak, cliff, and glacier, rising in terrace above terrace and pyramid above pyramid, divided by mysterious valleys and shadowy recesses, the forms growing more delicate as the)' rose, till they culminated in the grand contrast of the balanced cone of the Silberhorn and the flowing sweep of the loftiest crest. A chaos of grand forms, it yet suggests some pervading design, too subtle to be understood by mortal vision, and scorning all comparison with earthly architecture. And the whole was formed, not of vulgar ice and earth, but of incarnate light. The darkest shadow was bright against the faint cliffs of the shadowy gorge, and the highest light faint enough to be woven out of reflected moonshine. So exquisitely modulated, and at once so audacious and so delicate in its sumptuous splendours of design, it belonged to the dream region, in which we appear to be inspired with supernatural influences.

But I am verging upon the poetical. Within a few hours we were again struggling for coffee in the

THE STAUBBACH, LAUTERBRUNNEN From ;i phut'.-iMph by Sommers, Naples

buffets of railway stations and forgetting all duties, pleasures, and human interests amongst the tumbling waves of the "silver streak." The winter Alps no longer exist. They are but a vision—a faint memory intruding itself at intervals, when the roar of commonplace has an interval of stillness. Only, if dreams were not at times the best and most solid of realities, the world would be intolerable.

CHAPTER XIII

THE REGRETS OF A MOUNTAINEER

I have often felt a sympathy, which almost rises to the pathetic, when looking on at a cricket-match or boat-race. Something of the emotion with which Gray regarded the "distant spires and antique towers" rises within me. It is not, indeed, that I feel very deeply for the fine ingenuous lads who, as somebody says, are about to be degraded into tricky, selfish Members of Parliament. I have seen too much of them. They are very fine animals; but they are rather too exclusively animal. The soul is apt to be in too embryonic a state within these cases of well-strung bone and muscle. It is impossible for a mere athletic machine, however finely constructed, to appeal very deeply to one's finer sentiments. I can scarcely look forward with even an affectation of sorrow for the time when, if more sophisticated, it will at least have made a nearer approach to the dignity of an intellectual being. It is not the boys who make me feel a touch of sadness; their approaching elevation to the dignity

of manhood will raise them on the whole in the scale of humanity; it is the older spectators whose aspect has in it something affecting. The shaky old gentleman, who played in the days when it was decidedly less dangerous to stand up to bowling than to a cannon-ball, and who now hobbles about on rheumatic joints, by the help of a stick; the corpulent elder, who rowed when boats had gangways down their middle, and did not require as delicate a balance as an acrobat's at the top of a living pyramid—these are the persons whom I cannot see without an occasional sigh. The) T are really conscious that they have lost something which they can never regain; or, if they momentarily forget it, it is even more forcibly impressed upon the spectators. To see a respectable old gentleman of sixty, weighing some fifteen stone, suddenly forget a third of his weight and two thirds of his years, and attempt to caper like a boy, is indeed a startling phenomenon. To the thoughtless, it may be simply comic; but, without being a Jaques, one may contrive also to suck some melancholy out of it.

Xow, as I have never caught a cricket-ball, and, on the contrary, have caught numerous crabs in my life, the sympathy which I feel for these declining athletes is not due to any great personal interest in the matter. But I have long antici-

pated that a similar day would come for me, when I should no longer be able to pursue my favourite sport of mountaineering. Some day I should find that the ascent of a zigzag was as bad as a performance on the treadmill; that I could not look over a precipice without a swimming in the head; and that I could no more jump a crevasse than the Thames at Westminster. None of these things have come to pass. So far as I know, my physical powers arc still equal to the ascent of Mont Blanc or the Jungfrau. But I am no less effectually debarred—it matters not how—from mountaineering. I wander at the foot of the gigantic Alps, and look up longingly to the summits, which are apparently so near, and yet know that they are divided from me by an impassable gulf. In some missionary work I have read that certain South Sea Islanders believed in a future paradise where the good should go on eating for ever with insatiable appetites at an inexhaustible banquet. They were to continue their eternal dinner in a house with open wickerwork sides; and it was to be the punishment of the damned to crawl outside in perpetual hunger and look in through the chinks as little boys look in through the windows of a London cookshop. With similar feelings I lately watched through a telescope the small black dots, which were really

men, creeping up the high flanks of Mont Blanc or Monte Rosa. The eternal snows represented for me the Elysian fields, into which entrance was sternly forbidden, and I lingered about the spot with a mixture of pleasure and pain, in the envious contemplation of my more fortunate companions.

I know there are those who will receive these assertions with civil incredulity. Some persons assume that every pleasure with which they cannot sympathise is necessarily affectation, and hold, as a particular case of that doctrine, that Alpine travellers risk their lives merely from fashion or desire of notoriety. Others are kind enough to admit that there is something genuine in the passion, but put it on a level with the passion for climbing greased poles. They think it derogatory to the due dignity of Mont Blanc that he should be used as a greased pole, and assure us that the true pleasures of the Alps are those which are within reach of the old and the invalids, who can only creep about villages and along highroads. I cannot well argue with such detractors from what I consider a noble sport. As for the first class, it is reduced almost to a question of veracity. I say that I enjoy being on the top of a mountain, or, indeed, half-way up a mountain; that climbing is a pleasure to me, and would be so if no one else

climbed and no one ever heard of my climbing. They reply that they don't believe it. No more argument is possible than if I were to say that I liked eating olives, and some one asserted that I really eat them only out of affectation. My reply would be simply to go on eating olives; and I hope the reply of mountaineers will be to go on climbing Alps. The other assault is more intelligible. Our critics admit that we have a pleasure; but assert that it is a puerile pleasure—that it leads to an irreverent view of mountain beauty, and to oversight of that which should really most impress a refined and noble mind. To this I shall only make such an indirect reply as may result from a frank confession of my own regrets at giving up the climbing business—perhaps for ever. I am sinking, so to speak, from the butterfly to the caterpillar stage, and, if the creeping thing is really the higher of the two, it will appear that there is something in the substance of my lamentations unworthy of an intellectual being. Let me try. By way of preface, however, I admit that mountaineering, in my sense of the word, is a sport. It is a sport which, like fishing or shooting, brings one into contact with the sublimest aspects of nature; and, without setting their enjoyment before one as an ultimate end or aim, helps one indirectly to absorb and be penetrated by their

influence. Still it is strictly a sport—as strictly as cricket, or rowing, or knurr-and-spcll—and I have no wish to place it on a different footing. The game is won when a mountain-top is reached in spite of difficulties; it is lost when one is forced to retreat; and, whether won or lost, it calls into play a great variety of physical and intellectual energies, and gives the pleasure which always accompanies an energetic use of our faculties. Still it suffers in some degree from this undeniable characteristic, and especially from the tinge which has consequently been communicated to narratives of mountain adventures. There are two ways which have been appropriated to the description of all sporting exploits. One is to indulge in fine writing about them, to burst out in sentences which swell to paragraphs, and in paragraphs which spread over pages; to plunge into ecstasies about infinite abysses and overpowering splendours, to compare mountains to archangels lying down in eternal winding-sheets of snow, and to convert them into allegories about man's highest destinies and aspirations. This is good when it is well done. Mr.

Ruskin has covered the Matterhorn, for example, with a whole web of poetical associations, in language which, to a severe taste, is perhaps a trifle too fine, though he has done it with an eloquence which his bitterest antagonists must freely

acknowledge. Yet most humble writers will feel that if they try to imitate Mr. Ruskin's eloquence they will pay the penalty of becoming ridiculous. It is not every one who can with impunity compare Alps to archangels. Tall talk is luckily an object of suspicion to Englishmen, and consequently most writers, and especially those who frankly adopt the sporting view of the mountains, adopt the opposite scheme: they affect something like cynicism; they mix descriptions of scenery with allusions to fleas or to bitter beer; they shrink with the prevailing dread of Englishmen from the danger of overstepping the limits of the sublime into its proverbial opposite; and they humbly try to amuse us because they can't strike us with awe. This, too, if I may venture to say so, is good in its way and place; and it seems rather hard to these luckless writers when people assume that, because they make jokes on a mountain, they are necessarily insensible to its awful sublimities. A sense of humour is not incompatible with imaginative sensibility; and even Wordsworth might have been an equally powerful prophet of nature if he could sometimes have descended from his stilts. In short, a man may worship mountains and yet have a quiet joke with them when he is wandering all day in their tremendous solitudes. Joking, however, is, it must be admitted, a dan-

gerous habit. I freely avow that, in my humble contributions to Alpine literature, I have myself made some very poor and very unseasonable witticisms. I confess my error, and only wish that I had no worse errors to confess. Still I think that the poor little jokes in which we mountaineers sometimes indulge have been made liable to rather harsh constructions. We are accused, in downright earnest, not merely of being flippant, but of an arrogant contempt for all persons whose legs are not as strong as our own. We are supposed seriously to wrap ourselves in our own conceit, and to brag intolerably of our exploits. Now I will nut say that no mountaineer ever swaggers: the quality called by the vulgar "bounce" is unluckily confined to no profession. Certainly I have seen a man intolerably vain because he could raise a hundred-weight with his little finger; and I dare say that the ■'champion bill-poster," whose name is advertised on the walls of this metropolis, thinks excellence in bill-posting the highest virtue of a citizen. So some men may be silly enough to brag in all seriousness about mountain exploits. However, most lads of twenty learn that it is silly to give themselves airs about mere muscular eminence; and especially is this true of Alpine exploits—first, because they require less physical prowess than almost any other

sport, and secondly, because a good amateur still feels himself the hopeless inferior of half the Alpine peasants whom he sees. You cannot be very conceited about a game in which the first clodhopper you meet can give you ten minutes' start in an hour. Still, a man writing in a humorous vein naturally adopts a certain bumptious tone, just as our friend Punch ostentatiously declares himself to be omniscient and infallible. Nobody takes him at his word, or supposes that the editor of Punch is really the most conceited man in all England. But we poor mountaineers are occasionally fixed with our own careless talk by some outsider who is not in the secret. We know ourselves to be a small sect, and to be often laughed at; we reply by assuming that we are the salt of the earth, and that our amusement is the first and noblest of all amusements. Our only retort to the good-humoured ridicule with which we are occasionally treated is to adopt an affected strut, and to carry it off as if we were the finest fellows in the world. We make a boast of our shame, and say, if you laugh we must crow. But we don't really mean anything: if we did, the only word which the English language would afford wherewith to describe us would be the very unpleasant antithesis to wise men, and certainly I hold that we have the average amount of common-

sense. When, therefore, I see us taken to task for swaggering, I think it a trifle hard that this merely playful affectation of superiority should be made a serious fault. For the future I would promise to be careful, if it were worth avoiding the misunderstanding of men who won't take a joke. Meanwhile, I can only state that when Alpine travellers indulge in a little swagger about their own performances and other people's incapacity, they don't mean more than an infinitesimal fraction of what they say, and that they know perfectly well that when history comes to pronounce a final judgment upon the men of the time, it won't put mountain-climbing on a level with patriotism, or even with excellence in the fine arts.

The reproach of real bona fide arrogance is, so far as I know, very little true of Alpine travellers. With the exception of the necessary fringe hanging on to every set of human beings— consisting of persons whose heads are weaker than their legs— the mountaineer, so far as my experience has gone, is generally modest enough. Perhaps he sometimes Haunts his ice-axes and ropes a little too much before the public eye at Chamouni, as a yachtsman occasionally flourishes his nautical costume at Cowcs; but the fault may be pardoned by those not inexorable to human weaknesses. This opinion, I know, cuts at the root of

the most popular theory as to our ruling passion. If we do not climb the Alps to gain notoriety, for what purpose can we possibly climb them? That same unlucky trick of joking is taken to indicate that we don't care much about the scenery; for who, with a really susceptible soul, could be facetious under the cliffs of Jungfrau or the ghastly precipices of the Matterhorn? Hence people who kindly excuse us from the blame of notoriety-hunting generally accept the "greased-pole" theory. We are, it seems, overgrown schoolboys, who, like other schoolboys, enjoy being in dirt, and danger, and mischief, and have as much sensibility for natural beauty as the mountain mules. And against this, as a more serious complaint, I wish to make my feeble protest, in order that my lamentations on quitting the profession may not seem unworthy of a thinking being.

Let me try to recall some of the impressions which mountaineering has left with me, and see whether they throw any light upon the subject. As I gaze at the huge cliffs where I may no longer wander, I find innumerable recollections arise— some of them dim, as though belonging to a past existence; and some so brilliant that I can scarcely realise my exclusion from the scenes to which they belong. I am standing at the foot of what, to

my mind, is the most glorious of all Alpine wonders —the huge Oberland precipice, on the slopes of the Faulhorn or the Wengern Alp. Innumerable tourists have done all that tourists can do to cocknify (if that is the right derivative from cockney) the scenery; but, like the Pyramids or a Gothic cathedral, it throws off the taint of vulgarity by its imperishable majesty. Even on turf strewn with sandwich-papers and empty bottles, even in the presence of hideous peasant-women singing" Stand-er auf" for five centimes, we cannot but feel the influence of Alpine beauty. When the sunlight is dying off the snows, or the full moon lighting them up with ethereal tints, even sandwich-papers and singing women may be forgotten. How does the memory of scrambles along snow aretes, of plunges—luckily not too deep—into crevasses, of toil through long snow-fields, towards a refuge that seemed to recede as we advanced— where, to quote Tennyson with due alteration, to the traveller toiling in immeasurable snow—

Sown in a wrinkle of the monstrous hill The chalet sparkles like a grain of salt;—
how do such memories as these harmonise with the
sense of superlative sublimit\'7d'?

One element of mountain beauty is, we shall all admit, their vast size and steepness. That a
mountain is very big, and is faced by perpendicular walls of rock, is the first thing which strikes everybody, and is the whole essence and outcome of a vast quantity of poetical description. Hence the first condition towards a due appreciation of mountain scenery is that these qualities should be impressed upon the imagination. The mere dry statement that a mountain is so many feet in vertical height above the sea, and contains so many tons of granite, is nothing. Mont Blanc is about three miles high. What of that? Three miles is an hour's walk for a lady—an eighteen-penny cab-fare—the distance from Hyde Park Corner to the Bank—an express train could do it in three minutes, or a race-horse in five. It is a measure which we have learnt to despise, looking at it from a horizontal point of view; and accordingly most persons, on seeing the Alps for the first time, guess them to be higher, as measured in feet, than they really are. What, indeed, is the use of giving measures in feet to any but the scientific mind? Who cares whether the moon is 250,000 or 2,500,000 miles distant? Mathematicians try to impress upon us that the distance of the fixed stars is only expressible by a row of figures which stretches across a page; suppose it stretched across two or across a dozen pages, should we be any the wiser, or have, in the least degree, a clearer notion

of the superlative distances? We civilly say, "Dear me!" when the astronomer looks to us for the appropriate stare, but we only say it with the mouth; internally our remark is, "You might as well have multiplied, by a few more millions whilst you were about it." Even astronomers, though not a specially imaginative race, feel the impotence of figures, and try to give us some measure which the mind can grasp a little more conveniently. They tell us about the cannon-ball which might have been flying ever since the time of Adam, and not yet have reached the heavenly body, or about the stars which may not yet have become visible, though the light has been flying to us at a rate inconceivable by the mind for an inconceivable number of years; and they succeed in producing a bewildering and giddy sensation, although the numbers are too vast to admit of any accurate apprehension.

We feel a similar need in the case of mountains. Besides the bare statement of figures, it is necessary to have some means for grasping the meaning of the figures. The bare tens and thousands must be clothed with some concrete images. The statement that a mountain is 15,000 feet high is, by itself, little more impressive than that it is 3000; we want something more before wc can mentally compare Mont Blanc and Snowdon.

Indeed, the same people who guess of a mountain's height at a number of feet much exceeding the reality, show, when they are cross-examined, that they fail to appreciate in any tolerable degree the real meaning of the figures. An old lady one day, about ii a.m., proposed to walk from the ^Eggisch-horn to the Jungfrau-Joch, and to return for luncheon—the distance being a good twelve hours' journey for trained mountaineers. Every detail of which the huge mass is composed is certain to be underestimated. A gentleman the other day pointed out to me a grand ice-cliff at the end of a hanging glacier, which must have been at least ioo feet high, and asked me whether that snow was three feet deep. Nothing is more common than for tourists to mistake some huge pinnacle of rock, as big as a church tower, for a traveller. The rocks of the Grands Mulets, in one corner of which the chalet is hidden, are often identified with a party ascending Mont Blanc; and I have seen boulders as big as a house pointed out confidently as chamois. People who make these blunders must evidently see the mountains as mere toys, however many feet they may give them at a random guess. Huge overhanging cliffs are to them steps within the reach of human legs; yawning crevasses are ditches to be jumped; and foaming waterfalls are like streams from penny

squirts. Every one knows the avalanches on the Jungfrau, and the curiously disproportionate appearance of the little puffs of white smoke, which are said to be the cause of the thunder; but the disproportion ceases to an eye that has learnt really to measure distance, and to know that these smoke-puffs represent a cataract of crashing blocks of ice. Xow the first merit of mountaineering is that it enables one to have what theologians would call an experimental faith in the size of mountains—to substitute a real living belief for a dead intellectual assent. It enables one, first, to assign something like its true magnitude to a rock or a snow-slope; and, secondly, to measure that magnitude in terms of muscular exertion instead of bare mathematical units. Suppose that we are standing upon the Wengern Alp; between the Monch and the Eiger there stretches a round white bank, with a curved outline, which we may roughly compare to the back of one of Sir E. Landseer's lions. The ordinary tourists—the old man, the woman, or the cripple, who are supposed to appreciate the real beauties of Alpine scenery— may look at it comfortably from their hotel. They may see its graceful curve, the long straight lines that are ruled in delicate shading down its sides, and the contrast of the blinding white snow with the dark blue sky above; but they will probably

guess it to be a mere bank—a snowdrift, perhaps, which has been piled by the last storm. If you pointed out to them one of the great rocky teeth that projected from its summit, and said that it was a guide, they- would probably remark that he looked very small, and would fancy that he could jump over the bank with an effort. Now a mountaineer knows, to begin with, that it is a massive rocky rib, covered with snow, lying at a sharp angle, and varying perhaps from 500 to 1000 feet in height. So far he might be accompanied by men of less soaring ambition; by an engineer who had been mapping the country, or an artist who had been carefully observing the mountains from their bases. They might learn in time to interpret correctly the real meaning of shapes at which the uninitiated guess at random. But the mountaineer can go a step further, and it is the next step which gives the real significance to those delicate curves and lines. He can translate the 500 or 1000 feet of snow-slope into a more tangible unit of measurement. To him, perhaps, they recall the memory of a toilsome ascent, the sun beating on his head for five or six hours, the snow returning the glare with still more parching effect; a stalwart guide toiling all the weary time, cutting steps in hard blue ice, the fragments hissing and spinning down the long

straight grooves in the frozen snow till they lost themselves in the yawning chasm below; and step after step taken along the slippery staircase, till at length he triumphantly sprang upon the summit of the tremendous wall that no human foot had scaled before. The little black knobs that rise above the edge represent for him huge, impassable rocks, sinking on one side in scarped slippery surfaces towards the snow-field, and on the other stooping in one tremendous cliff to a distorted glacier thousands of feet below. The faint blue line across the upper neve, scarcely distinguishable to the eye, represents to one observer nothing but a trifling undulation; a second, perhaps, knows that it means a crevasse; the mountaineer remembers that it is the top of a huge chasm, thirty feet across, and perhaps ten times as deep, with perpendicular sides of glimmering blue ice, and fringed by thick rows of enormous pendent icicles. The marks that are scored in delicate lines, such as might be ruled by a diamond on glass, have been cut by innumerable streams trickling in hot weather from the everlasting snow, or ploughed by succeeding avalanches that have slipped from the huge upper snow-fields above. In short, there is no insignificant line or mark that has not its memory or its indication of the strange phenomena of the upper

world. True, the same picture is painted upon the retina of all classes of observers; and so Porson and a schoolboy and a peasant might receive the same physical impression from a set of black and white marks on the page of a Greek play; but to one they would be an incoherent conglomeration of unmeaning and capricious lines; to another they would represent certain sounds more or less corresponding to some English words ; whilst to the scholar they would reveal some of the noblest poetry in the world, and all the associations of successful intellectual labour. I do not say that the difference is quite so great in the case of the mountains; still I am certain that no one can decipher the natural writing on the face of a snow-slope or a precipice who has not wandered amongst their recesses, and learnt by slow experience what is indicated by marks which an ignorant observer w T ould scarcely notice. True, even one who sees a mountain for the first time may know that, as a matter of fact, a scar on the face of a cliff means, for example, a recent fall of a rock; but between the bare knowledge and the acquaintance with all which that knowledge implies—the thunder of the fall, the crash of the smaller fragments, the bounding energy of the descending mass—there is almost as much difference as between hearing that a battle has been fought and being present at it

yourself. We have all read descriptions of Waterloo till we are sick of the subject; but I imagine that our emotions on seeing the shattered well of Hougomont are very inferior to those of one of the Guard who should revisit the place where he held out for a long day against the assaults of the French army.

Now to an old mountaineer the Oberland cliffs are full of memories; and, more than this, he has learnt the language spoken by every crag and every wave of glacier. It is strange if they do not affect him rather more powerfully than the casual visitor who has never been initiated by practical experience into their difficulties. To him, the huge buttress which runs down from the Monch is something more than an irregular pyramid, purple with white patches at the bottom and pure white at the top. He fills up the bare outline supplied by the senses with a thousand lively images. He sees tier above tier of rock, rising in a gradually ascending scale of difficulty, covered at first by long lines of the debris that have been splintered by frost from the higher wall, and afterwards rising bare and black and threatening. He knows instinctively which of the ledges has a dangerous look—where such a bold mountaineer as John Lauener might slip on the polished surface, or be in danger of an avalanche from above.

He sees the little shell-like swelling at the foot of the glacier crawling down the steep slope above, and knows that it means an almost inaccessible wall of ice; and the steep snowfields that rise towards the summit are suggestive of something very different from the picture which might have existed in the mind of a German student, who once asked me whether it was possible to make the ascent on a mule.

Hence, if mountains owe their influence upon the imagination in a great degree to their size and steepness, and apparent inaccessibility—as no one can doubt that they do, whatever may be the explanation of the fact that people like to look at big, steep, inaccessible objects—the advantages of the mountaineer are obvious. He can measure those qualities on a very different scale from the ordinary traveller. He measures the size, not by the vague abstract term of so many thousand feet, but by the hours of labour, divided into minutes—each separately felt—of strenuous muscular exertion. The steepness is not expressed in degrees, but by the memory of the sensation produced when a snow-slope seems to be rising up and smiting you in the face; when, far away from all human help, you are clinging like a fly to the slippery side of a mighty pinnacle in mid-air. And as for the inaccessibility, no one can measure

the difficulty of climbing a hill who has not wearied his muscles and brain in struggling against the opposing obstacles. Alpine travellers, it is said, have removed the romance from the mountains by climbing them. What they have really done is to prove that there exists a narrow line by which a way may be found to the top of any given mountain; but the clue leads through innumerable inaccessibilities; true, you can follow one path, but to right and left are cliffs which no human foot will ever tread, and whose terrors can only be realised when you are in their immediate neighbourhood. The cliffs of the Matterhorn do not bar the way to the top effectually, but it is only by forcing a passage through them that you can really appreciate their terrible significance.

Hence I say that the qualities which strike every sensitive observer are impressed upon the mountaineer with tenfold force and intensity. If he is as accessible to poetical influences as his neighbours—and I don't know why he should be less so—he has opened new avenues of access between the scenery and his mind. He has learnt a language which is but partially revealed to ordinary men. An artist is superior to an unlearned picture-seer, not merely because he has greater natural sensibility, but because he has improved if by methodical experience; because

his senses have been sharpened by constant practice, till he can catch finer shades of colouring, and more delicate inflexions of line; because, also, the lines and colours have acquired new significance, and been associated with a thousand thoughts with which the mass of mankind has never cared to connect them. The mountaineer is improved by a similar process. But I know some sceptical critics will ask, Does not the way in which he is accustomed to regard mountains rather deaden their poetical influence? Doesn't he come to look at them as mere instruments of sport, and overlook their more spiritual teaching? Does not all the excitement of personal adventure and the noisy apparatus of guides, and ropes, and axes, and tobacco, and the fun of climbing, rather dull his perceptions and incapacitate him from perceiving

The silence that is in the starry sky, The sleep that is among the lonely hills?

Well, I have known some stupid and unpoetical mountaineers; and, since I have been dismounted from my favourite hobby, I think I have met some similar specimens among the humbler class of tourists. There are persons, I fancy, who "do" the Alps; who look upon the Lake of Lucerne as one more task ticked off from their memorandum

The Regrets of a Mountaineer ,^6;

hook, and count up the list of summits visible from the Gornergrat without being penetrated with any keen sense of sublimity. And there are mountaineers who are capable of making a pun on the top of Mont Blanc—and capable of nothing more. Still I venture to deny that even punning is incompatible with poetry, or that those who make the pun can have no deeper feeling in their bosoms which they are perhaps too shamefaced to utter.

The fact is that that which gives its inexpressible charm to mountaineering is the incessant series of exquisite natural scenes, which are for the most part enjoyed by the mountaineer alone. This is, I am aware, a round assertion; but I will try to support it by a few of the visions which are recalled to me by these Oberland cliffs, and which I have seen profoundly enjoyed by men who perhaps never mentioned them again, and who probably in describing their adventures scrupulously avoided the danger of being sentimental.

Thus every traveller has occasionally done a sunrise, and a more lamentable proceeding than the ordinary view of a sunrise can hardly be imagined. You are cold, miserable, breakfastless; have risen shivering from a warm bed, and in your heart long only to creep into bed again. To the mountaineer all this is changed. He is beginning

368 The Playground of Europe

a day full of the anticipation of a pleasant excitement. He has, perhaps, been waiting anxiously for fine weather, to try conclusions with some huge giant not yet scaled. He moves out with something of the feeling with which a soldier goes to the assault of a fortress, but without the same probability of coming home in fragments; the danger is trifling enough to be merely exhilatory, and to give a pleasant tension to the nerves; his muscles feel firm and springy, and his stomach—no small advantage to the enjoyment of scenery—is in excellent order. He looks at the sparkling stars with keen satisfaction, prepared to enjoy a fine sunrise with all his faculties at their best, and with the added pleasure of a good omen for his day's work. Then a huge dark mass begins to mould itself slowly out of the darkness, the sky begins to form a background of deep purple, against which the outlook becomes gradually more definite; one by one, the peaks catch the exquisite Alpine glow, lighting up in rapid succession, like a vast illumination; and when at last the steady sunlight settles upon them, and shows every rock and glacier, without even a delicate film of mist to obscure them, he feels his heart bound, and steps out gaily to the assault—-just as the people on the Rigi are giving thanks that the show is over and that they may go to bed. Still grander is the sight

The Regrets of a Mountaineer 369

when the mountaineer has already reached some lofty ridge, and, as the sun rises, stands between the day and the night—the valley still in deep sleep, with the mists lying between the folds of the hills, and the snow-peaks standing out clear and pale white just before the sun reaches them, whilst a broad band of orange light runs all round the vast horizon. The glory of sunsets is equally increased in the thin upper air. The grandest of all such sights that live in my memory is that of a sunset from the Aiguille du Goiitcr. The snow at our feet was glowing with rich light, and the shadows in our footsteps a vivid green by the contrast Beneath us was a vast horizontal floor of thin level mists suspended in mid-air, spread like a canopy over the whole boundless landscape, and tinged with every hue of sunset. Through its rents and gaps we could see the lower mountains, the distant plains, and a fragment of the Lake of Geneva lying in a more sober purple. Above us rose the solemn mass of Mont Blanc in the richest glow of an Alpine sunset. The sense of lonely sublimity was almost oppressive, and although half our party were suffering from sickness, I believe even the guides were moved to a sense of solemn beauty.

These grand scenic effects are occasionally seen by ordinary travellers, though the ordinary travel-

37° The Playground of Europe

ler is for the most part out of temper at 3 a.m. The mountaineer can enjoy them, both because his frame of mind is properly trained to receive the natural beauty, and because he alone sees them with their best accessories, amidst the silence of the eternal snow, and the vast panoramas visible from the loftier summits. And he has a similar advantage in most of the great natural phenomena of the cloud and the sunshine. No sight in the Alps is more impressive than the huge rocks of a black precipice suddenly frowning out through the chasms of a storm-cloud. But grand as such a sight may be from the safe verandahs of the inn at Grinclelwald, it is far grander in the silence of the Central Alps amongst the savage wilderness of rock and snow. Another characteristic effect of the High Alps often presents itself when we have been climbing for two or three hours, with nothing in sight but the varying wreaths of mist that chase each other monotonously along the rocky ribs up whose snow-covered backbone we have been laboriously fighting our way. Suddenly there is a puff of wind, and looking round we find that we have in an instant pierced the clouds, and emerged, as it were, on the surface of the ocean of vapour. Beneath us stretches for hundreds of miles the level fleecy floor, and above us shines out clear in the eternal sunshine every

The Regrets of a Mountaineer 371

mountain, from Mont Blanc to Monte Rosa and the Jungfrau. What, again, in the lower regions, can equal the mysterious charm of gazing from the edge of a torn rocky parapet into an apparently fathomless abyss, where nothing but what an Alpine traveller calls a "strange formless wreathing of vapour" indicates the storm-wind that is raging below us? I might go on indefinitely recalling the strangely impressive scenes that frequently startle the traveller in the waste upper world; but language is feeble indeed to convey even a glimmering of what is to be seen to those who have not seen it for themselves, whilst to those who have it can be little more than a peg upon which to hang their own recollections. These glories, in which the mountain Spirit reveals himself to his true worshippers, are only to be gained by the appropriate service of climbing—at some risk, though a very trifling risk, if he is approached with due form and ceremony—into the farthest recesses of his shrines. And without seeing them, I maintain that no man has really seen the Alps.

The difference between the exoteric and the esoteric school of mountaineers may be indicated by their different view of glaciers. At Grindel-wald, for example, it is the fashion to go and '"see the glaciers"—heaven save the mark! Ladies in costumes, heavy German professors, Americans doing the Alps at a gallop, Cook's tourists, and other varieties of a well-known genus, go or! in shoals and see—what? A gigantic mass of ice, strangely torn with a few of the exquisite blue crevasses, but defiled and prostrate in dirt and ruins. A stream foul with mud oozes out from the base; the whole mass seems to be melting fast away; the summer sun has evidently got the best of it in these lower regions, and nothing can resist him but the great mounds of decaying rock that strew the surface in confused lumps. It is as much like the glacier of the upper regions as the melting fragments of snow in a London street are like the surface of the fresh snow that has just fallen in a country field. And by way of improving its attractions a perpetual picnic is going on, and the ingenious natives have hewed a tunnel into the ice, for admission to which they charge certain centimes. The unlucky glacier at his latter end reminds me of a wretched whale stranded on a beach, dissolving into masses of blubber, and hacked by remorseless fishermen, instead of plunging at his ease in the deep blue water. Far above, where the glacier begins his course, he is seen only by the true mountaineer. There are vast amphitheatres of pure snow, of which the glacier known to tourists is merely the insignificant drainage, but whose very existence

they do not generally suspect. They are utterly ignorant that from the top of the icefall which they visit you may walk for hours on the eternal ice. After a long climb you come to the region where the glacier is truly at its noblest; where the surface is a spotless white; where the crevasses are enormous rents sinking to profound depths, with walls of the purest blue; where the glacier is torn and shattered by the energetic forces which mould it, but has an expression of superabundant power, like a full stream fretting against its banks and plunging through the vast gorges that it has hewn for itself in the course of centuries. The bases of the mountains are immersed in a deluge of cockneyism—fortunately a shallow deluge—whilst their summits rise high into the bracing air, where everything is pure and poetical.

The difference which I have thus endeavoured to indicate is more or less traceable in a wider sense. The mountains are exquisitely beautiful, indeed, from whatever points of view we contemplate them; and the mountaineer would lose much if he never saw the beauties of the lower valleys, of pasturages deep in flowers, and dark pine-forests with the summits shining from far off between the stems. Only, as it seems to me, he has the exclusive prerogative of thoroughly enjoying one and thai the most characteristic, though by no means only, element of the scenery. There may be a very good dinner spread before twenty people; but if nineteen of them were teetotalers, and the twentieth drank his wine like a man, he would be the only one to do it full justice; the others might praise the meat or the fruits, but he w T ould alone enjoy the champagne; and in the great feast which Nature spreads before us (a stock metaphor, which emboldens me to make the comparison), the high mountain scenery acts the part of the champagne. Unluckily, too, the teetotalers are very apt, in this case also, to sit in judgment upon their more adventurous neighbours. Especially are they pleased to carp at the views from high summits. I have been constantly asked, with a covert sneer, "Did it repay you?"—a question which involves the assumption that one wants to be repaid, as though the labour were not itself part of the pleasure, and which implies a doubt that the view is really enjoyable. People are always demonstrating that the lower views are the most beautiful; and at the same time complaining that mountaineers frequently turn back without looking at the view from the top, as though that would necessarily imply that they cared nothing for scenery. In opposition to which I must first remark that, as a rule, every step of an ascent has a beauty of its

The Regrets of a Mountaineer 375

own, which one is quietly absorbing even when one is not directly making it a subject of contemplation, and that the view from the top is generally the crowning glory of the whole.

It will be enough if I conclude with an attempt to illustrate this last assertion; and I will do it by still referring to the Oberland. Every visitor with a soul for the beautiful admires the noble form of the Wetterhorn—the lofty snow-crowned pyramid rising in such light and yet massive lines from its huge basement of perpendicular cliffs. The Wetterhorn has, however, a further merit. To my mind—and 1 believe most connoisseurs of mountain tops agree with me—it is one of the most impressive summits in the Alps. It is not a sharp pinnacle like the Weisshorn, or a cupola like Mont Blanc, or a grand rocky tooth like the Monte Rosa, but a long and nearly horizontal knife-edge, which, as seen from either end, has of course the appearance of a sharp-pointed cone. It is when balanced upon this ridge——sitting astride of the knife-edge on which one can hardly stand without giddiness—that one full\'7d 7 appreciates an Alpine precipice. -Mr. Justice Wills has admirably described the first ascent, and the impression it made upon him, in a paper which has become classical for succeeding adventurers, behind you the snow-slope sinks with perilous steepness

towards the wilderness of glacier and rock through which the ascent has lain. But in front the ice sinks with even greater steepness for a few feet or yards. Then it curves over and disappears, and the next thing that the eye catches is the meadow-land of Grind el wald, some 9000 feet below. I have looked down many precipices, where the eye can trace the course of every pebble that bounds down the awful slopes, and where I have shuddered as some dislodged fragment of rock showed the course which, in case of accident, fragments of my own body would follow. A precipice is always, for obvious reasons, far more terrible from above than from below. The creeping, tingling sensation which passes through one's limbs—even when one knows oneself to be in perfect safety—testifies to the thrilling influence of the sight. But I have never so realised the terrors of a terrific cliff as when I could not see it. The awful gulf which intervened between me and the green meadows struck the imagination by its invisibility. It w T as like the view which may be seen from the ridge of a cathedral roof, where the eaves have for their immediate background the pavement of the streets below T ; only this cathedral was 9000 feet high. Now, any one standing at the foot of the Wetterhorn may admire its stupendous massiveness and steepness; but, to feel its influence enter in the very marrow of one's bones, it is necessary to stand at the summit, and to fancy the one little slide down the short ice-slope, to be followed apparently by a bound into clear air and a fall down to the houses, from heights where only the eagle ventures to soar.

This is one of the Alpine beauties, which, of course, is beyond the power of art to imitate, and which people are therefore apt to ignore. But it is not the only one to be seen on the high summits. It is often said that these views are not' 'beautiful" —apparently because they won't go into a picture, or, to put it more fairly, because no picture can in the faintest degree imitate them. But without quarrelling about words, I think that, even if "beautiful" be not the most correct epithet, they have a marvellously stimulating effect upon the imagination. Let us look round from this wonderful pinnacle in mid-air, and note one or two of the most striking elements of the scenery.

You are, in the first place, perched on a cliff, whose presence is the more felt because it is unseen. Then you are in a region over which eternal silence is brooding. Not a sound ever comes there, except the occasional fall of a splintered fragment of rock, or a layer of snow; no stream is heard trickling, and the sounds of animal

life are left thousands of feet below. The most that you can hear is some mysterious noise made by the wind eddying round the gigantic rocks; sometimes a strange flapping sound, as if an unearthly flag were shaking its invisible folds in the air. The enormous tract of country over which your view extends—most of it dim and almost dissolved into air by distance—intensifies the strange influence of the silence. You feel the force of the line I have quoted from Wordsworth—

The sleep that is among the lonely hills.

None of the travellers whom you can see crawling at your feet has the least conception of what is meant by the silent solitudes of the High Alps. To you, it is like a return to the stir of active life, when, after hours of lonely wandering, you return to hear the tinkling of the cow-bells below; to them the same sound is the ultimate limit of the habitable world.

Whilst your mind is properly toned by these influences, you become conscious of another fact, to which the common variety of tourists is necessarily insensible. You begin to find out for the first time what the mountains really are. On one side, you look back upon the huge reservoirs from which the Oberland glaciers descend. You see the vast stores from which the great rivers of

Europe are replenished, the monstrous crawling masses that are carving the mountains into shape, and the gigantic bulwarks that separate two great quarters of the world. From below these wild regions are half invisible; they are masked by the outer line of mountains; and it is not till you are able to command them from some lofty point that you can appreciate the grandeur of the huge barriers, and the snow that is piled within their folds. There is another half of the view equally striking. Looking towards the north, the whole of Switzerland is couched at your feet; the Jura and the Black Forest lie on the far horizon. And then you know what is the nature of a really mountainous country. From below everything is seen in a kind of distorted perspective. The people of the valley naturally think that the valley is everything—that the country resembles old-fashioned maps, where a few sporadic lumps are distributed amongst towns and plains. The true proportions reveal themselves as you ascend. The valleys, you can now see, are nothing but narrow trenches scooped out amidst a tossing waste of mountain, just to carry off the drainage. The great ridges run hither and thither, having it all their own way, wild and untameable region.-, of rock or open grass or forest, at whose leet the valleys exist on sufferance. Creeping about amongst the roots of the hills, you half miss the hills themselves; you quite fail to understand the massiveness of the mountain chains, and, therefore, the wonderful energy of the forces that have heaved the surface of the world into these distorted shapes. And it is to a half-conscious sense of the powers that must have been at work that a great part of the influence of mountain scenery is due. Geologists tell us that a theory of catastrophes is unphilosophical; but, whatever may be the scientific truth, our minds are impressed as though we were witnessing the results of some incredible convulsion. At Stonehenge we ask what human beings could have erected these strange grey monuments, and in the mountains we instinctively ask what force can have carved out the Matterhorn, and placed the Wetterhorn on its gigantic pedestal. Now, it is not till we reach some commanding point that we realise the amazing extent of country over which the solid ground has been shaking and heaving itself in irresistible tumult.

Something, it is true, of this last effect may be seen from such mountains as the Rigi or the Faul-horn. There, too, one seems to be at the centre of a vast sphere, the earth bending up in a cup-like form to meet the sky, and the blue vault above stretching in an arch majestical by its enormous

extent. There you seem to see a sensible fraction of the world at your feet. But the effect is far less striking when other mountains obviously look down upon you; when, as it were, you are looking at the waves of the great ocean of hills merely from the crest of one of the waves themselves, and not from some lighthouse that rises far over their heads; for the Wetterhorn, like the Eiger, Monch, and Jungfrau, owes one great beauty to the fact that it is on the edge of the lower country, and stands between the real giants and the crowd of inferior, though still enormous, masses in attendance upon them. And, in the next place, your mind is far better adapted to receive impressions of sublimity when you are alone, in a silent region, with a black sky above and giant cliffs all round; with a sense still in your mind, if not of actual danger, still of danger that would become real with the slightest relaxation of caution, and with the world divided from you by hours of snow and rock.

I will go no further, not because I have no more to say, but because descriptions of scenery soon become wearisome, and because I have, 1 hope, said enough to show that the mountaineer may boast of some intellectual pleasures; that he is not a mere scrambler, but that he looks for poetical impressions, as well as for such small glory as his

achievements may gain in a very small circle. Something of what he gains fortunately sticks by him: he does not quite forget the mountain language; his eye still recognises the space and the height and the glory of the lofty mountains. And yet there is some pain in wandering ghostlike among the scenes of his earlier pleasures. For my part, I try in vain to hug myself in a sense of comfort. I turn over in bed when I hear the stamping of heavily nailed shoes along the passage of an inn about 2 a.m. I feel the skin of my nose complacently when I see others returning with a glistening tight aspect about that unluckily prominent feature, and know that in a day or two it will be raw and blistered and burning. I think, in a comfortable inn at night, of the miseries of those who are trying to sleep in damp hay, or on hard boards of chalets, at once cold and stuffy and haunted by innumerable fleas. I congratulate myself on having a whole skin and unfractured bones, and on the small danger of ever breaking them over an Alpine precipice. But yet I secretly know that these consolations are feeble. It is little use to avoid early rising and discomfort, and even fleas, if one also loses the pleasures to which they were the sauce—rather too piquante a sauce occasionally, it must be admitted. The philosophy is all very well which recommends

moderate enjoyment, regular exercise, and a careful avoidance of risk and overexcitement. That is, it is all very well so long as risk and excitement and immoderate enjoyment are out of your power; but it does not stand the test of looking on and seeing them just beyond your reach. In time, no doubt, a man may grow calm; he may learn to enjoy the pleasures and the exquisite beauties of the lower regions--though they, too, are most fully enjoyed when they have a contrast with beauties of a different, and pleasures of a keener, excitement. When first debarred, at any rate, one feels like a balloon full of gas, and fixed by immovable ropes to the prosaic ground. It is pleasant to lie on one's back in a bed of rhododendrons, and look up to a mountain top peering at one from above a bank of cloud; but it is pleasantest when one has qualified oneself for repose by climbing the peak the day before and becoming familiar with its terrors and its beauties. In time, doubtless, one may get reconciled to anything; one may settle down to be a caterpillar, even after one has known the 1 pleasures of being a butterfly; one may become philosophical, and have one's clothes let out; and even in time, perhaps,—though it is almost, too terrible to contemplate,— be content with a mule or a carriage, or that lowest depth to which

human beings can sink, and for which the English language happily affords no name, a chaise a porteur: and even in such degradation the memory of better times may be pleasant; for I doubt much whether it is truth the poet sings—

That a sorrow's crown of sorrow is remembering happier things.

Certainly, to a philosophical mind, the sentiment is doubtful. For my part, the fate which has cut me off, if I may use the expression, in the flower of my youth, and doomed me to be a non-climbing animal in future, is one which ought to exclude grumbling. I cannot indicate it more plainly, for I might so make even the grumbling in which I have already indulged look like a sin. I can only say that there are some very delightful things in which it is possible to discover an infinitesimal drop of bitterness, and that the mountaineer who undertakes to cut himself off from his favourite pastime, even for reasons which he will admit in his wildest moods to be more than amply sufficient, must expect at times to feel certain pangs of regret, however quickly they may be smothered.

THE END

Printed in Great Britain
by Amazon

24441352R00084